ONE BLOOD RUBY

ONE BLOOD RUBY

melissa marr

HARPER

An Imprint of HarperCollins Publishers

Library of Congress Control Number: 2016938977
ISBN 978-0-06-208417-0

Typography by Jenna Stempel
18 19 20 21 22   PC/LSCH   10 9 8 7 6 5 4 3 2 1
❖
First paperback edition, 2018

To Youval—somewhere between silent hikes in Scotland, midnight whiskey in Paris, and dipping our toes into several seas, you've been a revelation.

The queen kept her troops safe in solace, until a time came when she finally gave birth to a child. The troops believed that this was the start of a new era, but when the babe was born, her skin broke like glass.

—Iana Abernathy, *The Last of Our Secrets*

PROLOGUE

The air in the theater grew thinner gradually. A few people squirmed. They looked around. Some rubbed their temples as headaches set in; others blinked and yawned. A few put a hand to chest or throat, as if they felt it sooner than the hundreds around them. He figured they were the ones with weaker lungs.

One of the performers collapsed, tumbling to the stage in a heap of feathered costume. The light that should've been on the dancer darted away, but not quickly enough. Some of the audience members, even as sluggish as they were becoming, started to panic.

Unfortunately, panic resulted in breathing faster. That only accelerated their death. So too did the attempts to stand and walk away. They had so little oxygen left, and they wasted it.

But, in truth, that's what humanity was doing every day—turning their atmosphere to poison. He was simply demonstrating the effect of their actions in a shorter time, minutes rather than decades. Nacton was under no illusion that he was doing them a kindness, but it was a choice, and like most choices he made, this one was about getting what he wanted. He wanted war to continue; he wanted them to suffer. Mostly, he wanted the fae to remain separate from the monstrosity of humans. They were, by the very virtue of their births, guilty. If he didn't kill them, they'd kill themselves slowly. They ate toxic food, inhaled filthy air, destroyed the very water and soil that the whole planet needed—that the *fae* needed.

Despite that, the rulers of the Hidden Lands wanted to declare peace. The Queen of Blood and Rage was so desperate for her half-human granddaughter's acceptance that she was going to end the attacks on humans. For all of his reasons to dislike the woman, he'd supported her guerrilla war against humans. He'd even fathered one of her so-called Sleeper agents, the Black Diamonds.

At his side, his companion murmured, "Are we simply going to watch them die?"

Nacton drew more of the air out of the room. There wasn't anything they could do if they wanted to escape. They sat in their finery and suffocated.

"No need to drag it out," his companion said.

The dancers on stage were still, fallen flowers that were only beautiful for an instant. They, at least, told Nacton that humanity had some qualities worth saving. He felt a sliver of guilt, but at least they had died doing what they loved. It was the most he could give them, a parting gift.

"Burn it," he said, and then he walked away. There were others who would die yet this week. And in each case, there would be no doubt that the fae were responsible.

one

EILIDH

Eilidh debated going to check on her niece, Lily, but Torquil had only been awake for a few days. She couldn't yet stand to leave her betrothed for very long. He was healing, but not as quickly as she'd like. Being stabbed made for a slow recovery, and she was trying to stay at his side as best as she could.

She'd feel better once the crown princess and her cousin Zephyr moved to the Hidden Lands. For now, Eilidh was trying to not let her worries consume her. The growing strife in the Hidden Lands would only increase when her people began mingling with humanity.

So many things could go wrong. Some inevitably would, no matter how carefully Eilidh planned. She'd been working toward this for most of her life, but no amount of preparation would ensure that everything went perfectly. She stared out from her tower and purposefully set aside her plans for a moment. If all one did was plot and scheme, madness would surely come calling. So every day, Eilidh chose to take a quiet moment to breathe and take in beauty.

The glass tower where she stood reflected just enough moonlight onto the waves that they seemed to shimmer and wink at her. The sounds of sea and air were a constant soothing symphony in her home, and the sheer beauty of the water from her vantage point was often all she needed to find a moment of peace. There was something in her affinities that made her less and less *separate* from sea and soil over time. Maybe it was simply being the child of both courts. Maybe it was the way she'd shattered as a child.

When she'd been born, the touch of air against her skin had literally fractured, like a spiderweb crack through a pane of glass, like dry earth in a drought. Every bit of flesh and bone had tried to separate, but vine and soil enclosed her in their embrace, and the fire that lived deep in the core of the world had surged to her so that she was as a phoenix. Water rushed to quench fire as fast as it burned, and her infant body was reborn of the elements. Born of fae, of Seelie and Unseelie both, and born *again* of nature.

Eilidh didn't remember, of course, but sea, soil, and fire were a part of her in ways that were more than fae. She was unable to go very long without giving herself over to the elements. The king and queen knew. They alone held her secret. Neither spoke of it, and so Eilidh knew that it was to be unspoken—even as it changed and grew within her.

She would sacrifice anyone or anything, including the truth of her nature, for the courts. It was why she'd been born: for them. It was not a decision greeted well by many of the fae. Her Seelie brothers were among those in protest. They and many of their kind saw only the maze of scars that covered her skin. They knew only that Eilidh lived in a tower built for the daughter the queen had truly wanted and loved—the child that had died—and that Eilidh was a replacement. They couldn't understand that the tower was a prison that her father was afraid to enter and in which her mother saw only ghosts.

"Princess?"

The voice that lifted to her tower from the rocks wasn't loud, but the glass walls had been enchanted to let her hear as if there were no barrier. She walked to the edge of the vast circular room where she'd been pacing and glanced to the sea.

She'd hoped that making it possible for LilyDark to become the new heir of the Hidden Throne would be enough to ease sentiment against her, but there were continued rumblings of discontent. Her Seelie brothers were embarrassed that they'd been bested by half-humans, and the younger fae who'd been born after the courts had withdrawn from contact with the human world were nervous at the idea of being among humans once again. The fae weren't a people known for accepting change gracefully, and it seemed that suddenly everything had begun to change.

After Eilidh checked to see that her injured fiancé was still resting, she descended the steps and went to do as she must.

WILL

Will stared out at the sea while Roan got dressed. It wasn't about modesty. When his boyfriend swam, he did so as a seal. That transition back to humanity was sometimes an adjustment for Roan. Will often carried a bag with Roan's things, and tugging on wet clothes took a few moments so Will marveled at the sea within the Hidden Lands while Roan dressed.

They'd come together, falling into the sea and swimming through a gateway into the Hidden Lands. There was a kind of trust required to simply drop into the inky black water, but Will trusted Roan with his life.

That didn't mean that he trusted the faery princess. He had whispered her name upon arrival and yet he *was* afraid. Anyone raised by the Queen of Blood and Rage was worthy of fear.

He wasn't shocked when Roan had told him they had an errand. He wasn't even alarmed when Roan revealed that they were going to the Hidden Lands. Not much surprised him at this point. He'd been to the Hidden Lands in secret a few times, but this time, it was the princess who had summoned him. Will had never met her, nor had Roan. Three of the others had.

Of the seven Black Diamonds only Alkamy hadn't gone to the Hidden Lands at all.

"Will?" Roan's voice made him turn away from the sea. It was then he saw the princess approaching.

She walked across the jagged rocks as if they were sand. They seemed to move out of her way or simply melt as she touched them. The waves, on the other hand, reached out for her. The sea rushed past their feet, climbing higher until it soaked them to their hips. They were, of course, already dripping from the trip across the water, but the urgency of the sea's reach was disquieting.

Roan whispered, "She doesn't even notice, does she?"

Will shook his head.

The wind had picked up, gusting toward them as if it too had to touch the fae who walked over an earth that moved to accommodate her. Sea, earth, and air were all attuned to the fractured princess.

She walked in the way of the Unseelie prince who was Zephyr's father. Rhys had the same disconnectedness that Eilidh had. Perhaps it was a result of having lived their whole life with the Queen of Blood and Rage. Will was fairly sure having *her* as a mother would make every parent he'd known—except possibly Lily's father—seem relaxed.

"You stare," Eilidh said.

"You are the princess," Roan replied.

"And we've never been summoned," Will added, not mentioning the way the elements were buffeting them. "Your mother sent tasks but . . ."

Eilidh met his eyes. "You lie well."

"The queen has never summoned us. Nor have you." Will didn't look away, didn't change his posture. He felt Roan tense at his side, but that was to be expected. Wind and water were battering them, and he *was* lying to Eilidh.

She smiled before saying, "You're very Seelie. No wonder my father likes you."

"The king doesn't know us," Roan said carefully.

Will knew that his boyfriend was trying to draw the princess' attention. He also knew that things were going to be tense when Eilidh pressed her lips together in a disapproving way. There were times for silence, and there were times for admissions. The princess knew the truth, and Will disliked keeping secrets from Roan anyhow.

"Roan?" he said. Will didn't add more, but they didn't typically need a lot of words between them. His confession was in his tone.

"And you never told me?" Roan's temper wasn't as bad as Creed's or Zephyr's, but he was of the sea, and anyone who thought the sea was calm, had missed two thirds of the moods that water could have.

"We all have secrets," Will pointed out gently.

It was no time for a petty argument. Things were changing. The fae were about to declare peace—and sometimes a declaration of peace was scarier than a continuation of conflict.

The princess made a noise in her throat, drawing their attention back to her.

"I have need of information," she said when they were staring at her. "The coronation is coming soon."

"When?" Will asked.

Eilidh ignored him. "There are troubles in Lily's father's business. I don't know if they've reached her yet, but I know that fields are burning. There are officers watching her because of her father. I know, too, that someone of our blood is killing humans."

"What are we to do?" Roan asked.

Will hoped that the task she was going to set for them was more in line with those set by the Seelie King. It was the queen who had made them killers. Gathering information was far easier than ending lives. What he knew of the princess so far wasn't encouraging.

"Whatever necessary," she said. "LilyDark must not be arrested. Make use of whomever you must to see to it. Find out if the troubles are connected. Keep LilyDark safe."

The seriousness of that order made it worse. The queen's orders created chaos and fear; she sent the Black Diamonds to kill or destroy things. The king sent Will to discover things or transmit information.

This was . . . different.

"We're not investigators," Will pointed out as calmly as he'd ever said anything, using the tone of voice he often had to employ when Violet was in a mood.

"No, but you know LilyDark and Erik. You have resources in your reach through your parents. You can walk where the fae cannot . . . and where your frequently photographed friends aren't able to pass unnoticed." The princess reached a hand out to the sea, as if it were an animal to pet.

The waves lifted toward her, seeming for a moment to take the same shape as hers. Arms, legs, and a torso formed. Rivulets of water streaked upward until the sea had a face as well. It smiled at her before dropping again to its rightful form.

The sight of it made Will uncomfortable. So, too, did Eilidh's seemingly vacant eyes in that moment where the sea smiled at her. He would say she was asleep if she'd been anyone else, but she was the daughter of the two strongest living fae. Who knew what passed as commonplace for such a one?

Roan was staring at her. Perhaps being a water affinity made him hear or feel things Will couldn't. All Will could understand just then was that Roan was afraid.

"We'll go then," Will said to the princess.

Eilidh nodded and turned away. She didn't offer words of kindness or benediction. She simply walked back across the rocks as if she was a sleepwalker.

Once she was gone, Will and Roan exchanged a look. Will touched a finger to Roan's lips. Here was not the place to speak. The princess might seem to have drifted into a fugue state, but every element here was attuned to her. There was no privacy.

Roan nodded and took his hand. For the first time in all of the years they'd know one another, first as friends and then as more, Roan looked at the sea with a sort of misgiving.

"There are other ways back," Will said.

Instead of answering, Roan shifted forms and stared up at him. The site of his boyfriend as a seal didn't seem odd after all this time. Will had seen it the first time it happened, and although none of the rest of the diamonds had another form, this was normal for Roan.

Will scooped up the clothes that Roan would need on the other side, and tucked them into the bag he wore on his back. That the sea felt sentient was enough to make him hesitate, but when Roan dove into the waves, Will followed. Together, he was sure they could handle whatever came, and if not, he'd rather be lost together than survive apart.

three

LILYDARK

The sky was still dark when Lily's phone rang twice and stopped. Then it rang once and stopped. When it rang again, she answered. That was the pattern last agreed upon with Daidí. They switched the code up periodically, but the use of a ring pattern was a constant.

"I've sent Hector to bring you home," Daidí said when she answered his call.

"You know then," she said.

Her father's silence at the other end of the line wasn't one of denial. For most of Lily's life, they'd practiced the art of silent speaking—gaps while they both figured out the proper words to say what they must, yet those which could not be translatable to others who might be listening. Being the most notorious of crime lords meant that Nicolas Abernathy was often being recorded, spied upon, or otherwise scrutinized. Lily had learned the tools of dis-sembling and misdirection before she'd learned her letters.

"I know *some* things," Daidí admitted.

"From?" Lily closed her eyes.

Creed sat up and pulled her to him, not speaking but offering her the silent comfort of his touch. She leaned back into Creed's arms. It was a strange thing, how much safer she felt simply because his arms encircled her. He didn't need to speak or do anything. His *being* was enough.

She felt like a plant with roots sinking deep into pure soil. Stronger. Safer. Nourished. There wasn't a word she knew that was enough to explain that feeling. Love was the closest one, but it was small in comparison with the size and depth of the emotions she felt.

Daidí's voice was more guarded as he said, "Your . . . aunt."

"No one else, though? You didn't need to ask Cerise for help with any other guests?" Lily used their old euphe-mism for handguns, thinking back to the number of times police officers had asked *who* Cerise was instead of *what* she was when they'd arrested Daidí. They might listen in on Daidí's conversations, but they were still clueless.

"No, *but* from what I hear, your aunt is more of a peacekeeper than you these days. I heard about your argu-ments with other family members."

Lily tensed at the words, not wanting to talk about crossing swords with her uncles, the sons of the Seelie King. They were technically her blood, but they had no love or kindness to show her. They'd captured and held her, and her escape had required a level of violence she'd not expected. Although she'd been raised willing to draw blood, it wasn't ever an act without weight.

"You should've called me, Lily," her father chastised.

Creed had started swaying slightly as he held her. He didn't sing, but she felt him use the air to gently stroke her arms. It was his affinity, air. So she often had the unusual experience of being consoled, cajoled, or caressed by someone who could turn the air into the equivalent of innumerable hands. She liked it, but it was distracting.

Her eyes popped open, and she glared at her boyfriend before she could stop herself.

"Sorry," he mouthed.

Lily shot Creed an apologetic smile before telling her father the big news. "I was going to tell you about it . . . and my plan to create *more* peace, when I saw you."

"Your plan . . ." Her father paused, and in the next moment, his standard implacable tone failed. He sounded like the man he was in the privacy of their home as he asked, "Are you sure, Lilywhite? If you don't want—"

"LilyDark," she corrected gently, using the name she'd chosen as a way to announce that she was neither Seelie nor Unseelie, fae nor human. "I am the daughter of two worlds and two courts. I want peace, and my plan will bring it."

He sighed. Her father actually *sighed*. This was a man who—more than once—had ordered a guard "permanently removed" with nary a blink of the eye. He'd presided over a criminal enterprise that laundered money, bought politicians, and—at least twice—been a part of the overthrow of a government. Nicolas Abernathy wasn't a man to sigh. He was a man to speak and do.

"Daidí?"

"I need to see you, Lily."

"I thought you were with Señor Gaviria?"

"There have been some complications with work, and several obvious fae attacks on humans that are getting a lot of attention."

"I saw the news," Lily said carefully, "I wish I knew who was doing it, but . . . I *don't*."

There was a long pause before her father asked, "Have you heard from your grandparents?"

"I don't think so," she said, answering the question he was really asking. "They've been busy with other things. You know how my grandmother gets when she's focused."

Lily closed her eyes and tried to keep her worry in check. How was the queen to declare peace between the fae and humanity in the midst of such blatant and horrible attacks? No one would believe in the peace she was offering.

Lily did, though. The queen might slit throats. She might destroy entire towns, but she wanted Lily's willing cooperation. The queen knew that Lily's price was peace.

If the Queen of Blood and Rage wasn't ordering the attacks, who was?

When the silence went on too long, her father asked, "Will the rock star be joining us?"

Creed, who had heard the whole conversation, let out a brief laugh.

"Hello, Mr. Morrison," Daidí added drolly as he overheard Creed. "Well, there's that answer."

Gently, Lily told her father, *"Abernathy Commandment #17: Love is a risk, so if you embark upon it, do it with no reservations. Never halfway.* Creed will be with me."

At that, Creed's arms tightened around her. She hadn't ever outright said the words to him. Proclamations of love weren't always necessary. Still, she felt her cheeks burn at the realization that she'd just implied to both her boyfriend and father that she loved Creed.

"So be it," Daidí said. "Hector is already on the way to fetch you."

"Yes, Daidí."

When Lily disconnected, Creed tightened his arms around her, imprisoning her. She had to be careful of his still-injured hand. His leg cut had healed, but his wrist was still bandaged from his actions in the Hidden Lands. She was staring at the proof that he'd been hurt because of her, when he spoke.

"Lily?"

She shook her head. Implying things wasn't the same as admitting them. She'd become the heir to the fae throne a few weeks ago. Any talk of the future, or of love, or even of possibilities was far beyond her reach. Loving her was dangerous. She shouldn't forget that.

Carefully, she turned within the frame of his arms and reached up to pull him toward her in a kiss. It felt like a strange gift to be able to do so, to expect a world-famous singer, a rock star she'd followed in the tabloids, to kiss her. There had only ever been one sort-of-boyfriend before him, so receiving affection from Creed was surreal. She wanted to keep this, the oddly fragile love that she couldn't stop, even as she wondered if the right thing to do was to find a way to run from him.

He kissed her, lips first touching softly and then demanding the proof she wouldn't give him in words. There was something in the silence, the words not yet spoken and feelings not yet admitted. It made their kisses fiercer, rougher, as if the act could say the things she wouldn't.

Lily's fingertips trailed up the back of his neck to graze the slight stubble of his hair. He didn't completely shave this week, but he kept his hair cut close enough that she'd taken to tracing the contours of his head. Admittedly, she'd let her hands wander over other parts of his body as well. Touching Creed was addictive, and she was a willing addict.

"Go pack a bag," she told him when he pulled back.

"Done." He stared at her a moment too long, as if he needed to burn her into his memory simply to be able to leave.

It was things like that that made Lily willing to fight

more and more for him. She wasn't concerned about him finding her beautiful in a prideful way. In truth, she was still in awe that he'd noticed her at all. When he looked at her, he was so focused, as if the world could end around them and he wouldn't even notice. Lily knew he saw her, not the Abernathy scion or the heir to the Hidden Throne. Creed saw *her*.

And that was everything.

ROAN

When he surfaced on the other side of the sea, the human side, Roan glanced to his right. Will was with him. He'd felt Will's hand on his back. As long as they touched, Will could breathe under the waves too. It didn't work with anyone else. Years ago, that had been one of the first clues that they *both* felt the attraction and affection between them. The ability to share breath wasn't there with Violet or Zephyr or Creed or Alkamy.

Will was the one exception.

"Okay?" Will asked as he noticed Roan's stare.

Roan transitioned back to his normal shape, shivering a little at the feeling of the water without a seal's pelt for warmth.

"You lied," he said quietly.

"I omitted," Will whispered.

Even these few words felt weighty and loud as they floated in the harbor at Belfoure. They swam toward the pier where they could slip onto shore. Roan never minded the water, even when it was impure, but after the clean sea water in the Hidden Lands, the filth here felt wrong. He wasn't ready to abandon this world, but for someone who had a second form, the appeal of living in the Hidden Lands was undeniable. There, the water was incredibly pure. It had to be. After all, the queen swam. There, he wouldn't have to hide what he was. The only reason it hadn't appealed up until now was that the queen often seemed a touch mad.

"*You* didn't tell me when you were sent to the train station," Will reminded him. It was a subject that had become an issue between them. Roan had taken Violet instead of Will. She was their best friend, and they'd never felt like she was between them. This time, though, Will *did* feel that way. Roan had turned to her, not to him.

"I apologized." Roan stood there, naked and angry. "Will?"

"No more secrets," Will said, unzipping his bag and pulling out sodden clothes. "I'm sorry. I can give excuses, but the truth is that the king is scary. Not the same way the princess is . . . but still . . ."

Grimacing, Roan pulled on his jeans. Wet denim was gross.

"I'm Seelie," Will added. "If I ever doubted it, talking to the king would've clarified it."

Roan paused in buttoning his jeans and looked at his boyfriend in surprise.

"I don't know *how* I can say that for sure, but"—Will shrugged—"I knew. When I met him, when he ordered me, I knew."

"I could be Seelie." Roan held out his arm. He was darker than Will, but they were both lighter in complexion than Creed. When they were revealed to be half-human, Roan attributed his color to his human mother. It had been a conundrum over the years. He was Seelie dark, but he swam like the Unseelie Queen.

Will shook his head. "We both know you're not."

"So you were afraid I'd *mind* that you're Seelie-born?" Roan's temper rose. "Do I have a problem with Creed? With Vi?"

"You don't." Will reached out and caught his hand. "But you aren't considering living with them—"

Roan cut him off by kissing him. When he released him, he said, "You can be an idiot. Still. After years. It amazes me."

"Thanks." Will's voice was light though, and he stayed close enough that there was no doubt that his worries had been answered.

"*When* we get married someday, I expect you to remember that I would throw away family, friends, anything for us to be happy." Roan stared at him, not accusing but reminding. "I accept that you think you can't because of *the senator*, and I'm still here. I would go to the Hidden

Lands or wherever we needed to be together and happy."

"It's not that I *think* I can't. My mother's career . . ." Will started, but he didn't finish this time. It was a subject that used to lead to fights. Roan had stopped fighting about it for now. They had an agreement to wait until they graduated at the end of the year to make decisions on how to deal with it.

"Right," Roan said with a quick brush of lips. "We can discuss her political inconveniences later."

Roan stepped back to finish dressing. He pulled on a shirt and slid his feet into sandals, before he looked at Will and asked, "So, how do we deal with the princess' orders to watch over Lily?"

"We call Lily's criminal friend," Will said levelly.

"Whose number you already have?"

Will shrugged. "I have several. One of them will work."

five

EILIDH

To say that the Hidden Lands were in flux would be like calling the turbulent sea merely *unsettled*. The fae were growing no less fearful, no less angry, no less confused. They would with time, but those who live for centuries are slow to adapt. Ending a war and declaring a new heir . . . both were world-changing events.

Of course, Eilidh had her own changes to embrace. She'd never been other than the heir to the throne. She'd drawn her infant breaths under observation, taken her first steps knowing that all and each fae watched her for weaknesses. She'd learned at her mother's side, felt blood from the queen's wounds drip onto her skin. For many years, Eilidh had believed that the queen's natural scent was salt and copper, but now she knew those to be simply tears and blood.

So it was not an easy thing to see her lands under worsening strife. Fae of both courts waited outside her door at all times hoping for an audience. Some were there to wish her well before they asked her to intercede. Most, however, had little time for pleasantry.

"She's corrupted the king," one of the bolder fae men said by way of greeting. "He's drunk on her witchery."

Eilidh affixed a placid look on her face and said, "Mother is no more witch than you are."

"Threatened him then," another fae, this one Unseelieborn, suggested.

Stone and mud slithered under Eilidh's feet. She'd started wearing boots, as if the leather between her skin and the soil would mute the constant chatter of earthen things. She had no idea when it had become so cacophonous and constant, but there were days when the mere touch of earth made her head thunder in pain. She took to the sea more and more the past few weeks; barely a day passed without her diving from the cliffs into the depths. The water here was cold, and only those fae with water affinity could stand the sea's embrace very long. They weren't in it as often as Eilidh was, however. She couldn't bear a day without the silence of water surrounding her.

"What if one of us threatened you?"

Eilidh laughed in unexpected joy. Every few days one of them would suggest such foolishness. With laughter still on her tongue, she pulled the earth toward her, burying the fae woman up to her chin. She sputtered, a face atop a termite mound, as Eilidh stood in bemused wonder.

"I am *their* daughter," she said lightly. "Child of *two* courts. Brother to Rhys. Betrothed to Torquil. Aunt to the new heir . . ." She slid a short dagger out of her skirt. "Surely, you can't have forgotten the blood that runs in these veins."

With no further word, she traced one of the many scars on her arm, letting her blood flow to the ground. Soil reddened as if those few drops were a torrent. Fae soil had always been fed by blood offerings. The regents made offerings still, including Eilidh and all of the princes.

"My blood will nourish this soil as long as I live," she reminded the assembled fae. Fire appeared in the air over her wound. It sunk into her body, burning deep into her bones. "And I will serve the future queen of the Hidden Lands. *You* will serve her."

"Or?" a voice from the back of the crowds called.

"Or I will show you what the conjoined blood of our people can do," Eilidh said, still looking on them with a smile.

"Nacton says—"

"Nacton. Is *he* of both courts?"

"No, but—"

"Do you forget that he violated your queen mother and king father's wishes?" Eilidh felt like her voice was thicker and denser than it ought to be, like earth and stone fell from her lips as words. Her body sometimes felt as though it were merely a conduit for the earth and sea, uttering thoughts not wholly hers. These words, however, she held as true. "LilyDark, daughter of Iana and granddaughter of Endellion and Leith, will protect our home."

Come, child. Come and be quiet. Come home to the waves, daughter.

Eilidh frowned, trying to push the sea's summons back. The people needed assurances. Her tongue was heavy though as waves and soil vied for mastery over her.

Words grew less present by the moment. Still, she knew actions. In a blink, she had drawn and was raising her sword in her free hand. The broken princess held it as if she were as capable as her mother. In moments such as these, Eilidh suspected she was.

"If you see fit to create quarrels, I will let the earth drink." She drew the tip of the sword through the dirt prison holding the fae woman steady. She let the fae-wrought steel cut flesh.

Fresh blood stained the soil, fed the land.

"These are my lands to protect, heir or no, and I will not allow you to disrupt the peace we are entering." Eilidh repeated the same words she'd said in one way or the other most days. "Let it be known."

Then she turned her back and walked to the edge of the stone cliffs alongside her towering glass home. With no other word, she extended first her dagger and then her sword. Stone and soil wrapped around them as if the very hands of the Hidden Lands were accepting her blades. Though she was grateful, Eilidh was also confused by it.

Come, child. Come and be quiet. Come to us, daughter.

With no weapons left in her hands, Eilidh stretched her arms skyward and then leaped. For the space of a few breaths, she was as if suspended. Air held her there, even though it was not her affinity. Then fire seemed to coat her entire body, burned over every nerve, searing her skin until she thought pain was imminent.

Air released her, and sea accepted her. And there was peace. There was silence. Everything that was wrong was carried away by the sea.

When Eilidh resurfaced, her father stood at the edge of his part of the Hidden Lands. For all of the years that the king and queen had been wed, they still didn't share a home. The king would visit the queen as often as he thought she would allow it, and then a few times more. It was more combat than companionship with the regents. Eilidh couldn't even attempt to understand them. She'd given up trying.

"Daughter," he greeted as she stepped out of the frigid waters. He had a thick blanket to drape over her shoulders like a cloak. The queen would likely have shrugged or at best tossed a skin of some sort toward her. The king was civilized in ways the queen thought foolish.

As if intent on proving that very thing, he'd had a fine table brought to the sandy beach. White linen edged with golden lace covered the dark wood. Silver tea service and delicate cups with hand-painted flowers rested in the center of the table. Beside it was a multi-tiered silver serving dish with tiny sandwiches and treats.

"I expect you've not broken fast," the king said, pulling out her chair.

"I needed the sea."

He nodded. "The children quarrel still?"

Eilidh sighed. He knew as well as her mother that the fae were struggling with the announcement of LilyDark as their future regent. It was the right choice, and they had to act as if they were unaware of the distress it caused. If they drew blood or pressed the matter, there were many who would rebel. That left the task to the fae themselves.

Rhys was seen as the queen's hand, and the Seelie princes were unlikely to do much other than fan the discontent. That left Eilidh and those who would speak rationally to their kin and kind. It was not an easy task.

Mutely, Eilidh poured their tea. Her hand didn't even shake when her father noted, "I've not seen Calder of late."

"He keeps his own counsel," she said mildly. Calder and Nacton, her Seelie brothers, hated her. They weren't pleased that she had survived her infancy, and they certainly weren't fond of the queen. To them, the courts would be better served separately. Then *they* could rule as they wished, once their father was dead.

It wasn't the least popular theory in the Hidden Lands. There were those who thought the Queen of Blood and Rage had carried on her vengeful war too long. Of course, there were plenty of others who thought the declaration of peace was a mistake. The problem with the fae, in Eilidh's opinion, was that so few of them thought about the fae not born of their own court, and hardly anyone thought about the fae-bloods trapped in the humans' lands. Worse still, many of them failed to think about the first reason the courts had withdrawn from living with humanity so long ago: the earth was thick with toxins. *Humans* had done that. They were still doing it.

Of course, there were laws, attempts to stop the destruction of the environment, but as long as the fae hid and waged war, the humans would not understand the effect of their recklessness and nothing would change. Change required massive action. It required courage and a willingness to put everything on the table. It required sacrifice.

While Seelie- and Unseelie-born alike had the Hidden Lands to nourish them, the lands outside their small corner were growing sicker by the year. In time, that poison would infiltrate their home too. Sometimes Eilidh tasted it in the waters. Eventually, they would have even less space than they had now. It was unhealthy to expect eternity in the little land they'd claimed as their own. Something needed to be done.

On that, the King of Fire and Truth was her greatest ally. While the queen had thought much of blood and revenge, the king had planned for the future. The Queen of Blood and Rage had ordered fae males to impregnate human volunteers—women either desperate for a child, sympathetic to her cause, or willing to accept a payment—so that she could create half-fae, half-human soldiers.

The king had looked at the same Sleepers the queen had used for her warfare, and he'd sent them different orders—ones that moved his plans for legal and criminal acts that furthered the protection of the earth. He'd been working toward a society where the fae and fae-bloods could come out of hiding and affect change. In ways that no one realized, the King of Fire and Truth was fighting for their people *and* humanity.

"We destroyed another company," the king said in a cheerful voice. "Water polluters this time."

Leith had used the very tools that the queen had crafted for killing to do it, employing the Black Diamonds even though the queen had forbidden it.

"Mother will figure out that you're using her toys again," Eilidh told her father, as she always did.

He grinned cheerfully. "I do count on it. She does enjoy threatening me, and my borrowing her soldiers always makes her surly." He took a big drink of his tea. He might love the trappings of civility, but at heart, the king was no more civilized than any of the fae. "Your mother never quite mastered the idea of sharing, you know?"

Eilidh politely kept her mouth shut and studied the trays of treats on the table. She was genuinely hungry. The king might be a glutton for conflict with his wife, but he did attempt to be a kind parent.

"Do you suppose you have fewer scars these past few months or am I simply no longer as bothered by them?" Leith asked after selecting a biscuit for himself.

"I have no idea, Father." Eilidh bit the scone she'd pulled from the middle tier. A mouth full of tasty food was her best answer just then. The alternative was pointing out her father's rudeness.

He was a beautiful man, tall and handsome. It was no wonder that the queen glared so at the Seelie-born women who stood too near him. For all of her posturing at not caring, the queen was just as smitten as the king. She was terror, where he was loveliness. Eilidh, despite being born to be the best of both courts, was neither gorgeous nor terrifying.

She sat on the shore and ate in silence with her father. Tomorrow, she'd visit the queen. Being the child of two courts was not an easy burden.

six

LILYDARK

As Creed left Lily's room, she was still smiling. Kissing didn't fix everything; neither did his embrace. Yet, sometimes they made her feel invulnerable. It was an illusion, maybe because they were both fae-blood, maybe because they meshed so well. She didn't know. All she could say for certain was that it was a feeling she'd fight to keep now that she'd experienced it.

First though, she had to talk to her father about her new status. The Queen of Blood and Rage and the King of Fire and Truth hadn't yet announced her to the human world as their heir, but they would be doing so in the coming weeks. She had to prepare—and part of preparing was having a plan. So many humans had died during the war. Lily couldn't expect things to go smoothly for her, at least not if she were realistic. Her father was a wise man, one capable of ruling his own empire as a king of sorts, so seeking his counsel was something she should've already done.

The summons from him wasn't unexpected. Daidí might not have reached the point of embedding a tracking device in her body, but Lily was fairly sure he'd at least considered it. She'd thought him overprotective at the best of times, but now and again that veered into paranoia. After meeting her maternal grandparents, she thought she understood why.

They were intimidating even at their kindest, and Lily's mother was their missing daughter. The news was a surprise to her, but Daidí had always known. Even with a massive criminal network at his fingertips, he wouldn't have been able to withstand them if they'd come for her. No human could stand against a fae regent. Likely, very few fae could stand against her grandparents either. He had to have known that for her whole life.

Lily was sometimes grateful she hadn't known. Being the heir to the fae queen wasn't an enviable position. Although Lily had already been the heir to a criminal enterprise, this was . . . more deadly. She would be queen of the monsters, sole keeper of the Hidden Throne. Even if she took a spouse one day—which was inevitable—she'd be the one ruling. She'd be their *queen*. It wasn't a future she'd even imagined. Becoming a princess . . . it felt nothing like in the fairy tales that still existed in her world. In those make-believe stories, being a princess was a lovely thing. The stories about the *fae*, however, were altogether different sorts of tales, recounting a vengeful queen in blood-red armor, a faery mother whose loss of her daughter started a war against the world.

Lily's own story would also be a fae story, one filled with violence and lies, not with midnight dances and charming princes.

Carefully, she let her fingertips rest on the necklace that she'd been unwilling to remove since it had arrived. Even now, she preferred to think of it as a necklace, but she—and her friends—knew it for what it truly was: the crown of the heir to the Hidden Throne. At her touch and will, the stones became as ink of flesh, sinking into her skin as if they'd only ever been a tattoo. The crown was, by this very trait, nearly impossible to steal from her.

At a quick rap, Lily opened the door to her suite. She hadn't expected Hector so quickly, but he must've had someone in the area. Smiling, she yanked open the door. "That was fast."

"Excuse me?" a tall pale man in a wrongly cut suit replied.

She stared at the two strangers in the hall. Hector, her usual bodyguard, wasn't among them. Neither had the darker skin of those from the southern continent, either. Her father often used the Gaviria family's employees as escorts for her. The men at her door were strangers. They weren't an obvious part of either of her worlds, the fae one or the criminal one.

"Abernathy?" the same man who had spoken a moment

ago asked. He was presumably the leader.

Lily stared at him, trying to see who or what he was. These were not her father's men at all. Their suits weren't as fine as his top guards wore, and the accent in the speaker's voice lacked the rhythm of those who were accustomed to speaking in Spanish, as all Gaviria employees must.

A second man added, "Are you Nick Abernathy's daughter?"

The back of her neck tickled at his words. There was something in his cadence that felt familiar. She didn't quite hear the sea under those sounds, but there was enough of lilt of a wave in the air that made her meet the man's eyes. He wasn't *obviously* other, but Lily recognized him now as a fae-blood.

Since donning the crown less than a month ago, Lily had been able to tell, to feel the fae strands in people who passed as human. Sometimes, she suspected they didn't even know about their heritage, but she could tell. Without even a pause, she could look at or hear a person and simply *know* that they were of her kind. It made a certain sense that she couldn't deny. To rule a people, one had to be able to feel them, to find them and know that they belong to you. This man was one of hers.

"I have no comment," she dissembled, starting to push the door closed. As an Abernathy, talking to the police was never a good idea.

The first of the men raised his hand, stopping the door. "Lilywhite Abernathy."

Lily held her voice steady and said, "Unless you have an actual warrant for my arrest, you can go. *Now.*"

The fae-blood reached forward as if he'd grab her forearm. When his fingertips grazed her skin, he stopped. He withdrew so he was just shy of touching her, eyes widening, hand hovering over her arm.

"Attempting to arrest her would be a mistake," said a soft voice.

The men turned to watch as Alkamy strode through the hallway toward them, her tiny feet coming down hard with each step so that Lily could dance to the rhythm of her walk. Violet, who had spoken, was just behind her. For reasons Lily didn't want to guess, she was carrying a sword. She held it at her side, but it was far from subtle. The third of their group, Will, strolled up casually. He looked wet, like he'd either just stepped out of the shower or been swimming. Both were possible since his boyfriend was a water affinity.

"Hi," he said. "Officers? I'm Senator Parrish's son, William."

The fae-blood was suddenly watching Alkamy and Violet. Lily could all but hear the gears clicking. He'd felt Lily's lack of humanity in their almost-touch, and the sight of her companions gave him further pause. When his eyes dropped to the rapier that Violet held in her hand, there was no way he wasn't thinking of the Hidden Court. Fae-blood, open weapons, and now a senator's son . . . he was suddenly much more respectful.

"Parrish?" he echoed. Then, he cleared his throat and added, "And you're—"

"Violet Lamb." The flame-haired actress grinned at him as she slid closer to Lily. Her every acting skill came into play as she sounded and looked far friendlier than she undoubtedly felt. She'd moved so she stood between the presumed officers and Lily, the sword still in her hand.

At a look from Lily, Will nodded and walked away. Violet was more than defense enough against a single human and a fae-blood. Beside which, Lily was plenty adept at self-defense.

Alkamy said nothing, but she came to stand beside Lily. She was not the one who would start a conflict. That would be Violet. She was all fire. It was as much her affinity as her personality, volatile and stunning. Alkamy would draw blood only if absolutely necessary.

"I was practicing," Violet said, lifting her sword into position as if to demonstrate. "Fencing."

"We don't want trouble," the fae-blood stranger said calmly.

The other officer glanced at him incredulously, but he continued, "There are some questions we would like to ask you, Miss Abernathy, so—"

"Then you'd best talk to my *family*." Lily touched his wrist briefly, letting her fire affinity ease through her skin and warm him.

He stared at her, looking at her face more carefully.

"Nick Abernathy isn't even in the country right now,"

the oblivious first officer said. He glared at Violet. "Put that away, miss."

Violet ignored him.

"*None* of my family members are in this country," Lily said softly, her gaze fixed on the fae-blood officer. "That doesn't mean they would respond well to my being harassed. Some would be *enraged*, in fact."

The fae-blood's eyes widened as she let the air carry the word "rage" to sting his skin, trying to convey just *who* they would be crossing. There was a moment, a brief heartbeat of an instant, when she knew that he'd been to the Hidden Lands at some point. He studied her face again, and the horror of whom they would be angering filled his eyes. He swallowed visibly.

The other officer reached out, but Violet shifted her sword so the point of it was at his chest.

"Remove that," he ordered.

"You're frightening her," the fae-blood said. "She's not going to hurt you. Right, Miss Lamb?"

"Give me the word, Lily," Violet said in a low voice. Her flickers of flame weren't yet visible, but like everything else since Lily had donned the fae crown, the promise of the fire in Violet's skin was intense enough that she could feel it building. The embers grew warmer, and the crackle of burning coals seemed to resonate within her body.

"There is no threat here," Lily said levelly.

She extended her hand to touch Violet's back, pulling her friend's fire into her own body, letting the heating embers flow toward her to calm Violet.

"These men are leaving. Unless they have a valid warrant"—Lily paused and let her gaze drift over the two adult men—"there is absolutely no way I'm going anywhere."

"We have questions that need answers, Miss Abernathy. You could come with us on your own accord."

Lily shook her head. "You're welcome to risk the consequences of taking me in, but I'm not going anywhere with you by choice."

"Are you threatening us, Miss Abernathy?"

The fae-blood opened his mouth to speak, but the sound of footsteps interrupted him. Lily wasn't sure whether she was relieved or not when she noticed who it was.

Hector came toward them; he was half-grinning as he approached. His sheer size and bulk were intimidating, but that expression made Lily shake her head. Like Violet, Hector was primed for conflict, but she wouldn't be able to restrain him as easily.

She'd had no intention of going with the officers, but she'd hoped that it would be resolved without violence. Will followed Hector silently.

The human officer looked relieved. "Hector Adams. There are warrants for your arrest."

"Usually are," Hector said with a shrug. He looked at Lily again. "Call the boss? Tell him I was arrested."

She nodded.

He shucked his suit coat, unfastened his holster, and

removed it. His gun was still in the leather sheath, and Hector was carefully not letting his fingers even brush it. There was no mistaking his actions, no chance to say that he'd gone for his weapon. In truth, he was exceedingly refined in his movements. Slowly, he extended both the jacket and holster to her.

"Go inside, Lily." Hector ordered. "All of you. Keep the door closed until Raoul arrives."

Again, she nodded.

"Might as well enjoy myself," Hector pronounced. Then he proceeded to tackle the fully human guard.

Mutely, Lily led her friends inside her suite. Hector would handle the police. He'd done so more than once in his tenure with the Abernathy family. It was his job—and if she went outside, she might very well be arrested too, which would draw the ire of both Daidí *and* Endellion.

So she glanced once more at Hector and then closed the door on the brawl that was about to erupt in the corridor. She wanted to join in, to protect him, to make them admit that they had no just cause to even be there. None of that was an option, so she leaned on the closed door and waited.

seven

ZEPHYR

Zephyr wasn't accustomed to time alone the past few weeks. His world had been turned upside down. He'd discovered that his true father was the *son* of the Queen of Blood and Rage. Although Zephyr had always wanted to believe he was important in the Hidden Lands, being Rhys' son—and therefore the queen's grandson—was daunting.

Since discovering he had a son, Rhys had taken to training him. Zephyr was grateful, but longed for more time with Alkamy. Now that he'd been given leave to date Alkamy, he wanted to spend every possible moment with her. He wouldn't say he'd sold his soul for permission to be with the person he loved, but he understood that any bargain with the queen was somehow in *her* best interest.

Initially, the queen had intended that he would wed his cousin, LilyDark, but that had been set aside when Lily herself made clear that her dating life was not going to be managed by the regents of the Hidden Lands. It was her only point of negotiation that had to do with her *own* interests. Most of her concerns were for others.

As much as Zephyr was glad that he was free to be with Alkamy simply because he loved her, there was also an undeniable part of him that realized that his cousin, the future ruler of the fae and fae-bloods, was going to be a formidable woman. As a cousin, a friend, a queen he would one day serve, LilyDark Abernathy was remarkable. Dating her would have been a lifelong battle of wills, and the mere thought of it was exhausting.

So too was the life he *was* living. He'd already been skilled with swords, daggers, and guns, but apparently that skill was not enough.

"We don't have training for several hours," Zephyr said when he heard his father arrive in the walled garden. "What if I'd been here with a . . . girl or . . . busy?"

"Do you often have relations with girls in the garden?" Rhys asked the question in a tone that said he was more curious than concerned. "I'm never sure how fae your behavior is."

Zephyr shook his head. There was no way to answer that without sounding rude. Sometimes silence was the best choice. He watched his father, finding it oddly unsettling to see his own expressions and movements in another person—in a virtual stranger.

"It's been several centuries since I spent social time in

this world," Rhys continued as he unpacked a satchel of weapons. "I think the customs are different. Women were more at ease with nakedness out of doors than they seem now."

"I am not discussing this with you," Zephyr said.

His father stared at him. "It was your choice of topic."

There was a line that they sometimes neared in conversations when Zephyr couldn't tell if his fae father was joking or not. Truthfully, Zephyr wasn't sure he *wanted* to know. He'd decided to try to build a relationship of sorts with him, partly because it wasn't Rhys' fault that he was unaware he'd fathered a child.

"You dislike me," Rhys said after a moment. "I am not . . . good at familial things, but I am not without good qualities. I have killed many skilled enemies. I wrote a few books." He cleared his throat awkwardly. "Illustrations and explanations of combat tactics for humans."

Zephyr laughed suddenly, despite best intentions.

His father's answering scowl was clearly not what either of them hoped to have happen, but the way Rhys was explaining his strengths was ludicrous. He was the second most skilled fighter in the Hidden Lands. That alone was enough to make him worthy of respect. He was *also* the Unseelie prince.

Rhys stood statue-still, no longer speaking or moving.

"I know you are worthy of respect," Zephyr said carefully. "I've never had much expectation of having a fae father. We were told we were full fae, that we had families

45

who volunteered us for service to our people."

"You had no hopes as to your parents?"

Zephyr shrugged. Who didn't imagine their fantasy family? It was something that everyone had done at some point. Perhaps Zephyr hadn't had much cause to want to give up his human one, the people he'd thought of as foster parents. They doted on him, thought he was brilliant, talented, handsome. All things that made them realize that he had fae-blood. His mother, obviously, had always known. She was young and lovely, still starring in blockbuster films—more than a few either directed or produced by his father.

Zephyr never wondered if his parents were in love. He never questioned whether or not they stayed in love either. If anything, Zephyr found their mutual adoration proof of the good in a world where fairy tales were dead. So did the media who doted on their relationship, casting them as meant to be.

Growing up with them was proof that it wasn't all a lie. Zeke Waters had treated his delicate wife extra carefully when he realized Zephyr had fae-blood, assuming that his beautiful young wife must have fae-blood too. It made him treat her like she could be swept away from him at any turn, like their baby was the greatest miracle in history. Journalists remarked on how much Zeke Waters indulged his young wife and son, and it meant that no effort was too much or too expensive to protect Zephyr when his affinity blossomed.

Having even a drop of fae blood was grounds for arrest, and that bias meant there was an entire industry dedicated to hiding fae-blood, as well as mimicking it for scandal's sake. Both were a benefit to Zephyr.

"Arabella was good to you?"

Zephyr walked over and lifted a sword from those that Rhys had brought today. "Aside from lying to me my whole life, yes."

Rhys said nothing as he selected a different sword, a more beautiful one, and held it out. "*That* one is not for you."

"Why?"

"Because it is dull. This one"—he flipped it so he was holding it by the blade and extended it farther toward Zephyr—"is sharp."

Blood droplets slid along the blade, seeming to be absorbed by it. Rhys said nothing as the sword drank in his blood. He squeezed tighter, in fact, so that more blood dripped along the steel.

Zephyr wasn't so unfamiliar with the fae that he thought this was insignificant. "Does it *require* blood?"

"No. It's not hungry steel." Rhys met his eyes then, not quite speaking but nonetheless insisting that Zephyr take the sword.

Zephyr accepted the weapon then, feeling the weight of it in his whole body. This was fae-wrought steel, and something in it hummed as if it had found its way home. That wasn't reasonable for inanimate objects, at least not ones that were outside his affinity.

"It was the queen's," Rhys said. "She gave it to me when I was a child."

"It . . ." Zephyr looked from the sword to Rhys. There were really no words that were appropriate. If there were, he didn't know them.

"You are the first-born son of the Unseelie prince, Zephyr. I know that means less than—"

"No," he interrupted. "It means a lot."

"My son." Rhys seemed paternal in that instant. "You are my child, so this sword was meant to be given to you."

Zephyr felt like his throat was tight. It wasn't a familiar feeling. Sure, he got emotional sometimes about Alkamy or about his duty to the Hidden Lands, but that was it. Excess wasn't his norm.

"It drinks," Rhys added offhand, "so that if you are lost, I can find you if it's with you . . . so can she. Our blood is in the blade. Those who feed it by choice can find it. There are words you say when you nourish it. I will teach you. None other than the queen and I know the words."

"The creator of the sword?" Zephyr asked.

Rhys frowned. "Was killed upon completion of his work. Mother is very . . . thorough when it comes to protecting her family."

"Of course she is," Zephyr said lightly. Perhaps it was wrong of him to feel uncomfortable with his family's bloodied hands. He wasn't exactly innocent, but he couldn't help the shudder that he had to repress. Killing for a cause seemed different from killing as a payment for having done a *good* job.

The sword Rhys had lifted was, yet again, a dull sword, but Zephyr was well aware that most people wouldn't stand a chance against his father if he were wielding a sharp blade. This was a practice blade, one he could use when training. Doing so while Zephyr held a sharp blade was new, but there was no way Zephyr was going to suggest elsewise now that he understood that the weapon in his hands was his father's way of letting him know that he was valued.

In what Zephyr suspected was to be a casual voice, Rhys asked, "Have any of you slaughtered groups of humans lately?"

Zephyr shook his head. "I've heard about some attacks, but . . . it wasn't us."

"The queen believed it was not, but she asked that I inquire." Rhys frowned. "It is not good."

"The slaughter?" Zephyr reminded himself yet again that the fae did not speak with the same nuances that humans did.

"Going against the queen," Rhys clarified. "Her Sleepers have been culled, and your team is not behind it. The guilty are either fae or fae-blood, however, and acting in direct defiance of the queen. You will tell me if you learn anything of use . . . and be cautious."

At that, Zephyr realized that some of his father's

vigorous training was a result of fear. The tone in his voice was one Zephyr had heard from his mother and stepfather often enough. It was enough to make him smile. "I will. You have my word."

Rhys nodded once.

"Shall we?" Zephyr asked, hefting his sword into a high guard position.

Rhys said nothing, merely swung at him, and Zephyr couldn't help but smile again. It wasn't the way most people expressed their affection, but expecting his fae family to behave like humans would only disappoint everyone involved. His fae father was making him better able to stay alive. It was, all considered, exactly what good parents did all the time, only in slightly different ways.

eight

LILYDARK

When Lily heard the roar that came out of Hector, her instinct was to jerk the door open and lash out, despite her common sense telling her that action was unwise. He was *hers*. Her duty was to those under her protection, and while he was a guard, he was still *her* guard. And whether she liked it or not, the instinctual need to protect her own had intensified with the acceptance of the heir's crown. It was changing her, making her more driven by instinct than by the rational rule-based approach she'd learned as the daughter of Nicolas Abernathy.

Her hand was on the door when Violet blocked her way. "Let him do his job, LilyDark."

Lily stared at her.

"He is human, and the guards are arresting him because of Abernathy business," Violet said levelly.

Hector's arrival should have heralded an end to the trouble, but instead, the police arrested him. It wasn't the absolute worst thing that could've happened, but when the sounds of violence quieted, Lily's temper was still heightened. She paced farther from the door, partly to avoid the temptation to push past Violet and open it.

"Do you think this is about the attacks?" Violet asked.

Alkamy startled. She curled up on the sofa, seeming more fragile than usual. She didn't reply.

"Maybe," Will murmured. He stood at the open window of the suite's common room with his face tilted to the sky, as if the air were flowing to him. It could be, for all she knew. Will was sometimes difficult to read. They shared an affinity, but that didn't make him any more comprehensible to her. The nature of Lily's multiple affinities was that she shared one with every member of the group.

"It was none of us," Lily said. She knew they all had secrets, but this was more than a secret. Someone was killing people in ways that were obviously patterned on the attacks of the Black Diamonds.

"It was not," Will agreed.

"It's about your father," Violet said. "They said *his* name. They don't know about . . ."

Lily shook her head. "They won't until the queen outs me. When that happens, people will think we are guilty."

"We are," Will said quietly. "Maybe not for *these* atrocities, but we've done plenty."

Sparks glittered around Violet. "Not by choice!"

"Vi," Alkamy said softly. There was nothing more, only Violet's name, but it was enough to make the sparks lessen.

Will shrugged. "They are still as dead as the people dying now."

Violet's sparks flashed brighter, as if she couldn't contain all of her fire. That happened more and more lately. No one discussed it, but Lily was certain they'd all noticed.

Before the guilt in Will's voice or the anger in Violet's could lead to more troubles, Lily held up her hands. "This is not helping."

The usually at-peace friends were staring at one another, but they held their silence. Alkamy watched them, but she remained quiet.

Lily grabbed the phone and called her father. "Hector was arrested," she said as soon as Daidí picked up. "The police were here when he showed up and—"

"I'll handle it." Daidí sounded weary, but he didn't volunteer anything. Phone lines were never truly secure. "Stay at the school unless your . . . mother's family sends for you."

"I thought I was coming home to you."

"If Hector was taken and they're already bothering you, it's best for you to stay there. You know not to go with them." Daidí sounded increasingly agitated. "You've done nothing illegal, Lily. I'll have the lawyers handle this disturbance . . . once I wake them. It's too early in the day for so much trouble."

There was something in his voice that made her more afraid than she liked. The forced lightness was underlined with fear. She recognized it from the years of overprotectiveness, but it was worse than normal. She started, "If the police come, I have no choice but—"

"Yes, you do. There is *nothing* you should refuse to do if it keeps you out of their hands. *She* would not take well to your imprisonment, LilyDark. You must understand . . . She's accepting a new plan, but she's not without temper."

Lily laughed, despite the seriousness of everything. There were understatements, and then there was *that*. The Queen of Blood and Rage had spent so much time attacking humanity, the stories that were told in the dark of night claimed that the queen's now-dark hair had once been as white as new snow. They said that its black-red color had come from the blood of her victims.

Lily wasn't sure that she believed that her grandmother had blood-darkened hair, but the point was the same: Endellion was not to be angered.

"You know where to go if you need sanctuary," Daidí added. "Keep your singer near, too, if you're not going to allow Erik to come protect you."

"Are *you* safe?" Lily asked. It had been just the two of them for most of her life, and there was no ceiling on what she was willing to do to protect her father. "If you need me to come there, I can—"

"I am safe, and there is no way I will go *there* if at all possible. I kept your mother from her family. That's how they'll see it. It's not the whole truth, of course. Your mother chose this life, Lily."

"I believe you," she assured him.

After they exchanged words of affection and finished their conversation, Lily was left with her friends, who were watching her as if in anticipation of orders. There wasn't a manual on dealing with this sort of thing, juggling the risks of being an Abernathy on one side but still not doing anything to upset a woman whose very name was one of violence. All Lily had expected to find when she started school at St. Columba's was the awkwardness of trying to figure out how to have classes and live around strangers.

"Classes," she said. "Breakfast and then classes."

Alkamy finally stirred from her silence. "Is it a good idea? We could skip."

Violet rolled her eyes. "There are guards outside right now—fae and human. They stand in shadows, and they patrol the gardens, and . . . I see them. I *feel* them, Kam. They might not have stopped the police from entering the school, but there's no way they'll let anyone take Lily."

"She has a point about the guards," Will said mildly.

Alkamy looked at Lily. "Did you notice them?"

"They're careful, but yeah. I can sense that they're out there too," Lily said.

Alkamy looked down guiltily.

"I'm going to breakfast. The rest of you can come or not." Lily shrugged. They had food in the room, but she wanted to act like things were normal for at least a little while longer.

"Your dad's okay though?" Violet asked.

Lily flashed her a grateful smile. "He is."

"Things will get better," Alkamy said. "Peace is coming, and then . . . it'll be better."

Lily walked to the door and pulled it open, grateful that there were no armed men lurking to try to arrest her. She wasn't sure what would've happened to them if they had. Now that she thought about the nearby fae guards, Lily was grateful that the worst that would happen today was Hector's arrest.

nine

CREED

The following day, Creed watched the rest of the diamonds move through the school as if they expected violence at every turn. Violet, in particular, struggled with the twin desires to stay at Lily's side and to go with Will and Roan, who were more on edge than the rest.

"Are they fighting?" he whispered to Violet.

She shook her head slightly.

"Trouble with Will's mom?" He wasn't a huge fan of the senator. Will seemed okay with her overprotectiveness, but most of them had parents who were either absent or indulgent. The senator was both and neither at the same time.

Violet paused, looking at Will the way she'd typically study one of her forging projects. It wasn't the first time Creed had seen her gaze at one of them that way. Metal and fire she could understand. Others' emotions, less so.

Will, however, was rarely a puzzle to her. They seemed as close as siblings.

"He's keeping secrets," she said. "I'm not sure what . . . but there's something."

"Do you think he's the one who—"

"Killed people?"

"It wouldn't be the first time," Creed pointed out gently. They'd all done horrible things; pretending otherwise was foolish.

Violet looked like she wanted to argue but couldn't.

He let it drop.

They were finished with classes by early afternoon, and the weight of things unsaid was leading to short tempers and sharp words.

Zephyr asked, "Who wants to practice in the garden?"

"Vi and I can meet you there," Creed offered.

"I'm in," Will said at the same time.

"Pass," Alkamy said. "I just want to take a nap."

The confusion on Zephyr's face was priceless. He'd attached himself to Alkamy so tightly that, by comparison, it made Creed look like he ignored Lily. The only question was whether someone would take mercy on Zephyr or if he'd have to be the one to suggest that Alkamy needed supervision to walk to her suite.

"I need to grab a sword," Lily said after a moment of watching Zephyr struggle. "Why don't we walk Kam up to the suite, and then I can come with you to the garden?"

Zephyr looked back at Creed and Violet. "We'll meet you at the garden in twenty."

For the first time in hours, Violet didn't snap or sound tense. She simply said, "Got it."

And that was the strange beauty of how they worked: even when things were off, they were still able to function as a unit. No one needed to say that it was unwise to be alone and unguarded. No one needed to argue that they could look after themselves. They worked because they cared.

Creed kissed Lily quickly, and then he and Violet went to the garden.

Once they were alone, Violet asked, "If the fae attacks keep up, do we have a plan? She hasn't mentioned anything to me, but I thought she might've told you something."

He wished he could say that Lily had a plan, or that he thought that they were in the clear, but the truth was that the violence seemed to be getting worse. Two apartment buildings had been burnt to the ground in the sort of infernos that were impossible to stop. There were fae-bloods who might be able to do that, but Creed was starting to think that a full-blooded faery was more likely to be the culprit.

"Lily's not heard anything. I'm just hoping that things won't get worse."

"Hope isn't usually a great plan." Violet scaled the wall as they had on more than a few occasions on their own. It was easier with Zephyr or Lily there to part the vines, and of course, they could go *around* some of the obstacles, but Violet wasn't one for patience.

Creed shrugged and followed her. "It's not like our planning matters. The queen does what she wants. We're pawns. Even Lily. We're all disposable."

They landed in the center of the walled garden that had been their sanctuary at St. Columba's for years. There was a comfort to it, a sense that they were safe here. Creed was about to say as much when Violet kicked his knees out and sent him face-forward, tumbling to the dirt.

He tried to push up to his feet, but she shoved him back down.

Creed rolled over. "What in Ninian's name is your . . ."

Violet had a short sword out. He wasn't sure how she'd hidden it. It wasn't a proper length sword, but it was longer than a dagger.

The clash of steel on steel was loud enough to make him realize that the fae-blood boy trying to slice her was as angry as Violet.

"Stay out of the way," she snapped at him.

Creed snorted. He loved his friends, and he knew that her protectiveness was the way Violet said she cared. "I'm not useless. I could help . . ."

"Busy right now," she muttered as she dodged.

He let her fight. The boy wasn't obviously fae-blood, but Creed assumed he must be. He didn't have the uncanny beauty of the full fae, and he was too quick to be human.

There wasn't much likelihood that he'd trained in the

Hidden Lands. He was a more than adequate swordsman, but he had an arrogance that said he'd never crossed blades with the fae. Creed had been stabbed by one of them. He'd realized his own limitations after that.

Violet didn't have as many limitations though. There was a ferocity to her that he didn't see in any of the other diamonds. She was holding her own even though she was at a disadvantage with her too-short blade.

All they needed was to buy themselves another ten to fifteen minutes, and then Lily and Zephyr would arrive. He was sure Violet knew that, but he was also sure that unless she used her affinity, there was a good chance she'd get injured in the process. The fae-blood was lunging as if he was trying to do more than wound.

Unfortunately, Violet's affinity was fire, which was a bit of overkill. That left Creed to use his. An affinity to air was more versatile. Cautiously, Creed shoved a breeze toward the fae-blood, testing to see what his affinity was.

The boy grinned and ignited the air, using the gust as fuel for flash fire that he pushed toward Violet.

"Oh no," Violet said in a faux alarmed voice. "Fire . . . Whatever shall we do?"

The sudden blast of flame made Creed wince.

For a moment, the fae-blood didn't seem to realize that he was in danger. He looked at her and lifted his sword. There was little chance Violet would be able to avoid both the sword and the fire, but Violet didn't need to do that. If Creed was right, she'd learned something far more dangerous than sword fighting in the Hidden Lands.

She stepped into the fire and knocked the fae-blood aside.

For a flicker of a moment, the fae-blood thought he'd won. Creed saw it. There was a smile that said he'd defeated Violet, and he'd already decided that Creed was not a threat.

Then Violet started drawing the fire into her, pulling it out of the fae-blood until he was wide-eyed with pain. Creed saw it, watched the realization come, knew that what Violet was doing hurt. She was alight as if she was burning.

The sword fell from the fae-blood's hand, and Creed lunged forward to grab it. He shoved air at it, hoping to not burn himself too badly. Then he grabbed it, shoved it deep, and twisted.

It was hasty and crude, but it was quick. The thrust killed the intruder quickly, but the smell of burnt flesh lingered.

Violet was still drawing fire to her even as the fae-blood fell. She stared at him and inhaled.

Creed stumbled to her. "Let go."

"I . . ."

"Let. Go." Creed forced back the pain. It wasn't the worst he'd felt, or even the worst he'd felt recently. Being stabbed was far more painful. "Violet Lamb!"

He debated striking her, breaking her attention, but as

he reached toward her, she shuddered and exhaled.

A roar of fire rushed away from her, and the flames she'd stolen seemed to vanish.

He was dead. He'd come there and tried to kill them, and now he was dead. The reason didn't change the fact that every death was a loss, and briefly Creed wished him peace.

"Are you okay?" he asked Violet.

"Not yet." She dropped to her knees and was still there when Lily and Zephyr came into the garden.

"Vi? Creed!" Lily drew her sword, as did Zephyr. "Are you okay?"

"I am good enough." Violet was shaking. "Creed's hand . . ."

"Hurt. Not fatal." Creed was trying to decide whether the touch of soil was helping or hindering healing. Typically, the earth would help, but just then, Creed wasn't sure much other than time would alleviate the pain of his burns.

Zephyr's gaze glanced off the dead boy and was scanning the area. "Are there others?"

"Don't think so."

Zephyr kept his sword in hand, but Creed felt the rush as water surged through the earth to cool his hand. He met Zephyr's gaze and smiled gratefully. He wanted to say something, but he wasn't sure he could do so without vomiting from pain.

"What happened?" Lily asked. "Who was that?"

Violet looked at Lily and then at Zephyr. "I don't know who he is. He attacked us when we got here. We fought. He lost."

VIOLET

After the situation in the garden, Violet had spent the majority of the day feeling like there were threats at every corner. By evening, she was pretty sure Lily was going to either hit her and Creed or wrap them in gauze and shove them somewhere for safekeeping.

Zephyr had summoned his father, who removed the body with the terse pronouncement, "This is not pleasing."

Creed's hands were treated and bandaged, and Lily was fussing over him despite his repeated insistence that he was going to be fine. Violet felt charged, though, and guiltily she almost wished there *would* be another attack. She had released the fae-blood's fire, but felt a residual hum inside her.

There was a moment during the fight when she knew that if her affinity were anything else, he would've killed her. Using fire against her meant that he intended grievous harm. She had seen the surprise in his expression when it was clear that she was aligned with fire too. He hadn't counted on that.

If it had been any one of the others they would've been defeated. Roan had water, which was of some use, but Creed was air. Alkamy was earth. Neither of them were great at repelling fire, despite the times she'd practiced with them.

Without affinities, they weren't significantly better fighters than the boy had been. Lily was a better sword-fighter than most of them. Zephyr was better still. Violet was good enough to hold her own in the fight—and like those two, she was comfortable with violence. She was willing to die if necessary, but if at all possible, she was taking her attacker with her. She'd thought that earlier in the garden. If she had to die today, she would.

As they walked into the bar that night, she was still rattled by the fight and the residual fire under her skin. Lily and Zephyr steered the group toward the VIP room, but Violet slowed.

"We can order back there," Roan said, as if it was her first time in the Row House instead of her who-knows-how-many times. She couldn't even begin to count the nights they'd spent here already. It wasn't about drinking. It wasn't even about being seen, not for her. She liked the vibrancy of it.

"Go on," she said to him and Will both.

"Vi . . . ," Roan started.

Will touched his arm and met her gaze. Whatever secret he had was making him more protective of Roan. The two boys weren't fighting. They both knew whatever Roan was concealing.

"I know you're hiding something," she said baldly.

"And you aren't?" Will challenged. He always seemed so mild, played up the faux conservatism, but he was one of the strongest personalities in the group. His lighthearted demeanor was a mask.

Violet shook her head. "We're all keeping secrets."

Roan looked between them, seeming more torn by the moment. "Will . . ."

Will shook his head, and Roan looked down to hide what she knew was frustration. Whatever they were hiding, it was important enough to keep it from her. That didn't bode well.

"Are you in danger?"

"No more than usual," Will said cautiously. "You?"

"Same," she admitted. The danger for her was internal, but it wasn't new. She had always been her own worst enemy.

"Anything to do with the things on the news?" Roan asked.

Both of them looked at him suddenly.

"Valid question," he said.

"No," Violet swore. "You?"

Will shook his head, as did Roan.

They stood there for a moment, and Violet wished everything was easier. Their togetherness had felt fractured lately. Maybe the cracks had always been there, and none of them had noticed.

"I need space," she admitted. "The thing earlier . . ."

"It wasn't your fault," Roan assured her.

She nodded. Maybe it wasn't. She'd defended herself and Creed too. That didn't change the fact that she'd reached out and snagged the fae-blood's affinity with her own and jerked it from his body. If Creed hadn't stabbed him, what Violet was doing *would* have killed him . . . slowly and painfully. Being that out of control made her feel afraid. Killing someone by yanking their affinity from them was a horrible thing, and she hadn't been able to stop that impulse.

"We'll be over there," Roan said, pointing to the dance floor.

She knew they wouldn't dance together the way they did in private. For reasons she didn't get, they were both very conscientious about Will's mother's reputation. The attempt to hide Will's heritage had been more fierce for Senator Parrish than the rest of their families—not that *any* of them would be able to hide it anyhow after Lily's coronation.

"You could come too," Will said.

Violet nodded again. She could. Typically, she would. Dancing always made them feel better. Just then, however, she needed to be alone.

"Soon," she said. It was the best offer she had, and it was true as well.

They walked away into the crowd, and Violet watched. She let the music roll over her, but didn't move with it.

The fae had always been drawn to music, so much so that a few conservative politicians had argued for blood tests of dancers and singers about five years ago. History said that there had been balls nearly constantly when the fae were still living among humanity.

It made a certain sense though. Nature was their *source*, their requirement for living, and creativity flowed from nature. At least that was Violet's theory. Every last one of the diamonds was drawn to music and the arts. Alkamy and Creed were far from the only fae-blood singers, and she knew she wasn't the only fae-blood actress. Roan was all about surfing and snowboarding, which were arts of their own. In truth, Lily was peculiar in that she didn't embrace an art, but the way she enjoyed dancing made Violet suspect that she *would* have if she hadn't been raised to be a crime lord.

Violet stayed in the main room at the bar, glaring at anyone who looked like they might talk to her and watching Will and Roan dance with stranger after stranger. No one spoke to her. She'd been in this sort of dark mood often enough that her friends knew not to bother her when she was.

"Are you sulking?" asked a low voice near her ear.

Her hand went up as she spun to face the speaker. The fire inside her skin pulsed. When she saw Erik Gaviria there, she retracted the fire but was tempted to follow through with a slap for her own enjoyment.

Erik towered over her, and she tried not to admit to even herself that he looked good. He wasn't pretty in the way that fae or fae-blood were. There was a massiveness to him, a darkness that spoke of metal and bullets. He smelled like gunpowder. She preferred blades—or her fire—for any necessary violence.

"I thought LilyDark sent you packing," Violet said, lifting her voice slightly to be heard over the music.

Amusingly, they were playing one of Creed's songs. She wasn't sure if it was a coincidence.

Erik leaned down toward her instead of speaking louder and said, "Lily doesn't have the authority to send me packing. She's my friend, not *my boss*."

"She's a good boss," Violet replied with a shrug. She couldn't lie, but she could joke and Erik's appearance made her oddly lighthearted. "Gives out potted plants on National Lackey Day, and she doesn't mind my temper."

He peered at her curiously for several breaths before saying, almost casually, "When I realized Lily was what she is, I started paying attention to what she did and didn't say . . . and how she attempted to mislead people. It's a good strategy for those unable to lie outright."

Violet said nothing. Even now, there was no way she was admitting anything. Erik knew, no doubt, that she was fae-blood, but she still wasn't admitting her heritage aloud.

"Lily's beautiful too." Erik didn't move back at all, even as the crowd pushed in closer. He had his back to the room, and one arm on the bar behind her. It looked like he was protecting her, but it didn't feel that way to her.

"A lot of people are beautiful," Violet said, pushing away a tinge of jealousy and resisting the urge to duck under his arm and walk away.

"Including you."

Violet shrugged. "I'm an actress. It comes with the job."

"So are you saying that the group of you being as beautiful as Lily is merely a coincidence?"

Violet wished lying didn't hurt. She'd wished the same on numerous occasions. Life was easier with even the little fibs that people used so carelessly. For a fae or fae-blood, that wasn't an option—not without some degree of pain.

"I see no need to discuss this," she said, a snarl creeping into her voice.

"So . . . what are you drinking, Miss Lamb? I'll buy you another." He grinned at her and motioned the bartender over.

"Water."

"No alcohol? No soda?" Erik prompted from behind her. "Another coincidence?"

"Oh, piss off."

He laughed, ordered a beer for himself and water for her. When the bartender walked away, Erik closed the small distance so he was all but touching her.

"Mind yourself," Violet hissed. "I'm not someone you want to cross."

"So you're admitting that you're scarier than the girls I know," he said quietly, not retreating but still not physically touching her. "That you're someone to fear."

Violet looked over her shoulder at him. "Read the tabloids."

His voice became so low that there was no risk of being overheard. "I got over my fear of the fae when I learned that my best friend was one."

Without hesitating to think if it was a bad idea or not, Violet jabbed her elbow into his chest.

"Your temper is as bad as my *abuela*'s," Erik said wonderingly.

She snorted. "No wonder you're single. You're an idiot."

He grinned again. "Not really. I'm just very, very particular. I need someone who's not intimidated by me, someone graceful and lethal. All the things my *abuela* said my wife would be. Someone who makes me feel a . . . spark?"

Violet scowled at him. The temptation to show him a proper spark burned in the palms of her hands, but the thought of exposing her affinity over a bit of a mood was sobering. She was too hot-tempered to let people get close to her as a rule.

She glimpsed Will and Roan headed toward her. She shook her head. She could handle herself.

"You have all of those traits," Erik said blandly, and then he stepped back and turned to face her friends.

"What?" she asked in confusion.

He glanced over his shoulder at her. "You. You're perfect."

"*Excuse* me?"

"You, Violet Lamb, are perfect."

Violet frowned. There was something unsettling in his words, a vague awareness that she was missing something. It wasn't the admiration. Plenty of people had extolled her beauty or offered flattering words. It was simply a result of her job, or maybe her ancestry. Praise wasn't rare, but it didn't make her tense like Erik's words did.

"What are you doing?" Will asked as he and Roan reached the bar.

"I was talking to Miss Lamb." Erik motioned toward her.

"And?" Roan prompted.

"No 'and.'" Erik smiled as if they were all old friends, and Violet realized that there would undoubtedly be pictures. People knew who *she* was, and Erik was photogenic enough to end up in photos even *before* people put together that he was the eldest son of one of the most ruthless criminals in the world. In truth, it was just as likely that there were pictures being snapped because of *him* as because of *her*.

Violet snagged Will's arm and started toward the VIP section. It would cause chaos if the senator's son was photographed with a renowned drug dealer's son. By the time she'd gone three steps, Erik was at her other side like a bodyguard. It was impossible for her to pretend he wasn't with her *and* Will.

"I may kill him," she muttered. "Move away, Will. Your mother would have kittens if she had to explain why her son was seen with a thug."

Will gave her a curious look, but he stepped back.

They were halfway across the main room when Erik actually raised his arm, palm out, to stop someone from getting close to her.

"I don't need help," she said.

Erik shrugged, but he didn't give her any space. Instead, he reached for her arm.

The temper she struggled to contain in her best of moods escaped, and with it, a brief surge of heat shimmered just under her skin. It wasn't enough to send him in search of medical attention, but he flinched.

"Perfect," he repeated yet again. He smiled.

She blinked at the sheer perverseness of it, and then she shook her head. "No. Definitely not."

Erik continued to smile, as if he knew things she didn't.

Violet walked a little faster. It wasn't as if she'd been dateless her whole life, but she carefully chose who, and when, and why she allowed anyone close. A simple sharp word made most men cower and run. It didn't make them *smile*. Ever.

She glanced up at him, and he met her eyes without

hesitation. There were a thousand words she could use to explain why he needed to go away, but the look on his face made all of them escape. It also made her walk a little faster, not running per se, just walking toward the comfort of her friends and the ability to be done with the feel of his hand on her skin.

eleven

LILYDARK

Seeing Erik walk into the VIP section with Violet, Will, and Roan was far from expected. Violet looked like she was two seconds from slugging Erik. The boys didn't seem much calmer. To add icing to this particular mess, Creed grumbled, "What's *he* doing here?"

Lily sighed. He was allowed to be in a mood with as much pain as he was in. She was grateful he wasn't pouring liquor down his throat to numb it. "Hush," she told him.

Then she met Erik's eyes and asked, "Is there trouble at home? Or with Hector?"

"No. This is purely a social call," he said, sitting down on the empty loveseat. He glanced at Violet and then at the space beside him.

Violet made a rude gesture and shoved Roan toward a chair. He managed to look graceful as he half-fell in the chair, but he looked stunned a moment later when Violet perched on his lap and scowled at Erik. Lily couldn't help thinking she seemed more like a dainty bird of prey than anyone's girlfriend.

Will sat on the loveseat next to Erik. "You shouldn't upset Vi," he pronounced. "Especially tonight."

"What did you do to Violet?" Lily asked.

"I called her perfect," Erik said calmly. "Graceful." He glanced at her and prompted, "And what else?"

Violet glared.

"That's right," he said, as if she had replied instead of scowling at him. "Not intimidated by me. Maybe I was wrong about that one."

"Fuck. You." Violet smiled sweetly and then twisted so she wasn't facing him.

Lily sighed again. "Erik? Stop trying to provoke Vi, and tell me why you're here."

"Visiting my closest friend. Getting to know her schoolmates." Erik leaned back and looked around at everyone. It seemed like he watched Roan and Will, and Lily hoped that Violet putting the boys between her and Erik wasn't going to lead to trouble.

"He's sort of darling, isn't he?" Alkamy's pronouncement drew mixed reactions. Violet glared. Creed scowled. Roan looked at her like she'd begun speaking a dead

77

language, but Alkamy continued, "He strolls in here, knowing what we are . . ."

Alkamy paused and looked at him expectantly.

Erik nodded. "You're all just like Lily. Once you know the tells, you know."

"So he's got a *reason* for being here, and it's not unrequited love." Again Alkamy looked at Erik, as if she were granting him permission to speak.

Erik, however, looked at Lily. "You're my best friend, but it wasn't ever about romance."

"I know," she said, squeezing Creed's hand reassuringly. "So why are you *really* here?"

Erik shook his head. "I know what's going to happen. The coronation. I heard from Nick." The way he looked at her was as chastising as his father had done in years past, and it made her want to laugh despite the seriousness of his words as he added, "You can't honestly think that after all these years I'm going to let you walk into the public eye without being here to back you."

Lily gaped at him. In her mind, she'd kept fae and human concerns so divided that she hadn't even considered intertwining them. To deal with the fae, she had the other diamonds. If there were trouble with the Abernathy holdings, she'd go to Erik. The worlds were divided. It was tidy.

"You *did* think that," Erik said. "Why would you . . . *querida!* You wound me."

"You have your father's business to consider and—"

"And I have other brothers who could stand to learn about the business instead of assuming it is only my job to know how things work." Erik met her gaze. "My father and I discussed it. We stand by the Abernathy family. It would've been easier to protect you as my wife . . ."

"Not happening," Creed interjected with a little gust of air that pushed Erik backward.

"Obviously," Erik said mildly before continuing, "but I'm not turning my back on *you* any more than my father would turn *his* back on Nick. Gaviria and Abernathy. Our partnership continues, as does our friendship."

Lily felt almost tearful at what Erik was saying. He was offering her the same support her father had always had from the Gaviria cartel, the support she'd expected to lose when she rejected Erik's offer of marriage. She was grateful, but the kind of trouble before her as the heir of the Hidden Throne made his offer unrealistic.

"They . . . *we* aren't like you. You know about"—she lowered her voice until it was barely above a whisper—"affinities. Don't you?"

Erik gave her a familiar look of irritation. "I'm not stupid, Lily. I'm also aware that there is another concern you'll need to address. The *police* and the law. I've spent more hours than I can count studying that, making connections, gathering material for applying pressure. I come with my father's full arsenal at hand. We were prepared for this. Even though I wasn't aware of *who* exactly you were to them, I have always known your secret."

"Oh."

"With the rash of attacks, perhaps I can be of use here. Plus . . ." Erik then glanced at Violet, who was no longer refusing to look his way. "I am newly single."

For a moment, no one spoke. Provoking Violet so publicly was never wise. She was already in a temper after the attack earlier. Lily suspected that some of it was guilt. If Violet could've, she'd have been the one to handle it all on her own, but Creed had done so. He'd struck the final blow.

"You're as subtle as a fart," Violet pronounced. "And just as appealing."

Erik stared at Violet. "All fire and darkness."

Lily winced at what he was implying. Erik had told her years ago, one rare night when he'd been drinking, that his grandmother—a self-professed *bruja*—had prophesied his future wife. He'd confessed that he tried to date girls who matched her description, but he thought most of them as appealing as chewing glass might be.

Violet stood and snatched Roan's hand. She held her other hand out to Will. Without saying a word to anyone, the three of them left for the dance floor.

Alkamy all but slithered to her feet and said, "I've heard that formal dances are quite the thing at underworld parties."

"They are how we lie to ourselves about our civility." Erik shrugged. "Dress in tailored clothes. Parade around the ballrooms. We can pretend not to have a darker side."

"Excellent. Our sort does much the same. Let's parade then." Alkamy offered her hand to him imperiously.

He looked in the direction Violet had gone. "Refinement won't work with her, will it?"

At that, Zephyr finally spoke up. "No, but fortunately for you, Alkamy is as restrained as a hammer. Vi knows it. That's why she walked away."

"I love her like a sister, and she needs a distraction tonight," Alkamy said, tone growing sharp until Zephyr smiled at her.

Once they were gone, Zephyr looked at them and said, "My, umm, my *father* doesn't know who that was earlier or why they tracked us down or how." He met Lily's gaze. "Neither does our grandmother."

He said the word so easily, so comfortably. Lily almost envied his ease. These were her friends, but at times she still felt distant from them. They'd all been raised with the knowledge that the Queen of Blood and Rage knew them and would use them as she saw fit. They'd had loyalty to the Hidden Lands trained in them since childhood.

And even though she suspected all but Creed of keeping secrets of some sort, she knew that they were loyal to her now too. A boy died today—at Creed's hand. Fae or fae-bloods were attacking humans at an ever-increasing rate. Her father was on his way to see her. The police had been at her door, and Hector was arrested. This didn't feel like the peace she'd bartered for, and Lily wasn't sure what to do about any of it.

twelve

WILL

"You need to let Vi dance with Roan," Will told Alkamy when she cut in on his dance with Violet.

"But Erik seems good for her and—"

"He's here because I called him. I need to talk to him in private. I would've done it elsewhere, but after today . . ." He didn't need to specify that Lily's anxiety about the attack at St. Columba's made the idea of them all being apart untenable.

As he'd been speaking, Alkamy's face shifted into the sort of mask they'd all perfected. "Work?"

Will nodded, knowing she would assume he meant that he was acting on the queen's orders. It wasn't a true lie, simply a misdirection. Rather than explain anything, he said, "When Vi shoves him away, let her and Roan go.

Follow them. Steer them to the VIP room. Say whatever you need to keep her there."

A part of him hated lying to Alkamy, but he was counting on her sense of duty. Her loyalty was to Zephyr. First. Foremost. Always. That meant that she would follow his lead, and right now, Zephyr was sworn to the Queen of Blood and Rage. That meant Alkamy was, by extension, also loyal to the Unseelie Queen.

Will wouldn't go so far as to think that the *princess* was disloyal to the queen, but like everyone else, she had an agenda. He didn't want to know what it was, and he didn't care enough about Erik to feel regret for his actions. His priority had been finding a way to survive the price he had to pay for being born fae-blood—and protecting those he thought of as family. Erik wasn't family.

He waited while Erik and Violet danced. She was in a temper, so he doubted it would take long for her to jerk away from Erik. If it lasted much past the next song, Roan would cut in. Will looked up, unerringly finding his partner who was dancing with a random stranger nearby.

By the time the next song—one of Alkamy's—was only a few bars in, Violet's temper snapped.

"Dancing with you doesn't mean you can *touch* me!" Violet stepped away from Erik.

"How do propose we dance without touching?" Erik's voice was loud enough to be overheard by several people nearby.

Will glared at them, as did Alkamy, and they started

giving their small group more room. The girl who had been dancing with Roan stood there, obviously hoping she'd be asked to stay. Will couldn't blame her; Roan was easy to find fascinating. He said something to her that made her smile before going. Once she was gone, though, he shot Will an accusing look. It was Will's fault that Roan had to flirt with girls, and more than a few times, he'd pointed out to Will that doing so meant that, in essence, his love for Will meant he was left acting like an ass, flirting with no intention of following up. It was increasingly a point of contention for them, and Will knew that he'd have to choose to risk the damage coming out would do to his mother's career or lose Roan.

Right now, though, the more pressing issue was Violet. She had her hands on her hips. It was one of her tricks to keep from reaching out and burning someone.

Violet snapped, "You were . . . thinking about touching me."

"Thinking about it?" Erik echoed. "Really?"

"Don't pretend you weren't!" Her hand lowered from her hip, and Will knew there was likely a blade of some sort hidden on her. She was always armed more than any of the other diamonds—even though her affinity was the most dangerous weapon she could wield.

Roan was already there, wrapping an arm around Violet's waist, stopping her from temper. It had seemed worse since her trip to the Hidden Lands, as if whatever extra fire she'd channeled there still lingered. Today's events only added to that problem.

"Erik," Will said. He stepped between them, his back to Violet. For all of her temper, Violet wouldn't hurt him. He knew that with a certainty that he couldn't say he felt about most people.

Roan stepped in and steered Violet away. Alkamy trailed them quietly. It wasn't much different from the way she'd sulked in public over the years, so it was doubtful that Violet would question it.

Once they were far enough away, Will said, "I have questions."

"I came when you called," Erik said. "If Lily trusts you, I'm guessing you're . . ."

He didn't speak the word, but Will didn't need to hear it for them to both know what it was. He nodded once and said, "We're family of a sort."

Erik grinned. "We are too. A very different sort though. My father's family and hers . . ." He shrugged. "Is there a threat from *that* side of her family?"

"That's a good question." Will steered Erik closer to the wall, not the corner. Corners gave privacy, but they also made it easier to end up trapped.

"There were fires in the south," Erik said quietly. "Not natural."

"I didn't see that in the news."

"True," Erik agreed. "For some reason, it was not covered."

Will scanned the crowd as they spoke, realizing that

Erik was doing the same. Honestly, except for being human, he wasn't that different from the diamonds. He watched his surroundings the same way, and he worked around the law to do what he needed to do.

"Were they targeting Lily's father?"

Erik stared at Will for a long moment before saying, "You ask a lot of questions."

Will wasn't in the mood for subtlety, not right now. "I've been *ordered* to do so. I need to know anything you can find out about the attacks."

Still, Erik said nothing.

"You know the police were here today?" Will prompted.

Erik nodded.

After one more look around to be sure that no one was listening, Will added, "And that there was an ambush from a fae-blood on campus?"

"That, I did not know." Erik looked toward the VIP area. "She seems fine."

"*Vi* and Creed handled it before Lily arrived."

Erik met Will's gaze. "And?"

"They *handled* it."

This time, there was no mistaking the approval in Erik's expression or voice as he said, "She is remarkable."

Will opened his mouth to press for the information he needed, but the sudden scent of fire made him pause. He stepped forward and looked around. No one else was reacting, but Will's affinity was air. He could smell things before humans would, and *that* smell was one he was very used to.

"What?" Erik followed him.

"Get out of the building," Will ordered. "Get people out however you can."

"What's going on?"

Will stopped and said, "You want to help? Sometimes that means *following* orders. Get out. Get them"—he pointed around the dance floor—"out."

Erik looked like he wanted to argue, but instead, he walked away. Will wasn't sure what he intended to do, but it didn't matter. His first priority was the rest of the diamonds. He shoved through the dance floor with a rudeness that he didn't typically exhibit, but emergencies weren't a time to be polite.

As he went, he said, "There's about to be trouble. Get out."

A few people listened, but most didn't. He wasn't a celebrity darling like Creed, Violet, or Zephyr. He was a guy who was with them. He'd worked hard not to be memorable. He wore things that hid his physique and intentionally slouched. He even wore a pair of the ugliest glasses he could find. That had been his mother's strategy for his whole life—downplay his fae beauty—and he stuck with it. Unfortunately, right now that meant people weren't paying attention when he really needed them to listen.

"Get out of the building," he said to a group of girls as he pushed through them.

At the VIP barricade, Will stopped long enough to say, "I think something's going on. Maybe it was a cigarette . . . or something . . . but there's smoke on the dance floor."

Will knew it wasn't cigarette smoke, but whoever set this fire was working with someone who could steer air away from those sensitive alarms. That meant that there were fae-bloods about, and with the attack earlier today, he had no doubt that they were connected. Someone knew that the Black Diamonds were here, and more concerning, someone meant them harm.

Once he was in the room, he solidified the air around them, slowing the molecules so it was like a shield, and said, "Fire."

thirteen

ZEPHYR

Zephyr took a quick look at the group. The only one missing was Erik, but he wasn't one of *theirs*. His well-being wasn't a top priority.

"Where's Erik?" Violet asked.

"Handling the exit," Will said. "I sent him to start evac."

Violet and Lily both nodded, and Zephyr wondered if Alkamy had been right about Violet's interest in Lily's human friend. It wasn't logical to him. Fae-blood belonged with other fae-blood or with fae, not with a human.

"Where do we go?" Lily glanced at Zephyr, and he was surprised that she was deferring to him. She was the future queen of the Hidden Lands. He was likely to follow his father's path and defend the queen.

"You know the area," Lily said when she caught him looking at her. She flashed a wry grin before she added,

"And I don't think this is a guns or swords situation."

"We'll see." He looked around at them as he ordered, "Will and Roan, stick with Vi and Kam and get outside. Creed . . ." Zephyr shook his head. "You'll be where you always are."

Outside the room, some of the people had started to realize something was truly wrong. The smoke wasn't thick yet, and Zephyr couldn't help but think of the way the diamonds had been trained to keep people calm long enough to create the most devastation in an attack. Panic resulted in people escaping. When they'd been sent to create terror, the objective was maximum destruction. This—this was someone with ties to the Hidden Lands.

Creed glanced at Lily. "Are you leaving or staying with Zeph?"

"There are only three of us with water," Lily pointed out. "I stay with him."

Zephyr startled at that. "If the place burns, it's just a building. If you get hurt . . ."

"You think she'd be okay with *you* getting hurt?" Lily asked.

"Why is *anyone* staying?" Alkamy crossed her arms.

"Because the fire isn't an accident," Will said.

"Which is why I should stay." Violet pulled on a jacket and tapped the seam where he assumed she had a knife concealed.

"The building is on fire. Can we argue outside?" Roan suggested.

Zephyr looked at all of them. "Out. The *four* of you out. Creed, I know you stay with LilyDark, but you're more use outside too."

Creed looked at Lily who nodded, and in the next minute, everyone but Lily had gone. They joined the crowd moving toward the exit, and Zephyr could tell that someone—probably Creed or Will—was moving the air so the growing cloud of smoke wasn't as oppressive.

He and Lily were the last people in the VIP room. With the future queen of both the Unseelie and Seelie at his side, Zephyr stepped into the increasingly smoky main room.

"I hate the lack of a sword," she said.

He could smell the tinge of metal and gunpowder that said she'd drawn a weapon that no true fae would use. Zephyr didn't like guns, not the crudity or the quickness of them. Swords and affinities were deadly too, but there was less honor in pulling a trigger.

Zephyr drew on the water he could feel in the pipes in the walls. It was sluggish, as if there were blockages, but it was there. He'd been working on getting more comfortable with water since he'd discovered an affinity for it. It wasn't as intuitive as earth was, but it would be more useful at extinguishing fire.

"This way," Lily said, gesturing toward the corner where a DJ often sat.

Finding other fae-blood intuitively was an ability none

of them possessed, except Lily. Zephyr suspected it was because Lily was now tied to them as their future queen, or maybe it was a consequence of the crown she wore. All of her affinities were stronger since she'd let it sink into her skin like a tattoo.

The air was hazier by the moment. His affinities were earth and water, though, so he wasn't able to do much about it. He coughed and asked, "Air?"

A breeze of clean air surged toward them, like a ribbon of purity in the grayness that was starting to make his throat itch and eyes burn. He wasn't sure how much time they had to find the attacker. He looked for shapes in the smoke.

"This way," Lily announced, catching his hand and tugging him along with her.

Zephyr wasn't sure if she was leading him to the fire or the fae-blood. He was grateful that she steered him around tables and chairs that had been knocked down in people's haste to leave. He was even more grateful that there weren't any bodies on the ground—at least, not so far.

There was a person in the haze suddenly. Flames flashed upward, making the smoky air glow. Zephyr could see burn marks on tables and the floor where fires had ignited and been put out.

"You're slow," a boy said. He was pretending to be bored, but his voice betrayed his excitement.

Zephyr concentrated on the water in the old pipes in

the walls. He could feel the rust on the pipes, the bends and twists as they wound through the walls. There was an obstacle. He could feel it.

"I thought you'd *all* come." The fae-blood looked at them both and sighed. "Not just you two."

Unlike many of the diamonds, Lily was less inclined toward being a smart-ass and more inclined toward confrontation. Zephyr wasn't surprised when she released his hand and lifted a gun.

"There's no reason I shouldn't shoot you."

Instead of backing down, the boy laughed, albeit a little nervously. "You really are the Unseelie Queen's kin, aren't you?"

"We both are," Zephyr said. He glanced at the boy, but his attention was on the pipes. They'd been seared, so they were melted and impassable in various points. That was why the water was so sluggish.

"Who are you?" Lily asked. The gun was still unwavering in her hand.

Zephyr couldn't help wondering why a name even mattered. "What do you *want*?"

The fae-blood lifted his hand as if to indicate that he didn't know, but then he said, "To let *her* know that there's no way this truce is going to happen." The fae-blood grinned.

"Who *are* you?" Lily repeated.

He laughed, fire rolling out of his mouth like he was some mythical beast. It was a clever trick, using his own air to steer the fire kindled in his hand.

The pipes above them groaned. Zephyr felt Lily add her own force to his, and the pipes began to crack. They couldn't unmelt them, but they *could* break them. Water started to soak the walls, preventing them from burning. Soon the water would seep through the walls and onto the floor.

"You've been the one burning places?" Lily asked.

He smiled.

"You're just a fae-blood," Zephyr said. "Do you think you can stand against the *queen*?"

"She's not here, is she? No. She's safe in her little world while we are here in the filth, in the pollution they've created. She used us while she and her fae stayed where they're safe while we are left in this diseased world. She has no business declaring *peace*."

Lily lowered the gun and pulled Zephyr closer to her side. He felt the water rolling toward them as soon as she touched his hand. Whatever strengthening the crown gave her, Zephyr felt it too now.

But it wasn't only water that answered when they'd touched. Earth heard their summons, and soil followed water. In less than a moment, the fire was being extinguished by a wall of mud. The fae-blood was setting everything he could on fire, and the room grew thick with smoke, ash, and mud.

The wall started to shudder, and Zephyr couldn't decide whether it was better to release Lily's hand to stop the intensity of the call to their affinities, or if doing so would mean they'd be overcome.

His answer came when a wall started toppling.

The fae-blood shoved Lily toward the debris. She fell into the mud and water, and Zephyr scrambled after her.

"Thanks for the help," the fae-blood called out. "I couldn't have created nearly this much destruction on my own."

Then he was gone, clambering over the mess and vanishing as Zephyr pulled Lily to her feet.

She shoved him. "Go! Catch him."

But the idea of leaving the queen's heir alone was ludicrous at best. He'd far rather face Lily's anger than Endellion's if Lily were injured on his watch. He ignored his cousin, and together they left the wreck of the bar.

As they stepped outside, the rest of the diamonds gathered around them, and Zephyr saw his father standing off to the side. He handed Lily over to their friends and went toward the shadows where Rhys waited.

"You are intact?"

Zephyr nodded.

"And the princess?"

"Is fine," Zephyr said.

He filled his father in on everything that had happened. When he was done, Zephyr watched as his father's normally placid expression shifted to simmering rage.

"Father?"

Unexpectedly, Rhys clasped his forearm. "I would be

unhappy if you were grievously injured. You will be alert."

It was as much of an expression of affection as Rhys had managed in Zephyr's presence, and Zephyr smiled. He wasn't precisely *paternal*, but he cared.

"I will," Zephyr swore. "We all will."

Rhys nodded. "I will confer with the queen. Declaring peace will be difficult if there are attacks like the ones she's long ordered. The boy—and anyone working with him—will need to be contained."

Then he turned and left, and Zephyr went to join his friends. The cessation of war was turning out to be far more dangerous than he'd imagined.

Meanwhile, the Black Diamonds were sopping wet, dirty, or some combination of the two. Lily and Creed looked the worst. Roan, Alkamy, and Will were scanning the crowd attentively. Violet, not surprisingly, had a short blade barely concealed at her side. Erik was standing at their side with a hand under his jacket where a gun was hidden, and in that moment, Zephyr was grateful for the extra eyes and weapons.

Was the fae-blood part of another Sleeper cell? A radical unaffiliated with the queen? Maybe there was another answer. Zephyr had no idea, but he hoped that Rhys would find one.

fourteen

EILIDH

In the Hidden Lands, Torquil woke. He wasn't as weak as he'd first been after the fight with Calder, but it didn't take but a glance to see that he was weaker than he should be. Usually, he radiated dark light like a small star made flesh. Instead, he was ashy and drawn. His normal glow was dim, and Eilidh was doubtful that he could defend himself properly if there were a threat of any kind.

"I know you're here, Eilidh," he murmured, his eyes still closed. "I don't need to see you to know you're near me."

"I wasn't hiding." She studied him, wishing he'd let her use her affinity to heal him all at once. It would exhaust her in many ways, but so too did seeing him in pain.

"You're lurking in the doorway."

She stepped farther into the room. It was unnerving

to see him so still in the bed. She'd imagined him in her bed often enough, and she'd been there with him in their linked dreams, but this was something very different. Seeing him brought low—by her brother's blade no less—was terrifying.

"I wish you would let me heal you," she said for at least the twentieth time. It wasn't a skill she used often, but she could do it. She'd started to heal Torquil, but her father, the King of Fire and Truth, had pulled her away as soon as he realized what she was about.

When Torquil had opened bleary eyes that first day, he chastised her for taking his wound in any degree. She didn't pull it into her body, but she pressed her energy and strength into his so his healing would accelerate. Her affinity wasn't one that she could use lightly. It weakened her, and she was already physically weaker than many fae.

"I healed Lily's beloved. Why not my own?"

"Neither Lily nor the boy know it weakens you," Torquil argued. "If they did—"

"So if *you* didn't know . . ."

"But I do, Patches." He was one of the only people who used that name. Most people wouldn't overtly refer to her near-death as an infant. Torquil had been the first person to suggest that her many scars were beautiful, and he'd been the only one to ever make her feel like they truly were.

He held his hand out to her. It didn't tremble today.

That was progress. Eilidh took his hand and sat at the edge of the bed where he rested under a blanket stitched of sheepskins. It was the most comforting thing she owned, warm and weighty in a way that made her feel inordinately *safe*. When the injured fae was carried into her home at her order, she'd covered him with it in some silly hope that it gave him the comfort it had given her over the years.

She was silent with a twist of both guilt and determination. Each day when he slept, Eilidh sped his healing a little. She didn't *heal* him, not truly, merely helped him along. As with all things when it came to fae honesty, there were more degrees of truth than one.

"Has something else happened?" Torquil asked as she sat silently at his side.

Eilidh stared at the glass walls of the tower. On the ground below them, the always-watching fae couldn't see everything. Many details were obscured, making her seem like a shadow moving through the tower. But she could see them. Her entire life had been lived while the fae studied her, weighed her decisions, measured her failures.

They didn't see her patchwork skin as beautiful. To them, she was a broken princess, and right now, she was responsible for the fall of one of their shining lights. Torquil's injury had brought even more Seelie-born fae to stare up at the tower. Never mind that it was the Seelie princes who had almost killed him. They watched as if he needed their protection. As they came in greater numbers, more Unseelie-born watched *her*, most likely because Rhys, her Unseelie brother, or the queen had ordered it.

And in the middle of all of it, they watched because she had been their future queen and now was not. Many of them believed her to be unfit for the throne, but they'd accepted it. Now, however, a girl with the taint of humanity was to protect the Hidden Lands. In many minds, that was worse than a broken princess.

"Sometimes, I want to run away," Eilidh admitted quietly. "I want to find a silent corner of the Hidden Lands and live a life with you, away from all of them, away from court intrigue, away from murderous brothers and overprotective parents. Just us. You. Me. A little cottage where we're alone and safe . . ."

"They didn't kill me," Torquil reminded her quietly. "Your brothers aren't murderers."

Eilidh nodded and stroked his pale hair until he slept again. There were so many other things to worry over, but he worried over her. He'd been the only person to hold her time and again when the Seelie princes were awful to her. Torquil alone knew that what she wanted most in life was to be loved, to have a family, and to protect her people.

Eilidh was grateful he didn't know how far she would go for all of those things.

Silently, she stayed at his side, lulling him back to sleep with gentle strokes and soft words. Once he was asleep again, she nudged his wounds a little closer to healing. She was careful not to do too much too often, walking the line between helping him and getting caught doing so.

After she'd done as much as she could, coaxed muscles to heal and swelling to lower, Eilidh leaned back and took several deep breaths. Convincing the body to do as she willed was more difficult than any other affinity.

Quiet moments passed while she took comfort in being near Torquil, rejoicing that he was alive and growing stronger. Work could only wait so long, however. Eilidh sent a summons to her brother yet again. He would protect Torquil while she did what she must to ensure that injury to her loved ones was understood to be a bad idea.

"Stay with him," she asked when Rhys arrived inside the glass tower.

He met her gaze and asked, "Will you tell me where you go when he sleeps?"

With a regretful sigh, she looked past her brother to the sea that glittered so comfortingly below the tower. There were secrets more dangerous than others to know. This was, undoubtedly, one of them.

She shook her head.

"There is trouble," Rhys said. He told her of another fire that had threatened both Lily and Zephyr. Then he added, "Our mother sent me here to stay with you."

"I am safe from a fae-blood, Rhys." Eilidh shook her head. "I may be fragile, but a fae-blood? Truly?"

Rhys nodded. "I think she was more concerned about your . . . emotions."

At that, Eilidh paused. She worked hard to keep her feelings moderate. When she was overly emotional, the sea and soil responded. She wasn't sure if anyone else had noticed, but apparently her mother had.

Then, as if to point out that *he* noticed plenty too, he added, "One of the Seelie princes has been away."

Eilidh was grateful for the years of court training. Her expression was unchanged as she watched the sea writhe. It looked so gentle from the surface, but its depths were often raging. She'd felt them, letting her affinity tie her to the waves and currents, letting the undertow take her.

"Don't ask questions, Brother." Eilidh glanced at him. "I don't wish to attempt to lie to you."

Rhys didn't pause before offering, "Do you need anything?"

"Calder hurt what is mine, and I am our mother's daughter." Eilidh stepped around her brother and walked to the staircase.

"He is also your father's get," Rhys said softly. "Don't forget that."

Eilidh continued onward. There was nothing she forgot, not the risks or the costs. She pulled a hood up over her hair, letting it fall forward until it was like a cowl around her face, and she began to walk.

When she reached the sea, she shed her clothes and dove into the water. In a moment's time, she was gone from even the most astute of watchers. It wouldn't last forever. Her parents would find out. Questions would be asked. Tonight, though, as with the last several nights, she had a few brief hours of freedom, especially as the queen was undoubtedly interrogating anyone she suspected of undermining her plans for peace.

The Hidden Lands were smaller on the outside than on the inside. Technically, they were only a small series of islands near the Corryvreckan whirlpool, but the Coire Bhreacain was a magical space between the worlds that humanity knew as real and the world that the sky, soil, and sea offered to the fae when they'd been in need. The earth's natural fire, lava, rolled into the sea where the currents cooled it and thus more isles were made. The air and waves danced together to make the whirlpool that chased away humanity.

And Eilidh had affinities of earth, fire, and water. Here, at the edge of the Coire Bhreacain, she was able to vanish for just long enough to reach her secreted cave. Until she was caught or her task completed, she could do as she must.

The cave was only accessible via the whirlpool. Eilidh crossed the water until she reached a small cleft in the rock. If one didn't know it was there, finding it would be near impossible. The cliff had a ripple, a series of sea stacks that blocked the opening from view.

She pushed herself up and climbed up the cliff, scrambling over rocks that cut her hands and legs. Once she reached the ledge, she stood and walked inside. The only sounds were the steady drip of water within the cave and the battering of the sea outside.

Eilidh touched the pile of wood she'd left last night and it burst into flame. The flickering fire gave her light, and it offered a bit of heat. She didn't need it, but she enjoyed taking it away from her prisoner when she left again.

She liked heating the sword that rested in that fire too. Torquil's blood had long since been burned away, but it had been there. It had stained the blade. She thought it only fitting that the same blade be used to explain her upset to her Seelie brother.

"Did you rest?" she asked Calder.

He was held fast to the wall by the cave itself. Eilidh had explained to the stone that she was the daughter of the queen and king. She'd let the rocks feel her grief, and the cave had offered her aid. Stone had found Calder guilty.

Eilidh was justified in exacting her due blood price. She'd taken three days to do so, and tonight was her last night. After this, she'd dump him into the sea. If the sea thought him worthy of saving, it would take him to shore.

"The laws of the fae grant me blood rights," Eilidh said formally. "For the injury done me when you drew the blood of my beloved, my betrothed. Before I could be wed and bring a child of our union, you stabbed him. You risked my future child's life, the continuation of my parents' joined line."

Calder glared at her. He tried to remain silent when

she visited, but in the two prior nights, he'd failed. Something about pain seemed to encourage speech—even if it was of a vulgar sort.

Eilidh gripped the hilt of Calder's sword, welcoming the fire's warmth into her body. It wasn't something she would be able to do if she had different affinities, but she drew enough of the flames into her body that the hilt was cool in her hand. The blade, however, was heated, not as much as it would be later, but enough to hurt.

Slowly, Eilidh touched it to the bottoms of Calder's feet. For about ten seconds, he held his silence. Then, he screamed. As soon as he did, Eilidh removed the blade. Flesh came with it.

"You should've been drowned at birth like the weakest of the litter," Calder said in a rasping voice. "When the king hears—"

"He'll do nothing," Eilidh interrupted. She knew that to be true, was sure of it in the way that she was sure of the tides.

Calder stared at her.

"The land allowed me to take my price," Eilidh explained to her Seelie brother. He was the younger of the king's two sons, not known for skill with word or thought. Nacton, the elder Seelie brother, was the one to fear. Calder was simply the weapon Nacton wielded. If Calder wasn't so hateful toward her, she would feel sympathy for how he'd been used.

He hated her, though, and he'd stabbed Torquil.

"You didn't learn," Eilidh chastised Calder. "You weren't the eldest son, and so you never bothered to learn the old laws. I know them. Nacton and Rhys know them. I am within my rights to take these three days, Calder."

She shoved his now-cooled sword into his leg, careful to avoid the femoral artery. When he screamed again, she withdrew it—only to repeat the action on the other leg. As he bled, she heated the sword up until it glowed.

"It's important to cauterize these," she told him before pressing the flat of the sword to his bleeding leg.

"By the terms of the law, I cannot leave you still bleeding unless I know it is only minor blood." She pressed the flat to the other leg once he stopped shaking and yelling vulgarities. "His own daughter did this for him, you know. The half-fae girl Violet cauterized his wounds. The ones you gave to him. Torquil did not scream as you do. She told me that, as did the new heir. Torquil was brave."

While Calder was still shuddering in pain, Eilidh summoned the waves, drew them high up the cliff and into the cave, and then she let the water take him away. Softly she told the sea, "If you will it, deliver him to the shore safely."

And then she sat in the cave and wept until she thought she might be ill. This was not the person she wanted to be, but a weak queen—or princess—was as good as dead. Calder had drawn the blood of her husband-to-be; letting that go unanswered was tantamount to permission to do so again.

The cave curved around her, holding her in a basin where she curled up and sobbed. For herself. For her beloved. And for her brother-no-more.

fifteen

LILYDARK

When she heard the knock, Lily jumped. Her nerves were beyond tense. After the police, the attack, and the fire at the Row House, it felt like everything was a wreck. *She* was definitely a wreck.

Lily opened the door more cautiously than normal and . . . stared. The creature standing in the hall was obviously not here on Abernathy or Gaviria business. "What are you?"

"Not of the courts," the fae said with a bark-harsh voice. "No harm is meant to you, Heir. There are plenty of us who are outside the finery and ceremony of the royal ones. Too ugly or too human. Too"—he shrugged—"unnatural for the courtly fae."

Admittedly, the fae standing at the dorm suite door

was thinner than anyone strictly human should be, as if his body had been steadily and slowly stretched and extended over many years. It was an unsettling thing to look at him. His face had that peculiar beauty that only fiction or paintings could create. It was a matter of perfect symmetry: beautiful to behold but too . . . fae.

Lily didn't feel the urge to run, but regular humans often did.

"For you," the faery said, extending a hand with an envelope and a package. He had the beautiful dark skin of the Seelie Court, but his skin had fine pale green tracery that could've been the result of hours upon hours under tattoo needles.

Lily stared at the leafy pattern trying to recall what she knew about the faeries outside the two courts. He obviously would *not* be able to pass for human, and such faeries were rarely seen outside the Hidden Lands. It was a saddening realization. There was an incredible amount of beauty that the world was denied when the fae withdrew from the world.

"Sent by *them*," he added as if there would be any other fae so bold as to send her packages when she was carefully guarded.

Lily took the letter and package, and the fae man flashed her a smile. Then he was gone, sliding through the hallways with a grace that seemed as if he was swimming rather than walking on dry land. That, too, was a revelation. She wondered briefly if she'd ever be fae enough that she could move so elegantly.

"Lily?" Alkamy called from behind her.

She turned to look at her suitemate. Alkamy wasn't overprotective in any way that was uncomfortable or off-putting. However, she was, rather obviously, watching Lily's every move. Without discussing it outright, they had both acknowledged that Alkamy reported Lily's doings to Zephyr. It was something of an open secret since they'd returned from the Hidden Lands a few weeks ago, and as much as Lily found it irritating, she wasn't going to fight over it—at least not yet. Zephyr was beholden to the queen, and whatever she'd asked of him made him think that tracking Lily was essential. For now, she was letting it go.

"I'm right here," Lily told Alkamy. "I had a delivery."

"From . . . them?"

"Yes." Lily closed the door and walked over to the sofa. This was the second time now that one of the court minions had slid into her life with no pause or obstacles. It highlighted how vulnerable she truly was.

Lily held the leaf-wrapped package in her hands. When she'd touched it, the wrapping had looked like brown paper, but as she held it, the paper was revealed to be leaves. The shape of the package was oblong, and the weight of it was heavy enough that it spoke of the fae man's strength that he'd held it with barely one hand.

"What is it?" Alkamy asked as she came to stand near Lily.

Apprehensively, Lily turned it over in her hands. The other package from the Hidden Lands had been a crown. Lily wasn't entirely sure she wanted to open this one.

It wasn't that having a crown was awful. It was that this crown was changing her. She didn't mention it to the others, but she felt it. Her affinities were magnified, growing stronger by the day. In the few short weeks since she'd agreed to be the heir to the Hidden Throne, Lily had become so adept in her affinities that she felt certain that she could be mistaken for full fae already. It was terrifying. Opening another gift from her fae family was equally so.

As she started peeling the leaves back, the package shifted in size. Removing each layer of plants seemed to make the contents expand. By the time the third layer was removed, Lily knew what she held in her lap.

"A sword," she pronounced, removing the last few layers more quickly.

She slid it from the leaf-etched scabbard.

It was a beautiful weapon. The metal blade had a greenish-white tinge to it, and the edges glinted, making clear that neither side was dulled. The hilt was a thing of beauty, but not such that functionality had been sacrificed. The pommel was a metal fish-tail, not as blocky as some pommels, but still good for bashing if she needed to use it that way. The guard was elegant, if a bit elaborate for her taste, as if vines had become metal. The blade itself, however, was the finest part. It was light enough to let her fight for a while without tiring, but it was still carefully balanced.

Alkamy reached out. Her fingers grazed the sword. She flinched.

"Kamy?"

"Oops," Alkamy said in a fading voice.

And that was it. She didn't move, didn't speak further. Only her eyes moved, darting from the sword to Lily to the letter on the floor. Whatever had just happened was not good.

"Shit!" Lily tore open the letter and scanned it.

> *LilyDark,*
>
> *Our queen has instructed that I send you a sword attuned to your particular needs and size. Enclosed is the sword wrought for you. As an additional aspect of its usefulness, the Queen of Blood and Rage has enticed one of the plants from her poison garden to meld with the metal. Anyone attempting to lift the sword without your handing it directly to them will experience accelerated hemlock poisoning.*

Lily looked at Alkamy. "Hemlock. There's hemlock and . . . What does hemlock do?"

Alkamy couldn't reply.

And Lily had never seen anyone poisoned—or caused

it herself. It was an aspect of her affinity with earth that she'd never even considered. The queen, however, apparently had no qualms doing so. Hurriedly, Lily continued reading.

> The plant is a "devil's blossom" that will begin external paralysis that will numb the lungs. If a fae (or fae-blood) is exposed, they will be debilitated so they can be delivered to the Queen Mother for justice. Humans, of course, will be prone to dying as they expire so much more quickly than our people do.
> Yours in faith,
> Rhys.

Lily dropped the letter to the floor and went to Alkamy, who appeared to be in increasing pain. "I don't know how to stop it."

Carefully, she leaned Alkamy toward her. Her body was hardening, taking on the rigidity of a corpse. Simultaneously, she was becoming colder by the moment as if each exhalation eliminated her warmth and life.

"Poison," Lily muttered, trying to think of something, *anything* to do when someone was poisoned. Emetics were a bad idea when someone was paralyzed. Having Alkamy throw up would result in choking right now. Activated charcoal? That was used a lot, but it wasn't something they had lying around. What they needed was *help*.

"Come," Lily breathed into the air, sending her summons to whatever fae or fae-blood she could draw to her.

"Any of you who hear me and can heal, *come*. Please."

As gently but quickly as she could, Lily dragged Alkamy to the soil-filled sofa where they'd had to let Zephyr rest and heal recently. The soil alone wasn't enough, but it was something. It would help pull the toxins from Alkamy's body. Perhaps that would slow the progress of the poison.

"Kam? Lily?" Creed's voice came from the door.

Violet followed his words with the start of a question. "Where are . . ."

Creed and Violet walked into the room as Lily was hefting Alkamy into the vat of dirt. They stopped suddenly.

"What happened?" Creed asked.

If they were summoned by the words Lily had sent into the air, they wouldn't be so shocked. They'd know that she needed a healer. Lily didn't have time to worry about whether or not her summons would bring more help. Creed and Violet were present now, and their help was better than what she'd had a moment ago.

"She's been poisoned," Lily said, feeling somewhere between panic and idiocy. It looked like she was hauling a corpse to a dirt-filled box. If they weren't all fae, this would be the sort of thing that could send her to jail.

Alkamy was immobile and her lips were bluing. Rhys' letter gave her reason to think that Alkamy might survive, but Lily wasn't sure. How the poison would work on someone who was only half-fae might be different from how it affected someone who was wholly fae.

"I don't know what to do. She's stiff and freezing and—"

Violet was there next to her suddenly, her tiny frame seeming larger as it always did when she was in a mood. Her hands weren't filled with fire, but they were glowing. Warmth poured from them as she tried to stop Alkamy from frigidity.

For a moment, Lily watched, hoping, but not seeing any improvement. She repeated her plea, sending her words through the air, "I need a healer. This is the queen's heir, the king's heir, and I need aid."

She looked toward the door, willing it to fling open to reveal a faery healer.

"She isn't breathing," Violet said, voice edged with panic. "Someone—"

"Move." Creed shoved past them and bent to kiss Alkamy.

Violet and Lily both gaped at him.

Ignoring them, he kept his lips pressed to Alkamy's.

"Air," Violet pronounced in a soft voice. "Creed is air. He's breathing for her."

"Oh." Lily felt stupid for not thinking of it. The hemlock was making Alkamy's lungs falter, so Creed was pressing air into them, pushing the toxins back, and making her breathe.

Alkamy's hands started trembling, and her legs began to move. In another moment, her arms shot up in an oddly mechanic way and jerked Creed closer to her. She clutched

him, and it almost looked like a passionate embrace—
except that Creed was starting to struggle. He wasn't
pulling away yet, but he no longer seemed as willing to
hold his lips to hers. After several moments, the fight went
out of him, and he began to slump onto Alkamy.

sixteen

ZEPHYR

Walking into Alkamy's room and seeing Creed and Alkamy both slumped over filled Zephyr with the sort of fear that knew no sane word or act. He shoved Creed to the side in order to reach Alkamy. "What happened?"

Creed stumbled back, not speaking but making a raspy noise in his throat. Zephyr glanced his way, saw Violet restraining Lily, and shook his head. Whatever was going on here made no sense. But his first priority was Alkamy. Looking down at her, he saw that she was breathing shallowly and her lips were shaded bluish-purple. Her skin seemed tinged gray, so pale that a winding sheet would be brighter.

Never had she looked quite so much like the fairy tale Snow White as she did in that instant.

"Creed helping," Alkamy whispered. Her hand was

shaking as she gripped his wrist. "Hurt him."

Lily stepped closer to Alkamy and told her, "I'm so sorry."

Her tears were rolling down her cheeks and spilling onto Alkamy. Where the tears landed Alkamy's skin brightened, and the unhealthy gray cast lightened a little.

"Oh," Lily murmured, and then *she* leaned down and pressed her lips to Alkamy's too.

"For Ninian's sake! What's wrong with Kam?" Zephyr snapped as Lily kissed his girlfriend. "And why is everyone kissing her?"

"Sick," Creed murmured.

He glanced at Creed, who was sliding to the floor looking almost as unwell as Alkamy did. His usually night-dark skin was ashy, and his hands were trembling.

Zephyr went to the ground in front of Creed. He had just reached out to check Creed's pulse and breathing when a peculiar woman drifted into the room. Her feet logically had to be touching the ground, but she moved as if there was a cushion of air conveying her forward. There was something so alien about her that Zephyr knew that she was far more than merely fae-blood. This was a full fae, on the grounds of St. Columba, in Alkamy and Lily's suite.

With no thought beyond defense, Zephyr stood and put his back to Creed. Violet instantly came to his side. Together they weren't much defense against a fae if she was trained, especially as they were unarmed.

"LilyDark?" the faery breathed the word, letting it take shape and drift over them.

The fae woman was willowy, and not simply in the way humanity used the word. She was thin and flowing, her very movement like the draping boughs of willows in a breeze. It was an elegance humans could never replicate.

"That's Lily," Violet said, pointing but not moving to allow access.

"Ah." The willow woman slid closer to them. Myriad tiny pouches hung around her waist on cords of varying lengths. Bits of plant were tucked in her hair, and vials of liquids clinked together like glass chimes all over her. They were woven into her hair, affixed to her skin, made visible through the slits in her skirt as she moved.

"She summoned, and I came. You are witness to it," the willow woman said, lifting one hand to point toward Lily.

At the gesture, Violet stepped farther forward as if she wasn't entirely sure that the fae woman should be allowed nearer to any of them.

Creed stumbled to his knees. He lurched toward her, half crawling to pass them and reach the fae. He wasn't usually so awkward in his gait. In fact, the only time he *was* so lumbering was when he'd been exceedingly drunk or, more recently, when he'd been injured in the Hidden Lands.

"Test with me," he ordered in a stronger voice than seemed likely given his condition.

The willow woman drifted closer to him, her skirt shifting as she squatted in front of Creed. Tenderly, she touched his lips.

He jerked back forcefully, gasping like he was choking.

"Hemlock," she pronounced. With a visibly unfocused glance, she studied Alkamy and Lily before adding, "He took in the poison when he gave her"—she nodded toward Alkamy—"his air, then?"

Creed nodded.

The sounds of spring seemed to fill the air as the fae woman hummed. "Spider-legs, ash, and air."

Zephyr wasn't sure whether that was a recipe or a song. He met Violet's gaze and gestured for her to stay with Creed. She could inflict damage on the fae stranger if necessary.

As Violet went to Creed, Zephyr walked over to Alkamy and pulled Lily away. He hated that it might make Alkamy worse, that the air she was obviously providing his girlfriend would be stopped. He wanted to let her continue whatever she was doing to heal Alkamy. That wasn't his right though. Having the heir to the Hidden Throne suffocate in front of him wasn't acceptable.

"Poison," Lily said. "She was poisoned."

He nodded and looked at Alkamy. She smiled at him, but then her eyes drifted shut and she stopped moving.

"Kam!"

The willow woman *tsk*ed. "Let her rest. Her lungs must heal."

She reached out to Creed again, jerked open his mouth, and shoved some herbs and dirt in his mouth. For all her delicacy of form and motion, the willow woman was not gentle. Creed choked, but she forced his mouth closed and stroked her fingernails over his throat to make him swallow.

Once he did, she traced his lips again. "The devil's blossom is releasing you."

With a musical clatter of vials and sinuous sway of pouches, she went to Lily. "You summoned, and I came to your aid." She motioned over in the direction of Creed, who was looking better already. "I've undone the poison he took in and fixed his bone."

Lily nodded and opened her mouth.

Smiling now, the willow woman placed herbs and soil on Lily's tongue. She hummed as she did so, but she spoke no further words. When Lily closed her mouth, the willow woman stopped humming and nodded once.

Lily swallowed with visible effort.

The faery healer lowered a hand to trace the shape of Alkamy's lips. "She is un-poisoned, but there are better ways than taking it into yourself." She met Lily's gaze and then Zephyr's in turn before pronouncing, "When you come to the court, I shall expect to be made welcome there."

"If you do not harm or wish harm to me or mine, you will be," Lily promised.

"Next time, use this." She handed Lily a pouch. Then she turned and left in a musical cacophony of vials and spring birds.

"What was that?" Violet asked once the door was securely closed. She shook her head slightly. "I mean, she's fae but . . . that's not normal, right?"

Zephyr stroked Alkamy's face, feeling comforted when she sighed and shifted in her sleep. He had never seen her so ill that she couldn't stay awake, and the sight of it was far from comforting.

"She's outside the courts," Zephyr said, glancing briefly at Violet.

"The fae who delivered this was too," Lily said from behind him. "Fae-blood enough that he might've been able to pass, but . . . she couldn't have."

Zephyr nodded. The existence of the fae and fae-blood who refused to live in the Hidden Lands when the courts withdrew always seemed more myth than truth, but now and then, he'd seen one. They hid. They had no court protection, and too often they were the ones captured by the human police.

"Now that Lily's been found, there will be word of a new heir spreading to the fae that live in shadows or seas outside the regents' command. Word of Lily will lure them in."

"And of you," Creed added, rolling his newly healed wrist as he spoke. "She looked at *you* too when she asked for court welcome."

Zephyr didn't speak, but he didn't suspect he needed to do so. Creed, even weakened, was observant. For all of his flaws over the years, that was never an area of shortcoming.

The queen had warned him that the acknowledgment of his lineage and LilyDark's status as heir would draw attention from unexpected quarters. This wasn't quite what he'd imagined. After a lifetime in service to her majesty's bloodthirsty orders, he'd grown accustomed to ignoring most of the fears that threatened to pull him into despair. He'd always had the illusion of a safe haven though. He'd had the sense that here at the school or in their homes, all of the diamonds were safe. He'd believed—wrongly or not—that they had space to be freer. Not only had the campus been entered but the club had been torched. Now, Alkamy had been brought down by poison in her suite at St. Columba, a suite shared with the *heir*. The recent spate of events shook the foundations of his illusion of security.

"How did it happen?" He walked toward the sofa. It was either sit or hover at Alkamy's side. As he sat, he reached for the sword that was half propped there.

"No!" Lily heaved him aside. Her hand connected with his shoulder, and she shoved hard enough that he fell sideways onto the floor.

"Unless you want to be the next to kiss Creed, don't touch that!"

"Excuse me?" Zephyr glanced down at the sword. It wasn't that unusual in appearance. It was obviously well-made, crafted of fae steel with an odd greenish-white cast. He wouldn't say it was a match to his, but they were obviously crafted by the same artist.

"There's poison melded to it." Lily gestured awkwardly at the blade. "Touching it will make you numb or kill you if you're human."

"Alkamy was poisoned by *that*?" Zephyr asked dumbly. Alkamy wasn't injured in an attack. A *gift* had resulted in her near-comatose state.

Violet sighed, and when they looked at her, she said, "They never seem to understand that things in this world aren't like over there. What if the headmistress touched it? Or Lily's dad? Or"—Violet waved her hand toward the door that led to the hall—"what if we had guests who saw that happen to Kamy?"

Lily lifted the sword by the hilt. It was obviously fashioned for her. There was something inherently right when she hefted it. He could see that the weapon completed her in the same way that the queen's blade and blood-red armor did for her. It was as if Lily was slipping into her own skin more truly.

"It's the sword of a queen," he said. "And tainted for your safety. Obviously, the recent events are making our grandmother anxious."

His cousin—for that was the word they'd chosen, even though half-cousin was more accurate—startled. "It's not just that. She's readying me for the declaration, isn't she? For the public announcement that I'm not only a fae-blood, but . . . her heir."

Zephyr nodded, trying not to wonder if his own gift of a weapon was meant for the same thing. He was sworn to protect his family, even as the head of that family was hurtling them into peril.

"Crown and sword," Lily murmured, eyes still trained on the weapon in her grip. "She's sent me a crown, and now . . . this. It doesn't speak loudly of peace. What am I to do? Carry it openly? *Here?*"

"Her world is different, Lily. The queen of the Unseelie Court has always been a warrior," Violet said. She shrugged a little as she reminded them. Her own father, Torquil, was a fighter, but he was Seelie-born, and betrothed to the previous heir of the unified throne. Violet herself had always seemed the most war-ready of their group. She'd certainly taken more lives than any of the rest of the seven Black Diamonds.

They stayed silent for a few moments. Zephyr walked over to stand next to Alkamy, who was waking again. She sat up gingerly, and he was torn between helping her and insisting she stay in the healing soil.

"Take me outside," she half ordered, half asked as soon as she could speak. Her voice let on that she was afraid and weary.

So Zephyr scooped her into his arms. Dirt fell from her body as he lifted her, leaving a trail on the suite floor. "Someone grab the door. We're going to go soak up the sun."

seventeen

EILIDH

When Eilidh returned to her glass tower, she was no longer blood- or tear-stained. The sea had washed away the proof of her vengeance and her sorrow. She wasn't ashamed of either, but showing emotion wasn't something royals did in public. The sea understood whether she spoke it or not. There was rarely a need to explain anything to the salty waves. Water had rolled over her as she'd been carried aloft. She knew that the earth under her feet understood as well what she had done and what she needed. Her relationship with the Hidden Lands was stronger than she could explain, even now that she was heir no more. The land knew her as if she were an extension of it.

Eilidh's gait was slow as she walked up the spiral stairs of her tower. It wasn't that she didn't want to go home. She simply felt weary from the weight of the things she'd done.

Being the heir had never been easy, but she expected that once she was freed of it things would be easier. Reality was different.

"It is done then?" Rhys stood staring out the self-same window where she'd stood so many nights. There were no recriminations in his voice, no censure for the blood he knew she'd drawn.

"Three days."

"Calder lives?"

Eilidh wasn't sure, so she weighed her words. The sea had taken him, and that was all she could say. She walked over to her Unseelie brother and stood so close that his arm was touching hers. It wasn't a proper embrace, but it was what she knew he could offer: closeness and comfort akin to what the queen herself considered an "embrace."

"I woke and came back," she said cautiously. "When I dove into the sea, the Coire Bhreacain had no body floating in it . . . but there was no prince upon the shore either."

Rhys didn't look away from the now thrashing sea. Waves slammed the tower so ferociously that if it weren't wrought of magic, the glass would shatter. "If you need to rage, I can leave," her brother said, nodding toward the waves. "I believe they are yours."

Eilidh sighed, trying to pull anger back inside her skin. "There were no ships. I asked the sea before I gave over my mood."

He nodded.

"I broke no law," she said.

Again, he nodded.

"I would like an embrace." Eilidh spoke the request so quietly that even with fae hearing, Rhys wouldn't have heard if he'd been a few steps farther away. "If you would allow—"

"Brothers protect," he said, drawing her closer. "If you'd told me, I would've done what you required. I've done as our mother has required over the centuries."

At that, a sob escaped her. He would've tortured the king's youngest son for her. He'd undoubtedly done worse, but that didn't make it any less kind of him. She wasn't sure she could ever have asked him to do what was her responsibility. Their mother had, but she'd meted out justice for centuries already. Perhaps it wasn't any easier to endure after ages; perhaps the Queen of Blood and Rage sometimes needed the respite of sharing the burden.

Or perhaps she was simply trying to be certain that her own children were strong enough to do what must be done.

"The king wouldn't forgive *you*, and Nacton would've struck you," Eilidh pointed out. "I can handle my own responsibilities."

But she rested her head against Rhys' chest and let herself be comforted as if she were a child. Awkwardly, Rhys put his hand on the back of her head and held her still. He could crush her, and if anyone other than her parents or Torquil had held her thus before recently, she would expect injury to follow. A ridiculous laugh escaped her at that thought. Trust was a new thing.

"Shall I ask why you laugh?"

"Because I'm tired of crying." Eilidh stepped away from her brother. "I am her daughter, Rhys. I did as our mother would've, but I will be forgiven as neither she nor you would because I am the king's daughter as well."

"True." Rhys favored her with a genuine smile. "I would've taken pleasure in exacting your vengeance though, and there are laws I could cite to justify it. Remember that should the other son ever require a lesson."

This time when Eilidh laughed she woke Torquil. He walked out of the bedroom.

Rhys glanced at Eilidh and then at Torquil's healing abdominal scar. As the Queen of Blood and Rage's regular sparring partner, Rhys had been cut, slashed, and stabbed enough times to realize that Torquil was more healed than nature would allow. He barely pressed his lips together, but it was reason for Torquil to ask, "What?"

"We were speaking of my brother's dislike of Nacton," Eilidh said truthfully, if not completely so. Mildly, she took her betrothed's hand and led him toward a chair.

"He has admirable qualities too." Torquil sat, wincing a little less than yesterday when he did so. "Unlike Rhys, however, Nacton has never accepted the unification of the courts."

Rhys snorted.

Again, Eilidh had to smile. This new, more emotional side of Rhys continued to amaze her. For most of her life, her brother displayed less affect than a stone. Since he'd come to be closer to her, and then discovered that he had a half-human son *and* a niece, he was softening. In their limited meetings, it had been very clear that neither Zephyr nor LilyDark were at ease with Rhys, but he was going to try with them.

"Could we train tomorrow?" Eilidh asked. "I know I cannot go to the human world to check on our family, but . . . I am vexed and would benefit from the activity."

"If you can leave that one"—he nodded toward Torquil—"for a few moments."

Eilidh shot Torquil a fond look before telling her brother, "*That one* is my betrothed, who was stabbed defending our niece."

"A lot of fuss for a little wound," Rhys said lightly.

Torquil laughed, and Eilidh was grateful that he'd relaxed around her brother. Their need to posture with each other had been awkward initially, but over the past weeks as Torquil healed, the two seemed to have found a tenuous peace. She held hope that it would remain so, especially as everything around her was in disarray.

They brought Torquil up to speed, but his only worry was over the half-fae child he'd fathered. "And Violet is also safe?"

"She defended them against the first intruder," Rhys said. "She is a good fighter. Worthy of training."

Torquil smiled. There was no kinder thing Rhys could have said. He trained with so few fae that suggesting Violet would be worth training was high praise indeed.

Hours later, after Torquil was resting and Rhys had left, Eilidh curled up in the main room of the glass tower, staring out at the sea as if the waves could wash away the stain of what she'd done. She watched the waves and listened to their symphony until it lulled her to sleep. These moments, these rare times when the world was only theirs, made her often wish they could stay asleep. Torquil's affinity for dreams meant that they had a level of privacy when they shared sleep that no one else could invade. There were no illusions, no distances, and no reason not to touch as she wished they could in the waking world.

"You worry unduly," Torquil said as he took her hand and led her to a strange landscape that, as with many dreams since she'd learned that they shared dreamspace, was both delicate and familiar. A moss-covered forest floor stretched out like the finest rug. Her feet were caressed by the soft, stone and twig free, verdant green ground. Trees outlined the edges of a ballroom-sized clearing. Their branches stretched up as if they held a violet, star-scattered sky aloft. Other trees were scattered amongst the sturdiest ones; these had softly swaying branches that were moving in time with a music that only the finest of artists could replicate. In the middle of the clearing was a bed.

When the dance was done, she'd stretch out there with sky overhead and breezes on her skin like the softest kisses, and Torquil would touch her as he couldn't in the waking world. Here, there was no risk of pregnancy. Here, she was safe from the thing that they would one day struggle about. One day, in the future far from now, she *would* like to have a child. Not now. Not even soon. If her parents and her beloved had their way, though, she'd never take the risk of death that childbirth would present.

Eilidh was grateful to avoid that fight—and to avoid the risk for now.

In her shared dream with her betrothed, she danced barefoot on the mossy ground. She spun and dipped, swayed and paused. Torquil led her as they had never done in public. At the faery balls, she was treated as if she were made of the most fragile glass. Here, though, there was no risk of injury. It was but a dream.

It didn't erase the troubles waiting in the waking world, the unrest of both Seelie-born and Unseelie-born over the new heir. It didn't change the secrets she'd kept from Torquil. But it did give her a respite from all of that. Here, she wasn't Eilidh, daughter to the Queen of Blood and Rage and the King of Fire and Truth. She was just a girl in love with a boy who kissed her breathless.

"Make love to me under a rain of falling stars," she requested when the music started to slow.

And so he did.

And it was perfect.

eighteen

WILL

Will had figured that he didn't need to go rushing to the Hidden Lands last night. Zephyr had filled his father in on everything. Rhys would tell the princess about the attacks. He'd tell her about the fae-blood attacks.

"Anything?" he asked Erik when he walked up to the table.

"You're *all* impossible to sneak up on, aren't you? I used to plot how to surprise Lily when we were kids." Erik pulled out a chair as he spoke. As he did, his jacket flapped open briefly, and Will saw the gun holstered there.

Will closed his book and admitted in a very low voice, "The air told me."

"We should talk before we move on to business matters," Erik added just as quietly.

Will shrugged. He didn't see the need, but he wasn't

raised to deal with intricacies in the human world. He was more accustomed to stealth in action than in holding meetings to exchange information.

The waitress was at the table before another word was spoken. Will shook his head, expecting the menu to trip up the human. Somehow, Erik with his well-cut suit, barely hidden handgun, and high-gloss shoes didn't look like the sort to drink organic fruit smoothies.

"Anything with mango," Erik told the girl.

"We have a Mango Magic with açai and extra boost-ers," she started. "There's also the Fruit Fix with—"

"I trust your choice," Erik interrupted. He offered the girl a smile that made her all but sigh.

Will was amused. He'd watched Zephyr and Creed both do the same thing for years. They exuded charm to get their way too.

Once the waitress was gone, Erik looked at him and asked, "What?"

"You are more like Creed and Zephyr than I realized." Will glanced at the counter where the waitress was still smiling. "*You* are all human, but"—he shrugged—"you have charm."

Erik gave him a disdainful look. "Charm isn't *non*-human."

"Historically, as far as I understand it at least, the very word comes from non-human sources. It's sort of euphe-mistically connected to certain affinities, in particular persuasion and truth-evocation." Will sipped his drink, expecting Erik to interrupt him. When he didn't, Will was pleasantly surprised. "There are other words that derive from similar sources."

"Lily must be fond of you," Erik said musingly. "She doesn't seem the sort to fall for someone like the rock singer. You, on the other hand—"

"I'm gay," Will interrupted.

"Ah." Erik nodded. "Well, I guess she had to settle for the singer then."

Will laughed, as much from relief as in response to Erik's words. The thought of anyone finding Creed someone to "settle for" was oddly funny. He was splashed all over magazines and was quite the sensation on stage. Will was . . . just Will. He'd spent his life muting everything about himself. He'd been hiding in so many ways.

That was the main reason he'd pondered the possibility of a life in the Hidden Lands. This world, while not as rife with prejudice as it had been throughout more recent history, held enough pockets of hostility that he could understand his mother's concerns. More to the point, the same people who were homophobic were also, more often than not, racists. Being fae-blood *and* gay would make him a giant target. He knew that.

The waitress had returned and dropped off Erik's drink. "I made a Mango Magic, but with a little extra zest," she announced. "You let me know if you need anything else. I'm Liz, by the way."

"Thank you, Elizabeth." Erik gave her a slightly less

than simmering smile that had her beaming at him before she left.

"Violet isn't going to put up with you flirting all the time. You know that, right?" Will watched Erik until he was sure he had the other boy's attention. "Also I'd threaten you, but I assume you already understand that we'd all kill for her."

Erik pulled out an envelope and slid it across the table. "Reasonable."

Will tucked it into his book.

For a moment, they were quiet. There was a familiarity to it that made Will wonder how many other humans he could've found comfortable if he'd truly talked to them. He'd certainly never bothered to really get to know any of the assorted people that Creed or Violet had dated. It occurred to him that in that way, he was as prejudiced as some others.

Will looked directly at Erik. "I shouldn't judge you for being what you are. I'm sorry."

"A criminal?"

"Human," Will clarified in a low voice.

Erik laughed. "How about you help me figure out how to romance Miss Lamb, and we'll call it even?"

This time, it was Will who laughed. "We'll see."

"I'm staying downtown." Erik glanced at the book. "You have my new contact information."

Will stood, took his book in hand, and left.

There was something comforting in the walk back to

campus. If his mother knew how often he'd taken that walk, she'd have fits. Luckily, he wasn't hounded by photographers, so there was little chance of her knowing that he was accustomed to being on his own and outside the safety of campus.

Since he had privacy to do so, he opened the envelope from Erik. Inside were pictures of several of the scenes of attacks. Fire seemed to be the dominant method, as it had been at the Row House. There were police reports, coroner's reports, and then a scrawled note—presumably from Erik—that simply said, "No suspects. More than one attacker, though, since the timeline and distance makes one person unlikely."

Will saw the logic in that theory, but if the fae-blood knew how to access the Hidden Lands, he could conceivably enter and exit in different places. That, of course, would mean he had a fae accomplice. Maybe Princess Eilidh would have a theory as to whom. Once Will had shared what he learned with Roan, they'd decide whether to tell the princess first or share with Lily first.

When Will reached campus, he walked through the main building with the sort of ease that a lot of the students had.

"Mr. Parrish," one of the secretaries said, stopping him. It wasn't a rebuke though. She smiled. "How is the senator? Her interview last month about the new Clean Water Act was wonderful."

"I'll be sure to tell her." Will flashed his political smile.

The truth was that he was proud of his mother's work, and he was quite aware that her eco-platform was because of him. That was the part that the diamonds didn't get: his mother cared about the same things they did. She simply tackled it differently.

"You might mention to your friends that they ought to consider going to a few more of their classes," the secretary said. "Exams tend to be easier if one learns the material first."

Will nodded. He couldn't tell her that they would likely all be gone from the school soon, either in hiding or in the Hidden Lands. He wasn't optimistic that the pending declaration of peace would go well. All he said was, "I'll pass on the reminder."

That was enough though. At St. Columba's there was a tradition of looking the other way—unless one's parents paid for strict security. His mother didn't. Senator Parrish was very much a by-the-rules person. Aside from the one exceptionally massive rule she'd broken, having a child with a full-blooded fae, Will's mother's record was without the slightest smudge. That smudge, of course, was why he was entangled in guerrilla warfare. His mother had wanted a child—had wanted him—no matter who he was. It was hard to be angry for acts done in love, but sometimes Will still was.

For now, though, he needed to figure out what to do with the information Erik had delivered—and to whom to deliver it.

 nineteen

EILIDH

When morning came, Eilidh was almost startled to find Torquil still injured. The transition to the waking world was never easy. She frequently hated leaving their shared dreams behind. They were incredibly real, but they were still burned away by the daylight.

This world carried the parts that were harder to face, injuries and secrets and fears.

"I forget sometimes," she said, staring at his bandages.

"Forget?"

"That the dreams aren't the real world." She carefully touched his chest, aware that here they were always being watched.

"They're real, Eilidh, just not as complete as this world." He laced his fingers with hers and lifted her hand so he could kiss her knuckles. "I know your body here because I've touched you there. That's real."

"But . . . yours is *injured* here."

Torquil's smile was wicked. "Not so injured that I wouldn't take the same liberties here that I do when we sleep. If it wouldn't injure *you*, I would——"

"Hush!" Eilidh looked toward the window where she could see the already-watching fae. They couldn't hear her, but that didn't matter. She felt self-conscious speaking so when there were witnesses.

Torquil sighed. "I suppose I'm still banned from exercise?"

Tentatively she offered, "We could spar in dreams. . . ."

Her betrothed smiled again. "Then I should come watch what you are like with Rhys. I've seen you spar, but not often with him. He's a harsh fighter . . . unless he'll go easier on you."

"He'd better not." Eilidh scowled at the mere thought of being coddled, but then she realized that Torquil was teasing her. Rhys would consider it a waste of training if he didn't push her, and it would put her at a disadvantage when she fought an opponent intent on her injury.

She helped Torquil as much as his pride and their audience could permit, and in not too long they were in the courtyard where Rhys was fighting three fae fighters, one of whom was Seelie-born. The others were both Unseelie-born. Her brother was something beyond beautiful when he lost himself in the clash of steel. She'd seen human theater where the art of the blade was portrayed as if it were a crude hacking and slashing. In truth, it was akin to a dance—one that could end with bleeding, but if both parties were well matched it was more of an exercise than conflict.

There were occasions in which dancers and acrobats entertained the regents. It had always seemed as much a combat as an art. So too did Rhys' bouts seem as much an art as combat. There was something elegant and conversational to fighting, and something of the fight in the way the dancers or acrobats moved. She wanted to reach a point where she could fight with Torquil. Now that he shared her bed in their dreams, she thought they might be better matched with weapons too.

Torquil found a comfortable spot from which to watch her. The area where Rhys preferred to practice had no shortage of seats. Fae born of both courts regularly watched him fight. He might not be a future king, but Rhys was the queen's son, often considered second only to her in skill, and thought quite beautiful by many fae. He acted as if he didn't notice his constant audience, but now that she'd seen him relaxed, Eilidh knew better. Rhys was always aware of how he was presenting himself. He didn't have a glass tower as his home, but he was as on display as she was.

At the sight of her, Rhys dispatched his three dueling opponents within moments. He moved with speed akin to the great sharks that cut through the sea, but somehow with less aggression, despite the sharp-edged blade that clanged and slid time and again as it was used to beat back three attackers at once. He was barely visible at the speed he twisted and moved.

When all three defenders stood down, her brother dipped his head to them respectfully. It was the sort of courtly behavior that set him apart from her Seelie brothers. All three of the princes were of equal rank, but it was the *Unseelie* prince who was most courteous. Nacton and Calder, on the other hand, were known to stride away from a victory, as if winning were their birthright.

Of late, they weren't trained as stringently. The unification of the courts and the retreat from humanity meant that most of the fae had no need to draw a weapon. Eilidh, however, was raised not to forget the tenuousness of their safety or the need to defend it. She would be prepared.

"Brother," she said softly as she lifted the blunt longsword that she'd use for practice.

"Sister," he greeted, turning his back to the three fae he'd just defeated. Doing so was a testament to his regard for her. He was stating that he knew that she was watching his back. It was one of the many ways that he silently told anyone who saw them that he trusted her.

And Eilidh desperately wanted to be worthy of that level of respect.

Rhys set aside his sharp sword. He typically practiced with the same weapon he'd use to dispatch a threat, but he'd agreed to spar with her only if he didn't use sharps of any weapon. It was the one concession she'd had to make. Training with the second highest ranked fighter in the Hidden Lands was worth it.

Training with her eldest *brother* was even more worth it.

Silently, he took up the sword he used with her and waited for her approach. Unlike when he fought with their mother, Rhys believed in civility when he and Eilidh crossed blades.

She bowed and then lifted her sword into a high guard position and shifted through several other positions as if in a drill.

For a sliver of a moment, Rhys smiled at her, but then he moved to attack. "Never allow yourself to be on the defensive," he reminded her.

"Know your opponent," she countered as she parried his attack.

If she went on the offensive first, he tended to work her through every guard almost reflexively, as if assuring himself that she knew them all before he was willing to attack. He had more of a likelihood of relaxing out of his purely teaching attitude toward her if she could remind him she was *safe* to genuinely attack.

He smiled for real as he attacked again and then said, "So you remembered to study the enemy's habits."

"Never my enemy."

They continued sparring for almost half an hour before their peaceful combat was interrupted by a true enemy—the former Seelie heir, Nacton. He strode into the courtyard with his sword unsheathed and upraised. "Which of you did it?"

Torquil pushed to his feet and started toward them, but Eilidh darted forward to prevent him from reaching Nacton. She didn't need the clarification of words to know what had angered him so severely.

Neither did Rhys.

Her rightful punishment of Calder had been exposed.

The Unseelie prince looked at her, silently asking for her decision. He lowered his arm so his sword hung at his side. He'd take this fight if she wanted. Whether or not she was the heir, Rhys was at her disposal, still.

"Did what?" she prompted, wanting to hear the words said.

"Tortured my brother," Nacton said.

"There's no way that anyone here—"

"I did," Eilidh said firmly, cutting off Torquil's words. She met Nacton's gaze. "I broke no law. I held him three days, no longer, and I've left no debilitating injury. He'll recover."

"Scarred."

Eilidh shrugged. "So be it. He left a scar on my betrothed. He nearly *killed* what is mine, the fae who will one day make me a mother."

Laughter greeted her words. "You don't truly expect that you'll be allowed to breed. The mongrel might be their new heir, but you—"

"Mind your words about LilyDark." Rhys stepped forward, no longer simply holding a blunt sword. "To defame the heir is treasonous."

"You *tortured* your brother?" Torquil asked quietly from behind her.

Eilidh turned to face him. Typically, she wouldn't turn her back to Nacton, but Rhys was there. She was safe.

"I took the blood rights owed to me," she said as calmly as she could in the face of the disappointment in his eyes. "The *land* supported my rights. Soil held him, and sea removed him when I was done. There was no doubt of my right to vengeance."

For the space of several heartbeats, Torquil merely stared at her, and then he said, "Sometimes I forget that you are her daughter."

And then he limped away, not toward the tower where he had been staying with her, but in the opposite direction. It hurt like a fist to the face when he left her there, and for a blink, she felt her knees tremble. Had he gone for good? Had he finally seen her ugliness and left her? These were the fears that woke her far too often. There weren't words she knew to ask, not in any way that was true enough, so she watched him leave and clamped down on the cries that wanted to rise.

Schooling her emotions so she seemed in control, Eilidh turned back to Nacton. "Calder will recover. If you have issue with the actions I took, take it to the regents. Our father or the qu—"

"I have no need of *her* aid," Nacton interrupted.

Rhys neither spoke nor moved.

"The king will hear about what you've done," Nacton said before he, too, turned and left.

"I didn't hide it," Eilidh said in a soft but mostly steady voice.

As they watched him go, Rhys' hand came down gently on her shoulder. For him it was a very obvious sign of affection. "Not that I take death lightly, sister, but in this case it might've been wiser *not* to leave Calder alive."

"I did as needed done. No more. No less." She'd known that there would be repercussions, but there would've been *other* consequences of failing to act too. Weakness made one prey. Eilidh couldn't allow that. Her family was complicated. All of them were able to fight—including Lily and Zephyr—but they all deserved her support. If she'd let Calder and Nacton's actions go unanswered, they would think her too weak to be intimidating.

And under it all was the undeniable truth that because she was no longer the heir, she was no longer *protected*.

There had been too many reasons to strike Calder, and too few to spare him. More to the point of it all, Eilidh was doing what she must for those she protected and for herself. The Queen of Blood and Rage had taught her well.

twenty

LILYDARK

Lily kept her eyes closed even though she was awake. These few silent moments in the morning were hers. She wasn't Nicolas Abernathy's daughter or the Unseelie Queen's granddaughter or even one of the Black Diamonds. She was just a girl . . . who was snuggled up to a rock star. That thought made Lily fight back a laugh.

For some people, the thought that her roommate was poisoned or a club had burned around her would be shocking. Lily was used to violence. Truth be told, having a boy sleeping next to her was far more intimidating than her recent brushes with death.

That was the way for all people to some degree though. What any one person thought of as "normal" was someone else's strange. Every truth was relative, which was a fact that anyone with fae blood had to accept. The fae inability to lie easily—or in some cases, at all—meant that having any fae blood tied one intrinsically to the concept of "truth." It was far muddier than most people realized.

For instance, Alkamy wasn't angry about her near-death experience. She was simply healing from the poison in the place she felt safest—Zephyr's suite. The fact that she'd been poisoned at all made Lily feel guilty, but as she replayed the scene in her head, she realized that short of reading the letter before unwrapping the sword, there was nothing either of them could've done differently. Lily wasn't accustomed to poisoned gifts. There was no reason to expect such a thing. She'd opened her package, and Alkamy had touched the sword. That was all it took for potential disaster to hit.

Being the heir to the Hidden Throne seemed to come with a steep learning curve, and Lily wasn't certain she was ready for it. There weren't any other choices, unfortunately. This was her lot in life. She would master it, or she would falter until she couldn't continue trying. That was simply how the world worked, or more accurately, how Lily had been raised. Weakness wasn't an option.

"You are not to blame," Creed said. He was sprawled out in her bed, watching her.

She wasn't sure how long he'd been studying her, but it was a habit that she was trying to break him of. "Don't stare."

The sword was in its scabbard now, resting atop Lily's dresser. It was a beautiful weapon, and she was touched to have it as her own. Somehow that gift, more than negotiating with the queen or donning a crown, made the enormity of the role she was undertaking seem frightening. Swords were for those who expected to need to defend themselves. Lily had always known that she needed to be alert. It came as a consequence of her father's job and of her own fae blood.

This was more.

She'd already crossed blades with the former Seelie heir, her uncle, and she'd seen both Creed and Torquil injured for it. She'd watched Violet come near to murdering one of the princes. She herself had been more than ready to spill blood. Now she had to deal with the fact that her bodyguard—the human one—was arrested. She needed to know why the police were at her door, and whether it was fae or human influenced.

"I'm going to the police station," she pronounced.

Creed stared at her for a moment. Then he simply shrugged and stood up. He grabbed his shirt from where he had dropped it the night before and pulled it on. "Back exit or front door?"

"You don't need to come," she started.

His frown made abundantly clear that he disagreed. "Just us or . . . Vi? Zeph?"

"Erik," she added.

The frown morphed into a scowl. "He's only human."

She opened her mouth to explain to Creed that he was being unnecessarily difficult, but before she could speak, he continued, "But he's useful with this stuff, I guess."

"He is." Lily rolled out of bed and tried not to feel self-conscious that Creed was watching her. She wasn't painfully modest, and she knew he liked the way she looked, but she had been so sheltered that her only experiences of *any* sort were with Erik, and those hadn't gone too terribly far. Creed, on the other hand, had been in the public eye, on stages, in tabloids, and at innumerable parties. He'd taken advantage of the opportunities that presented. Often.

"Stop staring," she repeated.

"Can't." Creed waited until she met his gaze. "There are no other girls in the world . . . *either* world, since I met you. I have to stare to make sure you're really here."

Lily laughed. "You're ridiculous."

He grabbed her and dipped her back as if they were dancing. Her laughter shifted into a smile, and he leaned closer and kissed her. Like every other touch they'd shared, Creed's lips on hers felt like every right thing all compressed into one perfect moment. He was her *one*. They had that surprising *click* that made her sure that there was truth to the idea of soul magic. He was her soul mate. She knew it. Some people simply fit together in a way that no logic could explain and no words could capture. She wasn't going to call it fate, but she felt like her soul and his were intrinsically connected. Creed's very touch made her believe that two people could come together in a way that defied every obstacle or objection—and she'd certainly raised more than a few of them herself in an attempt to stay quit of him.

As he kissed her and brought her back to standing, she couldn't imagine her attempts ever succeeding. Creed felt like forever. He might not trust that yet, and her fae grandparents might not agree with it, but there were loves worth fighting for. She was more convinced every day that he was hers, and she'd raze the world if that's what it took to keep him.

"I *am* ridiculous," he admitted. "And yet somehow, you're mine."

She leaned against him. Spending the entire night tangled up in his arms, close enough that their hearts aligned and their breaths mingled, was not enough. Sometimes she feared that the more she had of him, the more she wanted.

One of the difficulties of growing up in the human world was that the fae approach to relationships vied with the human stance. The fae let themselves go; they let emotion and instinct guide them in matters of the heart and soul. Creed's steadfast devotion to her when she was trying to pretend that she was immune to him, Alkamy's unwavering devotion to Zephyr, Roan and Will's true compatibility, these were all very fae.

Lily was raised in a human home, with her human father, surrounded by human criminals. It made her see emotions as a liability more often than any faery would. It made her want to be *practical*.

Of course, her father had never suggested she do so. He'd certainly loved her mother with a passion that was illogical. Maybe, Lily had often wondered, it only took one person to be fae for that sort of magical connection to happen. Even in the human fairy tales—beautiful stories of adventurous princes and hidden princesses or of cursed princes and brave maidens—there was a tendency to pause in awe at the star-crossed lovers or the instant moment when a locked glance or the brush of a hand was enough to catapult a couple into complete surrender to love.

Lily knew that those stories were inspired by the fae way of loving or the fae-blood finding his or her true match. Creed was hers. She was his. There was no way to escape that kind of fate, and as she looked at him, she couldn't think of why she had ever tried.

Shaking her head, Lily stepped back and said, "I'm going to call Erik. He can meet us there."

Creed nodded and went to find his boots.

He needed reassurances, but she did too. It was odd to her that he could be insecure. She'd seen him in so many magazines with so many girls that she couldn't fathom how he had any insecurity at all, but that was the same thing he said about her. Maybe that was one of the secrets to being in love: both people were stunned that the other loved them.

She looked toward Creed as she got dressed. He knew

her. He'd heard her doubts even when she didn't speak them. The Queen of Blood and Rage was another matter altogether. Lily couldn't bring herself to trust her.

"Stop worrying," Creed said without looking at her.

"I don't know that I'm ready," she said.

"For?"

"Whatever is coming. And something certainly is. Daidí has taught me so much, but—"

"One crisis at a time," Creed interrupted. "We don't know what's going on with the attacks or the coronation, but you want to go check on your friend. We do that first."

Lily nodded, and Creed extended his hand toward her.

As she and Creed walked from the dorm to the main building, she called Erik and asked him to meet her. Aside from a brief and not at all subtle inquiry on Violet, he had nothing much to say when she called. He treated her like an equal, and he was doing that even more now that he accepted they would never be more than friends.

When she disconnected from the call, Creed glanced sideways at her. "Do you want to bring Vi?"

"A rock star, an actress, and the children of two international criminals walk into a police station. . . ." She shook her head. "Honestly, maybe you ought to stay here too."

Creed draped an arm over her shoulders. "Notoriety never hurts. I'm done ending up in the rags for being drunk or out with a new girl, so busting someone out of jail would be a welcome—"

"We aren't busting Hector out," she interrupted as they crossed the foyer to the exit.

"Right."

Dropping his sunglasses down as they stepped outside and seemingly becoming more languid as he walked, Creed looked every bit the "troubled boy" he'd been portrayed as for years. At the same time, her steps became more clipped, and her spine straightened. She was also acutely aware of her image, but in a very different way. That was the way of most people though: everyone was projecting something with the way they dressed, walked, and moved. Some people were simply more aware of it. Lily was very aware of it. She'd been trained to be so.

Outside, Erik zipped up in whatever expensive car he was currently renting—or had purchased on impulse. Lily didn't know one car from the other. This one was sleek, cherry-red, and low-slung. There was no doubt in her mind that it would be too fast and turn too quickly. She might not know the make or model, but she knew enough to know that those traits were essential to Erik . . . and that she loved *that* aspect of Erik's car addiction.

Creed let out a murmur of appreciation.

Erik got out of the car to greet them. He gave her a polite bow and kissed her cheeks. Creed he greeted with a nod and a polite, "Do you drive?"

"Sometimes, but nothing like that." Creed stared at the car the way most boys looked at beautiful girls. "Seemed like a waste of cash the way I dr— *used to* drink."

As Creed's words faded, he looked at her and added, "If I'm not drinking, I can buy a car."

Erik laughed, and they headed toward the tiny town center of Belfoure to see what the situation was with Hector's arrest.

twenty-one
CREED

Creed wasn't intimidated by much. For most of the years he remembered, including the fuzzier ones of late, his expectation of living to see twenty years old was low. It had been that way since he realized that he was, in essence, a tool for the Queen of Blood and Rage. She was a war queen, one who'd turned her anger away from the Seelie Court—the "more civilized" faery court—only to aim it at the humans a few years later. He understood her stated reasons: they'd not only polluted the land and sea, but caused her to lose her child to the sea almost a century ago. Under it all, though, the queen wasn't a figure of softness, but of terror. That meant that Creed knew he was unlikely to survive being her weapon.

He'd come to terms with that reality. He'd expected death, and so he'd lived accordingly. He'd ingested poisons upon poisons, alcohol and cigarettes both. On a few occasions, he'd taken street drugs. Creed had done all of it with the awareness that as a fae-blood, any toxin was multitudes worse for him. Even the things humans could ingest in small doses, caffeine or alcohol, were potentially deadly to him. That was the point: to die on his own terms as much as he could. He did as he was ordered, carried out her murderous intent as they all had done, but he was careening toward death as quickly as he could. It was the only rebellion he'd been able to conceive.

Sitting in Erik's car with Lily perched in his lap made him think about other possibilities. Survival was unlikely for different reasons now. He knew as well as the rest of them that his role in Lily's life made him a target. He'd already been injured once because of it.

She was also, quite simply, his savior . . . all of the Black Diamonds might live because she managed to wrest a declaration of peace from the queen of wars. He tightened his hold on her a little more and asked, "So what kind of car is this?"

"Lamborghini Aventador Roadster," Erik offered casually. "It's a V-12, seven speed, limited edition."

Creed said nothing.

"Over two hundred miles per hour maximum speed. Zero to sixty in under three seconds," Erik continued in the sort of awed voice Creed had typically heard when his friends were discussing pretty girls or good weapons.

"Erik?" Lily said gently but with an obvious laugh in her voice. "You're speaking another language."

He glanced at Creed inquiringly.

Creed shrugged. He had no idea what all of that was about beyond the obvious—it was fast.

Erik sighed.

"Vi likes to drive," Creed offered, feeling briefly guilty for failing at some secret human code he didn't understand. He'd had no friends that were purely human, ever.

On his lap, Lily beamed at his offer of friendliness to Erik. She hadn't been subtle about wanting them to be on good terms, but there was the discomfort that Erik had kissed Lily. He was a part of her human world that Creed didn't understand.

"What does she drive?" Erik asked.

"Oh. Something like this, sleek and fast. She's a bit more reckless, though, like she's trying to race a wild-fire." Creed had spent more than a few nights thinking he was going to vomit from Violet's terrifying driving. She took curves like she was hoping to roll the vehicle, and she abused the brakes, coming up on things too fast and stop-ping just shy of ledges. She might not admit a death wish, but he'd recognized it in her. It was only Alkamy, Will, and Roan who didn't push that edge over the years.

When he glanced at Erik, Creed saw that he was smil-ing widely. Again, he wondered if Lily's friend might actually have the reserves to court Violet. If he were determined enough, he might stand a chance. At the least, he'd be a distraction to her. At the best, he might actually make her happy.

Once Erik slid the car into the lot of the police station, he ruined any goodwill he'd earned in Creed's mind. "Nick is meeting us here."

Lily pressed her lips together and glared. "My father? Daidí is *here*?"

"He said not to tell you," Erik added with a not-at-all-covert glance at Creed.

Before anything more could be said, the man who was striding toward the car reached out and opened the door. With the sort of grace that made him seem more feral than human, Nicolas Abernathy extended a hand to his daughter and escorted her from the car—and Creed's lap.

"Daidí," she said softly, leaning up to kiss his cheek as if this entire moment was not a surprise. There were cameras aimed at them already, and Creed thought it interesting that Mr. Abernathy was allowing it. There was obviously a reason. He'd shielded her from publicity most of her life, so tolerating cameras now was exceptionally out of character.

Lily's father studied her in the way of wild things examining their young after a separation. Creed wouldn't have been shocked if he'd leaned in and sniffed her too. There would be no doubt after anyone saw the photographs that were being taken right now that Nicolas Abernathy adored his daughter.

Creed schooled his expressions to something less adversarial than he suddenly felt and stepped out of the car. He wasn't insecure enough to pull Lily closer, but he felt threatened.

"Mr. Morrison." Nicolas Abernathy did not smile or offer a hand. He merely nodded. "I hear you are healed."

"I am."

"Good." He greeted Erik with a hard shake hug combination, clearly more at ease with him than with Creed. The cameras recorded all of it.

Being dismissed stung even though it was subtle. It wouldn't change *any*thing though. Creed's place was at Lily's side. He'd had no doubt about that since he'd met her, and if the regents in the Hidden Lands weren't enough to dissuade him, nothing else would be. Sure, he knew that Lily harbored doubts, and he saw the urge to pull away that flittered in her gaze sometimes. Some creatures weren't meant to be tamed, and LilyDark Abernathy was one of them. She was more fae than human, and the longer she wore the crown of her heritage, the more obvious that became.

And he'd fight to be at her side until he was out of air and pulse. After a life of running toward what he'd thought to be certain death, having a reason to *live* was remarkable. Love was a gift he never thought he'd have, and he'd do anything to keep it for however long he could.

He stood at Lily's side, grateful when she slid her hand into his. A weight fell from him at that gesture. She wasn't rejecting him, despite her father's chill.

"Daidí," Lily murmured softly, seemingly drawing her father's attention to her alone.

"Does he truly want to be seen with all of us?" the elder Abernathy asked.

Creed startled slightly.

"He is with me," Lily said with a slight shrug.

"Erik and I are . . . *known*," Nicolas continued. "And not for the things Mr. Morrison is."

"You're both important to Lily," Creed answered before she could. He met her father's gaze. "And I am perfectly happy to be photographed at her side. That means *your* side too. It's Erik who is at risk when Lily's grandp—"

"I'll be by *her* side, as well as by yours and Violet's." Erik stiffened, but his voice lowered even further as he added, "The police can test my blood. I am not fae at all. I already had a test, years ago, to confirm it."

Lily looked at each of them, and again, Creed could see echoes of the Queen of Blood and Rage in her. "You're *all* already identified as part of my life. When the announcement comes, you'll all be targets. You're all also too stubborn to leave, which I *do* appreciate, so then . . . that's all resolved, yes?" She smiled at Erik, leaned closer to Creed, and grabbed her father's elbow. "Now, let's walk across the lot and into the station before we attract even more of a crowd."

Creed wondered idly if she had always been this regal or if that, too, was changing.

"So when will you be coming to the house again, Creed?" Nicolas asked in a voice sure to carry.

Lily squeezed Creed's hand slightly.

"We'll have to look at the schedule. Erik needs to take me car shopping too." Creed spoke casually, as if they were truly better acquainted than they all were.

Their purposefully light conversation continued as they passed into the police station—and were promptly stopped.

"Sir," a suit-clad man greeted. He bowed his head to Lily, and although he didn't greet Creed or Erik, there was no doubt that he'd noted them in his mental register.

"I trust that things are sorted."

The man's lips pressed together briefly, and he pulled Lily's father a little farther away. They spoke in quiet voices, and Creed could not have heard them if not for his air affinity. He could pull the sound toward him on currents no one else would notice, but he chose not to. Eavesdropping on the business conversations of Lily's father wasn't something to do lightly.

Instead he took a moment to solidify the air near them so *they* could not be overheard. An officer lingering near the desk frowned suddenly. Whatever listening apparatus he'd been using—or perhaps simply a more acute hearing owing to long ago fae ancestry—was thwarted by Creed's reflexive action. He made a mental note to tell Lily's father in the future he might want to employ a fae-blood with air affinity for that very task.

Lily caught Creed's gaze and gave him a beatific smile.

"What?" Erik asked.

"Later," she said, her sideways glance at her father and the lawyer saying enough that Erik nodded.

"Do you know what the trouble is?"

Erik sighed. "We've been trying to get Hector released since he was arrested. There's no reason to deny him bail. They've been absurd, testing his blood, interrogating him, misplacing him."

"No one told me." Lily crossed her arms imperiously. "I'm not going to keep tolerating secrecy, Erik, from anyone."

"Take it up with Nick," Erik said. "Or anyone else who wants to keep things from you."

There was something pointed in that remark, and Creed was sure Lily heard it. Quietly, he said, "Not me."

She nodded.

"Mr. Morrison?"

An older officer stood just to his side somewhat awkwardly. There could be fae blood in him or he could be all human. Creed had no idea. What he did notice was the tense way that the man held himself.

Creed offered him an easy smile, a disarming expression that he'd relied on for years. "What's up?"

"My daughter is a huge fan, and . . ." He broke off awkwardly, looking back at the desk where another of his colleagues was staring not-so-subtly at Lily and Erik.

Still smiling, Creed directed the officer farther away

from them, affording him privacy for his uncomfortable request for his daughter. "What's her name?"

"Lena."

"I'll tell you what. You figure out where my girl-friend's bodyguard is hidden, and I'll get you tickets for Lena for my next three concerts. Backstage for her and two friends."

The officer—whose badge said he was M. Adams—tensed. "I—I don't accept bribes. No one does."

"Not a bribe," Creed said carefully, nudging his charm a little more. He rarely used his fae charms like this, but spending the afternoon here or having Lily upset wasn't appealing. It was a small thing to push a little compulsion toward the man, and it didn't endanger Officer Adams. Gently, Creed said, "It's just an extra thank you gift if you can help my girlfriend."

After a moment, the officer turned and walked away without saying a word.

Disappointed that it hadn't worked, Creed rejoined Lily and Erik. He hadn't tried to use his skills for compulsion often. It was a mild affinity, barely there, but he felt it growing stronger since being healed in the Hidden Lands.

"What was that?"

Creed shrugged. "His daughter's a fan."

"Mr. Abernathy?" the officer at the desk said, pulling all of their eyes to him.

Nicolas inclined his head as if granting permission to speak.

"I am told that your associate is being brought up from holding." The officer's gaze darted toward Creed and narrowed. "They've located him."

The hostility in the officer's eyes was enough to make Creed want to draw a weapon and assume a guard position, but Lily's hand reached out and took his. She squeezed and whispered, "Thank you."

And at that, Creed no longer cared about one human's anger. He'd pleased Lily. That was enough for him.

twenty-two

EILIDH

Eilidh wasn't shocked when the half-fae boys came to her without being summoned. She'd been expecting them since she'd heard of the fire and of the attack at LilyDark and Zephyr's school. She knew she'd be late to meet her brother, and that he wouldn't respond well to that, but the only reason Will and Roan would come was if they knew things she needed to hear.

She would rather be finding Torquil to see if he would forgive her, but that wasn't an option when she'd heard Roan and Will speak her name. Duty before desire; that was how the world had always worked for her. Once she saw her unwilling spies, she could then seek out her beloved.

As quickly as she was able, she raced toward the tunnel where they'd entered this time.

"I'm glad you were wise enough to avoid a public entrance," she said when she saw them there.

"Here." Roan extended a thick envelope. "We need to get back . . . Lily will need to know this all too."

"She doesn't need—"

"Lily is the heir," Will interrupted. "She outranks all of us. All but your parents. I'm not keeping secrets from her, not even for you . . . your highness."

Eilidh flinched briefly. She'd become so accustomed to doing as she wanted that she hadn't thought much on her new reality. She could no longer hide as much as she'd like from Lily.

"I could solve the dilemma," she mused, staring at them. Was the information such that their deaths were justified? She wasn't sure, not yet. She opened the packet.

"She'd still find out. The information is waiting for her." Will met her gaze, and Eilidh had to wonder who had sired him. Her mother had only chosen the strongest of her fae for the small group that contained her grandson and granddaughter.

At his side, Roan made a choking noise and hastily added, "We're not trying to upset you, but Lily . . . She comes first for us."

Eilidh ignored them and started scanning the pages. The only thing she could say for certain was that the troubles in the human world were tied to *this* world. The fae-bloods who were striking out were not doing so without guidance. Her emotions grew unsteady as she thought about everything she'd planned, thought about the possibility of peace. It was so near, and someone was trying to snatch it from her grasp.

Abruptly, she turned and went toward her brother. She needed to think, and plan, and then, she'd need to tell both Rhys and the regents.

The weight of the years of planning was starting to wear on her. She knew not to let her emotions become unfettered. She needed to center herself so she sought her Unseelie brother first. Not surprisingly, Rhys was standing in the yard outside their mother's home. He wasn't standing guard per se, but it was often where he could be found when he was worried.

"Brother, I have need of your wisdom," Eilidh greeted him.

He looked vaguely frightened. It was a peculiar look for him, and for a moment, Eilidh worried that something else had gone wrong. Then, Rhys said, "If you need aid with Torquil, I could remind him of the laws that validate the blood debt you were claiming."

"No. I tortured Calder," she said gently. "Law or no law, Torquil disapproves. He was raised Seelie, friend to Calder and Nacton, friend to me . . . the then-heir of the Hidden Throne. He's innocent, or at least as innocent as one of our kind can be."

Rhys let out a grumble of disapproval and began wiping the blade he'd been using before her approach. "He is merely young."

"As am I," she reminded her brother. After a moment of hesitation, she decided that she was best served to not try to figure out this latest dilemma on her own—especially as he was as invested as she was. So, too, were her parents. They all deserved to know what she knew. Perhaps they already did. She extended the packet of pages. "Here. I need help with this . . . and telling the queen."

He took the pages.

She flashed him a grateful smile as she gave it over.

As soon as he started reading it, he paused and frowned at her. "Where did you get this?"

"Don't ask."

"I *did*."

Eilidh shook her head. "There is someone helping the fae-bloods stir trouble to stop the declaration of peace."

"Obviously," Rhys said. "You aren't to go over there, Eilidh. Our mother would be—"

"I didn't," she interrupted. "I asked for information. This is it."

Rhys stared at her until she felt like squirming, but after years of facing the Queen of Blood and Rage, Eilidh was well-practiced in hiding her discomforts. He sighed. "I will handle this. Go find Torquil and set that to rights."

"Yes, brother," she said gratefully.

"And sister? If I find that you are visiting that world again, I will speak to both of your parents about your security. It's enough that you're tempting safety by torturing Calder . . . and sending spies to the human world . . . and keeping secrets from the queen. . . ." Rhys paused, as if just realizing the extent of her list of misdeeds. He shook his head. "I would be unhappy if you were injured. Find your betrothed. Stay out of the other world *and* away from the Seelie princes."

Eilidh took a breath, wanting to argue, wanting to point out that she had single-handedly found the new heir and made it so peace could be decreed. But the voice of the trees told her in rustling words that she needed to come to them.

"I will do better next time," she promised, and then she went to find Torquil.

The sea murmured that he was not in the water. The air whispered directions. In the Hidden Lands, it was difficult to truly avoid being found by other fae. If one's affinities were strong enough, finding what was hidden was inevitable. Eilidh's affinities were exceptionally strong, perhaps as nature's apology for her lack of physical strength, perhaps as a result of the way the earth and sea had saved her in her infancy.

When she found Torquil, he was at the edge of the pathway to the human world that she'd used so often. The same tree where he'd waited for her time and again over the years was where he now sat. Unlike in the past, he was not perched on a branch, but leaning at the base of the tree.

"I knew who you were years ago, Patches." He didn't look at her as he spoke, and the simple absence of his gaze hurt. She'd never expected him to love her, never thought he could choose her. Having him turn away hurt.

"I've never asked you to be anything other than who you are," he continued. "When you were lying to our queen, I held your secrets. When you were pushing me away, I accepted it until I discovered your feelings . . . and then I *still* waited."

"I know." Eilidh watched him, not knowing what else to say or do. Torquil had small relationships before her. She'd had none. This feeling of discord was wholly new to her.

"You lied to me," he said, finally turning his gaze on her.

She opened her mouth to try to say that she hadn't, that when the subject was broached she'd admitted what she'd done, but he spoke again before she could force the words to come to suddenly parched lips.

"You didn't trust me," he added.

Eilidh stepped closer, not daring to touch him but wanting to do so.

He stared at her so intently that she would have flinched if not for years of training at her mother's side. Torquil's voice was low and harsh as he asked, "Do you think I forgot who your parents were? That I suddenly didn't know all of the lessons you had to learn to be the next queen? Do you think I would be left shocked that you are following the old laws?"

"I don't know," she admitted. All she'd truly thought was that she hated what needed doing, and she didn't want to let Torquil know. *Had* she thought he'd understand? She couldn't honestly answer that.

"When I was first invited to be your playmate, the queen and the king both pulled me aside to speak to me. The king asked me to look after you, to be a confidant. The queen . . . was less kind. She informed me that you needed to be strong and that I was not to weaken you, but she made clear that she trusted me to be a softening influence when your duties were too harsh. I was the one who was to let you weep or remind you to laugh or whatever you needed. She suffered my presence, my oh-so-Seelie nature, because she thought you would need to be fire-honed so you could be sword-edged, as she is."

Eilidh drew a shuddering breath.

"I expected that there would be worse before us if you had become queen. I expected that when I chose you as my wife, and I *accepted* that."

"Are you disappointed that I won't be queen?" She hated asking, but it was a thought she'd had more than once. She didn't believe that he cared about power, but she was still unsure as to why he'd chosen her when there were so many others more beautiful, more elegant, more everything. His loving her made no sense.

Torquil laughed, but not in true humor. His voice was just as bitter as his laughter as he said, "I am going to fear that you don't know me at all soon, Patches."

Tears blurred the edge of her vision. She had no idea how to do this, how to make him understand that she was trying to be what she must and what she was all at once. She didn't want to lose him, but she couldn't pretend to be other than who she was.

In violation of every rule of etiquette they'd observed so carefully up to this point, Torquil's hands gripped her hips. She let out a gasp as he pulled her closer. He was assertive in dreams, but never in the waking world. With daylight, he had been a proper Seelie fae, suitable to keep company with the daughter of his king. She preferred this.

Eilidh looked up at him. They were close enough that she could feel each of his breaths on her face as they stood together in silence. They'd shared closer space in their conjoined dreams, but in the waking world, propriety was the default.

"I wasn't interested in marrying the queen," he said. "I was . . . I *am* interested in marrying *you*."

"Still?"

"Still."

Eilidh felt like whatever had been holding her upright since he'd been stabbed snapped. All of the tears she'd tried to suppress rose up like the waves had done at her behest. Now, though, her tears called the rain.

As they stood there, they were soon drenched. She felt like the skies were soothing her, like they were weeping the tears that sometimes threatened to choke her. It wasn't the mad crashing of waves that she summoned when she was anger-filled, but it was a blissful feeling of release all the same.

Torquil pulled her tighter into his embrace, and she rested her face against his chest, clutching his shirt and holding him to her. His hands soothed her, stroking her hair and back as he murmured, "Shhhh. Everything is fine, love. Shhhh."

When she was finally able to speak, she told him, "I needed them to know that I was every bit her daughter, that I would not stop at an angry word if they hurt my own. Not just you but Lily too. I need to be able to keep you all safe."

"I know," Torquil assured her. "I am safe."

"And Rhys," she added. "I want to protect him too."

Despite how foolish that might be, Eilidh wanted to shelter Rhys as he did her. Her eldest brother was more than adept at protecting himself, and he'd undoubtedly be amused to think of her wanting to defend him, but he was her brother, her defender, and the only member of her fae family who had offered her acceptance and love.

"Of course," Torquil said in the same soothing tone, still caressing her comfortingly. "You did what you thought necessary to guard your loved ones. I have no judgment there, Patches. I understand why you—"

"It was awful," she blurted out uncharacteristically, but now that she was crying in his arms, she couldn't seem to keep anything back. "Hurting Calder was . . . awful. I hated it."

There weren't words enough to express the horror she'd felt, the pain it had caused her to know that he'd never forgive her, that she *shouldn't* be forgiven, but she couldn't let his action go unanswered. Unlike Calder, she was Seelie *and* Unseelie.

"No more secrets," Torquil said quietly. "That's all I need, Eilidh. You shouldn't hide things from me. You don't need to. Ever. You do as you must, and I will accept it. I did accept it long before I declared myself to you, but don't lie to me. Don't deceive me. *That* I won't accept."

Eilidh lifted her head from his chest and nodded. Then she stretched up onto her toes so she could reach and kissed him, not as fully as she did in their dreams but in a way that made her feelings clear to any and all who might be watching. She didn't *see* any fae nearby, but she knew as well as he did that they were as likely as not to be under someone's surveillance.

When she dropped back to the flat of her feet, he said only, "Have the rules changed?"

"Let them talk," she said. "If I want to kiss my intended, I should be able to do so. Everything feels so close to disaster. Everything but you. Us . . ."—she looked up at him—"*this* is what's good in my world. So kiss me."

He smiled and then he did exactly what she ordered.

twenty-three

LILYDARK

Lily watched Hector walk through the police station toward them with a mix of relief and fury. He had a swollen eye, a bandage around his arm where they'd obviously drawn blood, and he was limping. She leveled a glare at the human officer who'd been at her door and was currently escorting Hector out of wherever he'd been imprisoned within the bowels of the building.

"Stand down," Daidí said sternly.

At first, Lily glanced at Erik, who merely grinned and raised his brows at her. With a start, she realized that Daidí was talking to her. It wasn't a tone that allowed for any argument, however, so she held her tongue. She might be the future queen of faeries, but she was still her father's daughter. And this was Abernathy business, not fae. That made it his to manage. Perhaps, it always would be solely his.

With some sadness, Lily realized that she'd sacrificed his empire. She wasn't sure she could manage to rule the Hidden Lands and a criminal enterprise, and even if she could, she wasn't sure it was fair to anyone for her to try to do so. It broke her heart a little.

She leaned her head on her father's shoulder and said, "Yes, Daidí."

He sent her a sideways look that was full of questions, but they weren't anywhere where answers were possible.

"Abernathy," the human detective said as he released Hector's cuffs.

Daidí didn't deign to reply. He had a longstanding tradition of not answering the police in even the simplest matters if possible. It was well-documented.

"Mr. Abernathy is here to collect his employee, who was wrongfully detained without proper due process," the attorney supplied.

"And what does Mr. Abernathy have to say about the burning of one hundred and eighty acres in the South Continent?" the officer continued, staring at Daidí, not the attorney, as if he could read some hint there. He wasn't the first man she'd seen try to intimidate her father. It was sheer folly on their part every time. Nicolas Abernathy was implacable on even his worst days.

"Fires are a naturally occurring event," the attorney said mildly. "It's an unfortunate thing that such a large area was burned, but nature can be unpredictable."

"If a fae-blood were—"

"Are you accusing Mr. Abernathy of being fae-blood, officer?"

The officer said nothing for a long moment, but then he relented and said, "We have seen the records. He was not fae-blood in the tests."

"Then you know he was tested *voluntarily* several times," the attorney supplied smugly.

"A man with his sort of reach could just as easily hire one of them." The officer's voice was dripping with hostility at the mention of the fae-blood. He gestured at Hector. "That one might not be, but I'm certain he's harboring one of them."

Daidí turned away, steering her with him. Erik met his eyes and led the way, while Creed and Hector closed in behind them side by side. It was similar enough to how they'd walked in that it wasn't drawing undue attention. However, the feel of the air solidifying behind her was clue enough that Creed was uncomfortable.

Behind them the attorney prompted, "Are you filing any charges?"

"Not presently."

"Keep walking," Daidí ordered when she paused.

Lily didn't reply. There was no need. She kept her public mask in place, looking as bored as she could, and paused to wait when Erik opened the door. Typically, her father walked out first in case there was a threat. Today, he inclined his head toward the door and pressed lightly on her back to indicate that she should precede him. The threat behind them was reason enough for him to change his habit.

Outside, he scanned the lot. The photographers had multiplied.

Although it wasn't particularly newsworthy to see Creed at a police station, seeing her and Daidí was rare, and seeing Creed at their side was still new. The journalists might not know what the story was, but they knew that there was one.

Her father's black car pulled up, and she glanced at him. In front of them, reporters called questions and speculations, their voices mingling into cacophonies from which occasional lines stood out.

"Mr. Abernathy?"

"Creed! Hey, Creed!"

"Is Mr. Abernathy sponsoring a tour?"

"Or a new line of clothes?"

"Lily!"

"You can do better!"

Lily paused, not sure whether that last was directed at her or Creed. It didn't matter. It was untrue either way. No one would love Creed as she did, and she was sure she was lucky to have his love. She reached out for his hand.

"Raoul will ride with Erik," Daidí said as one of his other guards stepped out of the front passenger seat of the car.

Creed squeezed her hand in his.

No one argued with Daidí. As Hector took his

customary position at the door, Lily slid into the back of the long black car, followed by Creed, and then Daidí. Raoul escorted Erik to his little sports car, and they all left. Whatever remained to be done at the police station, the attorney would handle it.

The driver didn't raise the privacy divider, so Lily could see him and Hector both.

Once the car was sliding into traffic, Daidí turned to her and said, "I would have thought that my order to not allow yourself to be arrested would make it clear that going to the police station was foolhardy."

Lily sighed.

Hector turned around and looked at her. "You're not to come after anyone. Even if you have Cerise—"

"Who?" Creed interjected.

"A gun," Lily supplied. "That's the word for gun. For us, at least."

"She's not defenseless," Creed said loyally. Then he asked her, "Can I speak freely?"

There was no doubt in her mind that he was going to speak to her increased affinities, and she was certain that both Hector and Daidí were fine to tell. She darted her eyes toward the driver and then to Daidí, who wryly said, "Your *aunt* sent him to me. He's loyal."

The driver looked in the rear view mirror and said, "Your majesty."

At his speaking, Lily realized that Creed was still shielding her or she'd have felt the driver's fae-blood by now. She brushed past the solidified air that Creed had held around her and reached out her own air to study the driver.

"You're more fae than not," she said after a moment. There were definite threads of air and sea clinging to him.

"The princess thought your father might need a bit of looking after," the man said.

Nothing in the driver's appearance spoke of otherness. His mannerisms and his voice were of this world, as well. Most fae she'd met so far seemed so different from humans. She was at a complete loss. "You seem human. If I couldn't read you, I'd have thought you were."

He flashed her a wide smile. "The princess sent me here years ago. Clever at planning, she is. Most folk underestimate her. They see her as fragile, but she's a fierce one."

"She is." Lily was at a loss on how to proceed. Her father was . . . well, *the parent*. She was the one who was protected, and realizing that he was vulnerable because of her left her at a loss.

"I will keep him safe for you," the driver said, understanding her worries without her having to give voice to them. "As long as there is breath in me, he will be unharmed by those that question your rightfulness to lead our people."

His zealotry was unexpectedly comforting; in this case she couldn't object to it. Her father might be safe in a lot of ways, but he was defenseless against a fae like Nacton or his devotees. She wasn't sure why they would want to strike him, but she wasn't as clear on the fae reaction to her new role as she needed to be. For now, though, she was going to stick to the practical.

Lily shook her head. "I will be in your debt if you keep my father safe."

"No need, your highness. No need at all. The princess has seen to me and my family already. It's an honor to serve you both." He met her gaze again, gave her another wide smile, and then he returned his attention to the road.

"Speak freely, Mr. Morrison," Daidí said. "You've clearly got things on your mind."

Creed looked at her again, and she simply shrugged. If Eilidh hadn't already told Lily's father everything, it was only a matter of time until she did or Lily herself did. There was no reason for Creed not to fill her father in.

And so he did. Everyone in the car listened as Creed recounted their fights in the Hidden Lands and her subsequent negotiations with the regents. Then he ended with, "Lily's going to be the queen, and she's already been given a sword by them. She's going to be the one leading the fae, ruling the Hidden Lands, and she's already crossed blades with the Seelie princes and brokered a peace treaty. Even without her affinities, she's more than capable."

"And . . . my affinities are growing," she added quietly. "I think it's this." She showed her father the crown, touching the tattoo so it lifted out of her skin and became a solid circlet. "Or maybe it's being around so many fae and fae-bloods. I don't know, but . . . Creed's right, I'm not defenseless."

Daidí leaned back in his seat and was silent for several minutes. She wasn't sure whether it was disappointment or what in his eyes. Finally, he said, "I've never met your grandmother. I don't relish it ever happening either. Your mother and I talked about all the ways we could hide you, and I wanted that. We both did. Then we realized you'd never been unknown. Your aunt knew. Eilidh always knew who you were, and . . ."

"What?"

"I like her," Daidí said cautiously. "She's all fae, though. She's plotted for your discovery your whole life. We knew she was, that she was waiting to reveal you, that you'd end up in the queen's sight. The best we could do was try to prepare you."

No one spoke. It was clear that Daidí wasn't done even though he was staring out the darkened side window. He looked tired, and she could only hope that it was simply the jetlag wearing on him.

"You look like your mother," he said, turning back to her. "I understand from Eilidh and Torquil that you look even more like the queen."

"I do."

He nodded. "The Calvacantes torched one of my fields. They used a fae-blood to do it and were overt about it being fae related. No accelerant. During a storm that should've put out any fire. The only thing that would've burned that fast and hot in a torrential downpour was someone using an affinity."

"Why?"

Daidí shrugged, wincing a little as he did so. "We don't know. All we can say for certain is that the result is an international investigation that's tying our businesses to the fae."

"Which will make them look at Lily," Creed supplied.

"There are people who can fix tests," Hector pointed out.

Lily stared at her father, who was looking at her warily. She'd never seen such an expression on him before. "Daidí? Are you okay?"

"I was burned," he said mildly. "During the situation . . . it's tender."

"Let me see. What——"

"No." He took a deep breath and met her eyes, and in that instant, Lily knew that she didn't want to hear whatever else he was going to say. She shook her head. Everything was so unsettled. Hearing *more* bad news wasn't something she wanted, not even a little.

"I needed water, and I haven't . . . It's been a long time since I called it." Daidí looked at her as if willing her to understand him.

"No. You're not . . ." She didn't want to finish, couldn't even say the words that fit there. "You aren't."

Lily's father stared at her, his silence full of meaning.

She stared back, hoping she was somehow misunderstanding.

"Iana didn't want me to tell you, Lily. You need to understand. Your mother might not have been raised by them, but she was still their daughter." Her father smiled the proud and sad smile that he reserved for talk of Iana. "She was devious even in her sleep, you know. I wasn't ever planning to be as successful at the business, but your mother had plans."

"You were burned because you used an affinity," Lily said slowly, watching her father in hopes that he would laugh or explain or *something*.

Creed gripped her hand tighter, but no one spoke. No one stopped Daidí. No one interrupted to correct her interpretation.

"You need to understand, Lily. Iana thought it was best if you believed I was wholly human. She was always right. Everything we have came from her cleverness." Her father smiled again, a sad little expression that usually made her want to hug him but in that moment, she was feeling more like smacking him.

"But . . ."

"Iana wanted the best for us," he added.

Words wouldn't come to her as she looked at her father. She'd always known that her mother was fae, but she'd thought . . . she'd *known* her father was human. Feeling awkward in a way she never had, she reached out for his hand. She let her eyes close as she concentrated on knowing him, on finding what he was, or asking him to share.

It wasn't as obvious even now, but she could feel something there. It was muffled, though, as if a thick web was wrapped around him. Lily opened her eyes and frowned at her father. "You're . . . like hearing a radio underwater. If I didn't know . . ."

Her words faded, but he finished them for her. "You'd never realize. Eilidh helped us. There was a healer who did something or other. It took a lot of years to make it . . . undetectable."

Being fae-blood typically meant being Seelie- or Unseelie-born. If Daidí was fae-blood enough to need to be repressed by a fae healer, he wasn't one of the peculiar fae who lived outside of the courts. That meant that he was loyal to the queen or the king, and in some ways that was even worse than being human. It meant that *she* had more Seelie or Unseelie blood because of him.

Lily knew which of her grandparents claimed his loyalty even as she asked, "Which court?"

He looked at her, sighed, and said, "Not hers."

Creed muffled a curse. The driver raised his brows in surprise. Only Hector seemed unconcerned.

"Holy Ninian, Daidí."

He offered her a wry smile, but no further words. There *were* none. When Lily took the throne, there would be more Seelie blood than Unseelie ruling the Hidden Lands. Eilidh knew that, knew that the queen wouldn't allow it—just as she undoubtedly knew that it would come out in time. Lily had no idea what it would mean, but she knew she felt betrayed by her father, her aunt, and her mother. Anyone who thought it was a joy to be a royal heir wasn't paying attention. Her mother had hidden from it, and her aunt had worked to replace herself with Lily.

"Let me handle the Calvacantes," Daidí said, "and if you need me to come to that place, I will. I've never met my . . . in-laws, but perhaps one of them will not hate me overmuch."

Lily snorted. She knew there wasn't a perfect solution to the situation she was in, but she was still hurt that he'd lied to her. More than that, he'd gone so far as to deny a part of himself to do so. She felt like she'd stumble under the weight of how many people's lives were tangled up with hiding her, protecting her, defending her, and hating her.

"I loved your mother, Lily," Daidí said steadily. "That meant trusting her. We spent a lot of time trying to make you safe, trying to prepare you, and I don't regret any of it. She wouldn't either. We both loved you enough to risk your eventual anger in order to keep you safe."

Lily sighed, but she couldn't find any worthy words to even start to talk to him about how she felt. She was afraid and overwhelmed. Everyone was looking to her to be their savior, to know what to do. She didn't have half a clue most of the time. It was easy for everyone to say that it would be fine, but the part that they failed to say out loud was "because you'll make it so." She had so far. She'd accepted her role as the daughter of the dead heir, and she'd brokered a peace between the worlds.

Her father was a target. Her boyfriend was a target. Her friends were too. Somehow years of dealing with the criminal underworld was different from this new situation. The issues that would come with being the heir to the Hidden Throne felt heavier. Yet, they'd all conspired to make this very situation come to pass. Her parents, her aunt, the queen, the king, even Lily had been part of the long list of parties who had made choices that resulted in every single person she knew being in peril.

"Lily?" Her father gave her the sort of uneasy look that didn't belong on the face of a crime lord.

She shook her head. All she could do was tell him the one thing that was unchanged: "I love you, too, Daidí."

twenty-four
ALKAMY

There weren't any *bad* reasons that Alkamy was plotting to slip out of Zephyr's bed when he fell asleep. He was wonderful, and the past few weeks had been the best of her life. She wished it could last forever, but having it at all was more than she'd expected. They had a few hours alone, and he was relaxed enough to sleep. Being entwined with him wasn't going to help that happen.

Even though his eyes were closed, his hands were sweeping over her body with the sort of surety that said he would know her from any other person. He knew her curves and hollows, her edges and her swells. They'd always been in sync like that.

"What are you thinking?"

He did that more and more, caught her at the edge of a thought she couldn't share.

"That I like days when they are all gone," Alkamy told him. It wasn't a lie. She had thought it, just not at the *moment* he'd asked. Zephyr spent a lot of time worrying about them, and so she spent time worrying over him and trying to ease his stress. The rare moments when he was at peace were amazing, more so now that they were allowed to be together as they'd both wanted for so long.

"Vi's still moody, but Creed is better . . . and sober," she added. "It's like he finally thinks he can do anything."

She kissed the place where his neck and shoulder met. It wasn't about sex. Sometimes, they simply curled up and slept. Touching Zephyr was a lot like touching earth: it made Alkamy feel rejuvenated.

Zephyr opened his eyes and looked at her. "Being in love does that."

It still made her heart flutter when he admitted even in the slightest ways that he loved her. The hint of it was enough to make her feel like some foolish child who had been given every present under the moon and stars for her birthday. Growing up, she wasn't sure she'd ever had a birthday that was remotely satisfying. They were merely publicity stunts where she smiled for cameras, and her father pretended he had some part of selecting the presents she was opening.

Alkamy kissed Zephyr again and whispered, "I love you."

And the planned nap was no longer an option. Sometimes being with him made her best efforts futile. Touching him was as essential as breathing, and kissing him until she was unable to speak was the best idea she would ever have.

So she did just that.

When they were finally quiet and still again, Zephyr was smiling as peacefully as he ever had. "Lunch? We could grab some things and have a picnic."

"We haven't done that lately." Alkamy knew they weren't of the same court; there was no way she was anything other than Seelie-born. They did, however, share an affinity for earth. Picnics were an excuse to be together and close to soil and rock. "Back in ten."

She slipped into her clothes and went to her suite. Ten minutes became twenty as she gathered up a pair of sunglasses, water, and a tote. Twenty minutes became thirty as she changed into a sundress and sandals. By the time she was ready, Zephyr was in her doorway with food.

"You already . . ."

He laughed. "I know you, Kam."

"I reserve the right to be surly about your lack of faith later." She held out the tote for him to fill and carry.

"I have complete faith," he corrected. "Always. I knew you'd be here and you'd be beautiful."

Alkamy's gaze dropped to the sword hanging at Zephyr's side. Around campus, he'd started carrying it openly more and more often. Lily and Violet had too. No one said outright that they were expecting not to be here much longer. They didn't need to say it. Once Lily was announced as the heir to the Hidden Throne, they would all likely be openly identified as fae-blood.

They would be outlaws because of their birth.

It was ridiculous that things outside a person's control could make others hate you. The nature of your blood wasn't a choice, but humanity had a long history of killing, imprisoning, or fearing others for their race or religion. Hating fae-blood was just the latest manifestation of it.

"Do you really need to bring that?" she asked lightly.

"Maybe I'll practice when you nap in the sunshine." Zephyr shrugged like it was no big deal, like the constant reminder of war and violence wasn't upsetting. It was though.

But Alkamy knew a lost cause when she heard it. Safety was his obsession. He'd been willing to sacrifice them being together in some misguided attempt to protect her, so all things considered, this was mild.

"Maybe I ought to start practicing more," she said in a concession of sorts.

His answering smile was enough to make her debate grabbing a sword that instant. She wasn't exactly *bad* at swordplay, but she didn't love it the way he did. No one other than Lily seemed to like it that much.

"This week," Alkamy offered. "We could spend a little extra time practicing. Just us."

Zephyr nodded, and then headed toward the passageway out of the building. The door fell closed behind them,

and they started to walk. It was a walk they'd taken count-
less times, familiar enough that they could probably do so
without light.

"Are you okay?"

She squeezed his hand. "I am. I just know you worry.
I'm not as strong as them, and I don't want to let you down,
especially after the poisoning. . . ."

He leaned in and kissed her, silencing her litany of reasons. It wasn't a reaction she objected to at all. In public,
she was her father's daughter—pretty, cold, and maybe a
little icy. With the others, she was the one who made people relax. With him, she walked a line between supportive
and . . . relaxed. Being with Zephyr was like what she'd
heard people describe as being "home."

Alkamy let herself fall into his embrace. She could get
happily drunk on his kisses. Knowing that he was hers, truly
and completely *hers* to touch and kiss and hold made everything in the years before this okay. When he pulled away,
she told him as much. Both of them were breathing heavily.

"We could go back up to the suite," she said lightly.

Zephyr laughed. "We could. Let's get lunch first
though."

Alkamy couldn't remember the last day they'd had
that seemed so perfect. Later, there would undoubtedly be
things she'd rather not address. Later, there would be talk
of war and politics. Right now, though, there was only
this: a picnic with Zephyr.

She was giggling when she stepped out into the gardens. She slid off her sandals and bent to pick up them up. When she stood, something hit her stomach.

She felt herself lose balance and fall backward. "Zeph?"

He caught her and was in front of her somehow in the next moment.

Alkamy put one hand to her stomach and the other to the wall behind her. She slid down so her hand could touch the soil. Earth would help. It always did.

Absently, she noticed that the hand she pulled away from her belly was wet. She was bleeding. As she lowered her hand to the soil, she realized that maybe stretching out was better than trying to sit.

There was no hilt jutting out from her injury. There was only a searing pain, as if she'd been burned. There was no scent of burning flesh though. Alkamy looked at her stomach.

The skin was torn as if she'd been stabbed.

She closed her eyes and concentrated on the earth, asking stone for answers because her mind felt hazier with each passing exhalation.

Metal.

As soon as rock and soil answered her, she knew. She'd been shot. No affinity, no poison, no blade. None of the things that were her usual fears. This was a human cruelty, bullets tearing through flesh.

"Kam? Alkamy!"

Alkamy opened her eyes again and smiled at Zephyr as best she could.

There was a man with a sword, and Zephyr was fighting. The clang of metal connecting with metal had been a familiar sound for years, but the ferocity of it was different now. This wasn't friends sparring. Zephyr was angry, aggressive, and somehow more alluring for it.

"Pretty," she said, even though he couldn't hear her.

He was though. Whether it was his Unseelie ancestry or what, Zephyr was glorious when in a rage. It was always strangely beautiful to watch him fight. When they were younger, watching him was the spark that made her realize that she wanted more than friendship. It might be silly, but it made her a little less embarrassed by her fae blood. The Hidden Lands were a mysterious place to her, a sort of world where time had stopped moving. For years, her fantasy had been that the war would end, and she and Zephyr could move there.

It had seemed so close this morning.

But as the shock of being shot faded, she realized she'd never live there.

"Kamy!" Zephyr was there again, but closer now. He was on the ground holding her, talking to someone, yelling for help.

"Shhh." She reached up to touch his face, to make him look at her. "It's okay."

"No, Alkamy. No! NO!"

"I can't stay awake, Zeph." She blinked. Telling him

why seemed mean, but she *knew*. As she looked at his face, she was sure he did too.

"I need help!" he yelled. "Where is everyone?"

"Zeph?"

"You can't." Zephyr pulled her closer. It didn't hurt as much, even though he was taking her away from the soil. He wouldn't do that if he didn't know too. Somewhere inside, he knew.

And that made everything easier.

"I love you," she said.

Then she closed her eyes.

twenty-five

VIOLET

"Whoa!" Violet exclaimed as her door slammed open. She was on her feet with a knife in hand within a moment.

"And to think that people say you're high-strung," her suitemate Hailey murmured.

Without looking away from the unexpected trio in front of her, Violet flipped a rude gesture toward Hailey. She wasn't exactly high strung. She simply wasn't prepared to have Creed, LilyDark, and Erik come tromping into her suite.

Neither, obviously, was her roommate. Hailey was shy, studious, and aside from the discomforting tendency to wake up smiling, she was a perfect roommate. They weren't friends in the sense that she was with the diamonds, but she liked Hailey well enough to have lived with her for several years now.

Part of why that worked was that they had rules. The biggest rule was that they didn't let their social schedules in Violet's case or study schedules in Hailey's case inconvenience the other person. Creed hadn't ever endeared himself to Hailey, and Lily's criminal connections made Hailey—a future attorney—decidedly ill at ease.

"Whatever happened, don't say *anything* in front of me," Hailey announced. "Trials take forever, and I have too much work to do."

Erik grinned. Creed pantomimed sealing his lips. The diamonds were used to pretending to be far less serious than the situation required, so he slipped into lightheartedness easily most days. The only of the Black Diamonds who didn't was Lily, but Violet was fairly sure that was by choice.

It didn't take much to see that Lily needed her, though, and that outweighed peace with her roommate. It wasn't even about the fact that Violet had given LilyDark a vow. Lily was her friend. That mattered, vow or no vow.

"You had the light on until dawn studying last week," Violet said, spinning abruptly to look at Hailey.

Hailey crossed her arms and began to negotiate. "You weren't even here. That doesn't count. I'm not the one who's upended the schedule, Vi."

Violet sighed. Typically, she loved this. Hailey's tenacity was a treat, and the fact that she was undaunted by Violet's temper or her fame was awesome. Today, though, there wasn't time to bicker.

"Fine. You can have your next study session here, even if it's morning."

"Done." Hailey stood and shoved a few things into her bag.

Violet tossed a pen at her. "You were already headed to the library, weren't you?"

Hailey grinned and sauntered toward the door. "You tried to use my studying when *you weren't here* to bargain, too. Weak tactic, Vi. Weak."

"When I get arrested one of these days, I better get a discount on your legal fees." Violet caught the pen Hailey tossed back at her as she walked out. She might be quiet and studious, but she didn't lack in bravery or attitude.

Once Hailey left, Violet turned to her friends—and the interloper—and asked, "What happened?"

Between Lily and Creed, there was a quick debrief about the police station, the set-up against Lily's father, and the fact that he was fae-blood in hiding. Violet sat down with a lot less grace than normal. Then, she foolishly glanced at Erik to see if he'd noticed . . . not that she wanted him to, of course.

He had his back to her and was staring out the common room window. She didn't mean to, but she sent a surge of heat his way in her irritation. He glanced over his shoulder at her and smiled, but wisely said nothing.

"And Erik tells me that Will asked him to gather information on the attacks," Lily added.

"What?" Violet returned her attention to her friends.

That explained why he'd been acting peculiarly. She shook her head. "Do we know who asked him to get it?"

"We will," Creed muttered.

Violet's attention snapped to him as she reminded him, "We've all had to do things we weren't allowed to share."

Violet sighed. "It never gets less complicated, does it?"

"It will," Erik interjected. "Lily has both of you, and me, and her father. This will get resolved."

Creed glanced at him with a curiously friendly expression, but said nothing.

"We will keep you safe, Lily," Erik added in a tone that sounded a lot like a vow.

"I'm not worried about *me*," she pointed out.

Erik laughed. "Excellent. We'll handle worrying about you. You figure out what you need to do to get through all of this chaos."

"Stop the attacks. Declare peace . . . not get arrested." Lily rested her head on Creed's shoulder and met Violet's gaze. "Easy, right?"

"Not easy, but not impossible," Violet assured her.

Unfortunately, that didn't mean that Violet knew how to help with any of those things. She could kill the attacker once they found him. That was in her skill set, but the rest wasn't. The diamonds weren't exactly familiar with the legal system or gifted in politics. International travel? Currency conversion and fashion? All were easily managed. Poisoning, fires, and intrigue? Those were normal work.

Lily suddenly asked, "Can Erik stay here while I go talk to Zephyr?"

"What?"

"Can Erik stay with you?" Lily clarified.

There wasn't any fair reason to object. Violet simply didn't want him there. She didn't like the way he ignored her usually effectual distancing tactics. She certainly didn't like that she'd found him vaguely charming or thought about him more than she should already.

She shrugged. "Whatever you need, Lily."

Lily gave her a strained smile. "Thanks."

But then Creed turned to leave too. Violet should've known that he wasn't staying without Lily. He rarely separated from her if it was possible to be at her side.

"You're going?" she asked blandly. There was no practical *reason* to ask Creed to stay. Erik was no threat to her, and even if he had been, Violet was far from defenseless. She'd faced down armed fae with her affinities as her sole defense. There was nothing Erik could do that threatened Violet physically, but she still wanted to object.

"I'm going to go see Will," Creed said, vaguely gesturing to his left, in the general direction of the boys' suite.

"I could do that if—"

"Running *again*, Miss Lamb?" Erik interrupted.

"Violet doesn't run from harmless people," Creed answered before she could.

And there was nothing Violet could say to that. She motioned for him to go without saying another word.

202

Only a few moments later, her suite felt too small. It was illogical that fewer people would make a space seem to close in, but she felt like the space was too confining the moment that they were gone. It made her restless, which wasn't atypical. The need to constantly move was something that Violet suspected came with the affinity to fire. She felt better when she was flowing from room to room, space to space, without tether. They all had their quirks, of course. Those with air affinity needed open space; those with water or earth needed their element. For Creed, enclosed spaces were difficult because he was away from the vastness of air. Walls were difficult. For Alkamy, being too long with her feet not touching soil was unsettling. Her vat of soil was how she coped. For Roan, the lift and lilt of waves was essential. He coped with a lot of showers.

Violet had no recourse. There was nowhere she could go that made her feel quiet the way open space, bare soil, or flowing seas would soothe her friends. She could call flames to her skin when the pressure was too much, but the only way she'd found to truly keep the worst of her agitation at bay was to be constantly active.

She moved around the suite, absently reorganizing books on the shelves, folding a blanket she'd left on the sofa, straightening a picture that was tilted, and looking for something else to tidy. The suite wasn't ever messy though. Between Hailey's focus on study and Violet's need for motion, their room was as orderly as could be. Sometimes that need to move meant that she went to Will's room and

re-folded everything if her own space was beyond immac-
ulate. Putting things in place made her feel centered. It
channeled her need to move, and at the end she could see
results.

"Do I make you that nervous?" Erik asked in an almost
regretful tone.

She paused and looked over her shoulder at him. As
much as she'd like to blame her entire mood on him, she
wasn't going to try to lie. He wasn't a bad person, no more
so than the rest of her friends. It wasn't his underworld
connections or even his humanity that bothered her. It
was the way he looked at her as if every illusion she could
erect wouldn't stop him from seeing her. That terrified her
in a way that few things could, despite what she'd done in
service to the Queen of Blood and Rage already.

Slowly, Violet turned to face him. Sparks threatened
to fall from her hands as she struggled with the impulse to
run. He already knew what she was, though, and if he was
in possession of one more detail about her secret it was no
more or less damning than what he already knew. Without saying a word, she let the fire come. The first release
of the flames felt like a much-needed deep breath after a
long run. There was something infinitely satisfying about
that moment; the flicker of fire burned up some sort of
tension. Until the fire escaped her skin, she never realized
how much she'd been choking her stress back. Since she'd
harnessed her own affinity and borrowed her newly found
father's fire in the Hidden Lands, the pressure to let flames

free was a constant thing, pulsing at her like small birds were caught under the edges of her skin. When next she met her father, she might just have to ask if that insistence would ease in time.

Erik looked at the flames that were shivering across her skin and then at her eyes. "Anger?"

"Stress," she admitted.

"I can lie for you if it helps. Tell you it's definitely all going to be fine. Tell you that it's going to be easy." He didn't come any closer to her, but the way he watched her was the same as a touch. She'd had fans look at her that way, as if she were the only person in the world, but it was different. They were looking at award-winning actress Violet Lamb, not fae-blood Vi.

Having someone stare at her so intently made her fire sway toward him, not dangerously enough that she would accidentally hurt him. Quickly, she called it back into her body, feeling warmer for inviting fresh fire into flesh.

It reminded her, though, that he was human. Erik had no affinity, no way to smother her flames with earth, no gift of water to quench it, no skill with air to block it. He was vulnerable to her, to all of them. He was choosing this, and as one warrior to another, she owed him respect for that.

Carefully, she told him, "I don't need lies right now, but the offer is kind all the same." She walked over to a heavy box that held various blades she'd forged. "I like that you offered."

"I'd offer more if it makes you smile," he said lightly.

Violet didn't smile, but she gestured toward the box. It was an odd peace offering or maybe an unusual way of flirting, but it was *real* for her. *This* was the person she truly was, not the figment that she was on screens or in glossy magazines.

Erik walked over and stood at her side. When he glanced down, his lips parted on an appreciative sigh at the weapons stored there. "Yours?"

"I made them."

That same admiring gaze shifted to her. "With . . . your affinity?" He glanced at her hands briefly.

"Every last one," she said, with no small measure of pride. This time, she did smile.

But instead of seeming content, Erik stared at her as he had at the bar. He looked like he wanted to consume her, and she liked it. Maybe it was because fire was always close to her surface, but raw hunger always drew her near. She forced herself to step back. Humans were too vulnerable, even those who were raised on guns and lies.

"You're amazing," he said.

"No. I'm fae-blood." Violet lifted one of the knives she'd made more recently. It wasn't fae-steel, but it was stronger and lighter than anything but the finest blades in this world. "You'll need to carry something more than guns."

He accepted it reverently. "I'll treat it well."

"No," she corrected. "You use it. You bloody it. You keep yourself safe. Lily needs that."

Erik stared at the knife in his hand. It was good enough to be mistaken for the expensive fae-wrought ones sold illegally. In a way, it was. She wasn't full fae though. She'd *thought* she was, but that was a lie. Still, her blade was true. The edge wouldn't dull, and it would not grow slick if blood soaked it. Violet showed him the rest of the knives and swords she'd created as ways to harness her need to make use of her fire and learn control. She admitted to herself that it was an attempt to be friendlier to him.

"And you?" he finally asked, eyes lifting from a clumsy rapier that she'd tried and still kept as proof that there were things that were unwise to do in a truly foul temper.

"I could learn to tolerate you," Violet allowed after a moment.

Erik smiled widely. "I would like that."

"So be it," she said with a shrug.

"Friends is a start," he said with a far too happy smile.

Friends were fine. Friends weren't as dangerous. Maybe if she offered him her friendship, he'd see that anything more was a terrible idea. Most people only found her attractive until they got to know her better. After that, they had the good sense to realize that she was too much like her affinity to want to try anything other than friendship. Erik wouldn't be any different. They never were.

twenty-six

ZEPHYR

Zephyr held Alkamy long after she was gone. He was sure there were things he ought to do, but just then, none of them mattered. It was as if everything outside of them had vanished. There was a dead body in the garden, a stranger he'd killed. His sword was bloodied from it, and no one who came upon them would misread what had happened.

As the grandson of the Queen of Blood and Rage, Zephyr ought to be handling the details. He knew that. He couldn't. Letting go of Alkamy would mean that he'd never hold her again. She was dead, but he wasn't ready for the last moment of holding her.

His phone rang. He ignored it. Nothing anyone said would matter. He wasn't sure how long he stayed there before he heard someone approaching.

"Zephyr? Kamy? Are you . . ." Lily's words ended on a gasp. "Zephyr!"

"She's cold," he said.

Lily drew her sword.

Creed dropped down beside him. "Zephyr? We need to call someone or—"

"No." He tightened his hold on Alkamy. He wasn't ready to let go, wasn't sure if he ever would be ready.

"We need to move, Zeph." Creed didn't touch him, just crouched there. "No one needs to see her like this."

Zephyr nodded. "She wouldn't like that."

"Was anyone else here?" Lily asked. She stood like a guard surveying the area for threats.

Zephyr inclined his head toward the dead man. "Just him. He had a gun. It's . . . somewhere."

Lily nodded once. "You have them?"

"I do." Creed stood as Zephyr did. He didn't reach out though.

They stood in silence. Creed didn't cry, but Zephyr suspected he would later. They all would. Right now, they couldn't.

After a few moments, Lily came back. "I've sent word to your father."

Zephyr swallowed. "He liked her."

"Everyone did," Lily said softly. "She's . . . she was wonderful."

He nodded. "We stepped out. There was no time. No

209

warning. No fight. We just stepped out. She was bending down for her shoes, and when she stood, she was bleeding. It was . . . there was nothing I could do."

Lily heard the question before he even realized he was asking anything. She met his eyes and said, "That happens. Sometimes there's nothing. It just *happens*. You know that. Alkamy knew it."

"She's dead. She's *dead*." He said it, spoke that word, a word that should never have been said about Alkamy. She was vibrant and happy and giggling and . . . now she was gone. Between one heartbeat and the next, she was gone.

And he wasn't sure he wanted to go on without her. The only dream he'd ever had that was his own was her. She was all of his hopes and wishes given form, and this morning, she'd been kissing him. This morning, everything he could dream of was his.

Now, he had nothing.

He stared at her. She wasn't in there anymore. Zephyr knew as much. The things that made Alkamy uniquely *her* were gone. The way she giggled, the tone of her voice, her mind and her spirit, they were all silenced. All he had left was her body, and that was cold and motionless.

"Son?"

Zephyr looked away from Alkamy.

"I'll take her home." Rhys extended his arms.

But Zephyr couldn't. He shook his head. That wasn't her home. He'd hoped it would be, had hoped they would build a life there one day. "She doesn't belong there."

"It is your home, and she loved you." Rhys' words weren't as stilted as they often were. Dealing with death and loss seemed less foreign to him than most emotional things.

"She's gone. I would've stopped them if I knew. I would've. . . ." Zephyr's words broke. He'd have done anything for Alkamy, but she was killed, and he was powerless.

Rhys took Alkamy from his arms. "When you are ready, I will take you to the earth where her shell will be. Unless you want to come now?"

Zephyr allowed his father to take her body. He wasn't sure he could see the earth swallow her. He knew the way of death for fae and fae-blood. The earth sustained them, and the earth embraced them when they were no more.

"I can't," he said. "You'll take care of her, though, right? Maybe I should . . ."

"I will take her to her rest," Rhys said. "And when you are ready, you can see where the earth holds her."

Zephyr was vaguely aware that Lily and Creed were watching. Lily still held her sword, and Creed stood beside her. He looked ready to stab someone. The anger he'd seemed able to manage of late was all but radiating from him in burning bursts on the air currents.

"What do I do now?" Zephyr asked his father.

Rhys met his eyes and said, "Your duty. There are threats here. You keep yourself and the heir safe."

"I failed Alkamy and—"

"No. You did not," Rhys interrupted. "Was there any way you could've known there was an attack?"

"No, but—"

"The enemy outsmarted you. That will happen. *Death* will happen. It is not always avoidable." Rhys looked past Zephyr to Lily and Creed before adding, "You may not be safe enough here."

No one replied. There was no argument to make with Alkamy's dead body in his arms. Whatever else had happened before now seemed inconsequential to Zephyr. They'd had several attacks, and this one cost him the only thing that wasn't his duty.

Duty was all he had left.

"I will not fail the heir to the throne," Zephyr swore. "My cousin will be safe as long as I draw breath."

"As long as *we* do," Creed added.

When Zephyr glanced back at him, Creed added, "Alkamy was one of us, and even if we didn't love her the *way* Zeph did, we loved her. . . and we won't let him get hurt because she's not here to remind him to be careful."

Zephyr looked away. It wasn't that he'd intended to be foolish, but when he'd realized that he could get killed defending Lily there had been a flicker of dark interest. He knew that it was grief and desperation. He'd felt it before when he was weary of trying to keep all the Black Diamonds safe. Alkamy had been his way of keeping that at bay.

And Alkamy was gone.

"It is good to watch him carefully while he mourns," Rhys said. "My mother's grief has started rivers of dead.

I would not think that any of my family mourn gently."

"We will protect each other," Lily added. "You have my word, Uncle."

Zephyr walked several steps and lifted the sword he'd dropped after killing the man who'd shot Alkamy. It felt right to hold it. The blood on his hands soaked into the weapon. Alkamy's blood was within his sword now. That, too, felt right.

He glanced at his cousin, knelt and said, "I offer you my fealty."

"Zephyr!" Lily reached out to pull him to his feet, but he refused.

"I need a reason to live," he told her bluntly. "I will protect you as my father has protected the queen. I will give my life for you as I couldn't for . . . as I wish I could have."

"Zeph . . ."

"No." He shook his head. "The only thing that mattered more than the throne and our people is gone. *Give me a reason*."

Lily drew a sharp breath, but she nodded. "So be it. With Violet, you are my protector."

No one mentioned the fact that she didn't list Creed as such, but Zephyr understood. There was no way he would've let Alkamy die to protect him if he had a choice, and everyone standing there understood that Lily would not let Creed die to keep her safe either. Mutual love was the willingness to die for someone who would rather die themselves than see you harmed.

And the future queen did not love him enough to die before him. They both knew that. He would die for her safety because it was his duty and because there was no other person or cause he held above that duty now that Alkamy was gone. In that instant, he understood his father for the first time. The Unseelie prince had chosen his duty to the Queen of Blood and Rage above all else.

Zephyr would do the same with the new queen-to-be.

twenty-seven

EILIDH

Eilidh wasn't ready to face her mother, but she needed to update her. Matters affecting family were the top priority. It had always been so. The queen might be bloodthirsty, but she was more so in the service of those she held dear. Eilidh made it as far as the training courtyard before she found the Queen of Blood and Rage.

She was in her armor, sword in hand, feet bare. It was as close to comfortable as the queen ever appeared.

"Alkamy Adams was killed," Eilidh announced. "Zephyr is . . . emotional."

The queen was silent. Then—

"The coronation needs to happen *now*," Endellion said. "They need to know not to harm LilyDark. I don't know who is helping these traitors, but I will find out. Lily and Zephyr both need to come home."

"It's not as if there aren't threats here too." Eilidh didn't flinch despite the anger in her mother's eyes at her words.

Fortunately, Eilidh was saved from the queen's actual reply when a messenger approached them.

Before the young man could be chastised or worse, he said, "It's from the king, your highness! If it were anyone else, I—"

"Be gone," Endellion interrupted.

Eilidh opened the letter. It held only two words:

Come. NOW.

"What?"

"Father needs to see me," Eilidh said. Her summons to the king's court wasn't unexpected, nor was the arrival of said summons when she was with her mother. For all that the two courts were at peace, the regents were still creatures of habit. That habit had included spying long before it included carefully scheduled dinners where the king of Seelie and the queen of Unseelie traded barbs as they broke bread.

"He mentioned that, but wouldn't say why." The queen's sword sliced through the air as if there was a genuine chance that she'd allow it to knick her daughter. "I assume he didn't know about you gathering information before *I* did."

She glanced at Eilidh, who obediently agreed, "Of course not."

"Well, then what does he want?" Endellion's leather armor was bright in the early morning light, and the steel of her blade glinted. Despite all of that, the queen looked oddly childlike when she was vexed—not that Eilidh would dare to say such things.

"I tortured his son."

"Truly?" The sudden happiness in her mother's expression was no less childlike than her petulance.

Eilidh shrugged. "He injured my betrothed."

The Queen of Blood and Rage laughed, a beautiful pealing sound not unlike the sounds that divine beings might make. Endellion was far from divine, but she was ethereal and lovely in her many moods. The queen's sword flashed as she twirled it and re-sheathed it. "Well, then . . ."

"What?"

"I'll join you."

Eilidh stared at her mother briefly, but said nothing.

"Do not mention the girl's death," the queen said in that tone that was obviously an order. Then she looped her arm around Eilidh and started walking. Eilidh had no choice but to fall in step. The fae were watching, and even if they weren't, a happy queen was such a rarity that there was little that Eilidh would object to in the moment. Her mother wasn't gentle or doting; she wasn't prone to embraces or the affectionate cheek strokes that many a reserved parent found acceptable.

Just then, however, her mother bestowed a proud look on Eilidh. "I told him you wouldn't take it easily. I warned him. 'No, Dell, she's too busy fussing over Torquil,' he says. 'Don't think about what *you* would do,' he says. Ha! Can you imagine that I'd torture someone for stabbing that old goat?'"

Eilidh shook her head. Her parents had been together for centuries now, but her mother was no nearer admitting to loving her father than she was to taking up so-called women's arts. The queen was soundly opposed to what she considered the frivolous emotions.

Wisely, Eilidh kept her silence even when her mother, the typically surly Queen of Blood and Rage, started to hum. Admittedly, Eilidh's step faltered slightly, but she didn't say a thing. If anything, she concentrated on not hearing the queen's joyful little melody. It was disconcerting to hear such a thing come from her mother.

When they reached the king's bright palace, Eilidh wished she'd been able to delay her visit until evening. That really was the best time to be in the Seelie court. During the day, the brightness of the sunlight on the odd gold and bronze detailing was too jarring.

Where the queen favored vaguely medieval trappings and earth-hewn rooms, the king was forever updating his court to the latest human innovations. He didn't completely renovate, of course. That would be too consistent. Instead, he had animal print furnishings and stark white rugs, glittering stained-glass windows and ceiling fixtures of crystal that refracted and reflected light madly. Exotic animals that she couldn't even name napped in the lush thickets that were inside his palace, and on one occasion a lion caught and ate a human that the king had brought home. That was the last time Eilidh could recall her mother seeming so cheerful as they walked down a newly added hallway that was seemingly fashioned entirely out of opals.

"I have been thinking about birds," Leith said as he saw them enter the throne room, which was apparently modeled on some sort of chapel with high arches and a dome. "Hello, Dell. I don't believe I invited you."

The queen merely shrugged and walked up to him. Almost fondly, she shoved him so he was forced into his throne. The current week's throne seemed to be a sturdy wooden thing, remarkably mundane for the odd sur-roundings. He typically was a bit like a bird or perhaps ferret, gathering things he thought interesting or repli-cating them if necessary. He collected things whereas the queen trained in new martial arts.

"What, no kiss?" Endellion asked as she sat on the arm of his throne. Unlike most of his thrones, this one had arms wide enough for one to sit on them comfortably.

He tilted his head upward so she could kiss him. Then he wrapped one arm around her back, not pulling her to him or even holding her. He simply let it rest around her as if they always sat thusly. In that moment, Eilidh was cer-tain that he'd expected his wife would be coming.

Eilidh looked at her father, wondering not for the first time if he manipulated the queen more than anyone realized.

When he caught her gaze, the king shook his head slightly. He winked at her, though, confirming her suspicions that the queen had been expected and behaved predictably. Her parents were so odd.

"I had a curious visit from my son," the king said.

"There's only the one now?" the queen asked mildly.

He ignored her, but he clarified as he continued, "Nacton tells me his brother is injured."

Eilidh stood unflinchingly before her parents.

"*Someone* tortured him," Leith said.

"And did your son tell you what fae would be so bold?" Endellion reached out and caressed the king's cheek almost fondly.

"Are you trying to distract me, Dell?"

Eilidh's temper slipped. "Honestly? You are both absurd. Mother, admit that you're fond of him. Father, admit that you know that I tortured Calder, that I was right to do so, and that this is a formality."

"She gets that from you," Endellion said. "I'm never so impatient."

The king laughed. "You ordered me to marry you, dear. That seems impatient."

The queen waved her hand as if to sweep away his words.

"You slaughtered scores of men—"

"They deserved it," the queen snapped.

"Or numerous occasions," the king added.

"And they *always* deserved it." Endellion wasn't quite

220

at the point of crossing her arms over her chest or drawing her sword, but she was no longer petting the king's face or hair.

"Now, Dell—"

"Father!" Eilidh caught herself then. She cleared her throat and tried again, this time in a softer voice. "Do you intend to punish me?"

"Of course he doesn't!" The queen scowled. "If he'd disciplined those sons of his in the first place, they wouldn't have behaved like that. Rhys never—"

"You have stabbed *that* boy more times than—"

"And does Rhys obey me?" Endellion's voice grew sharper. "Is Rhys safe from attacks? Could someone capture and torture *him*?"

"I bet our daughter could," Leith pronounced in a rather self-satisfied way. "She has efficiently instilled fear in both of my sons, and she taught Calder the value of knowing our history. If she wanted to torture your son—"

"I didn't want to torture anyone," Eilidh snapped. "It was terrible and messy and . . . I saw no other way."

Her parents exchanged a look. Then her father said, "You were brave, and your people ought to rejoice that one such as you is here to look out for them."

The queen rested her head against his in a very uncharacteristically affectionate way. "We make amazing children together, don't we?"

"We need to schedule the coronation," Leith said. "Bring our granddaughter home too."

"Dinner's cancelled, Eilidh. We'll have a family meal when LilyDark is home," the queen said happily.

Leith stared at the queen as she spoke.

And Eilidh steadfastly refused to think about why her parents were cancelling the meal . . . or if she had known there was a meal in the first place. She turned to go and was several steps away, when the king added, "If you keep healing Torquil, though, I'll stab him myself. You know not to use your affinity so freely, child."

"Would you really?" Endellion asked.

Leith didn't reply. Instead he said, "Eilidh?"

"Yes, Father." She shook her head and left, carefully stepping around a sleeping peacock and a baby jaguar that was curled up against it. As much as she often thought the Seelie palace odd, there was something fitting about it. Only her father could convince predators and prey to rest peacefully together.

Quietly, she wandered through the halls, marveling at the strange beauty that seemed pervasive here. It wasn't *home* any more than the queen's palace was, but she could appreciate it . . . sometimes.

twenty-eight
ZEPHYR

When they were in the Hidden Lands, Zephyr had promised anew to be whatever the Queen of Blood and Rage wished. It wasn't a *new* vow. He'd been hers since before birth. Now, though, he knew that he was her grandson—and had sworn fealty to his cousin. Like his father had with the current queen, Zephyr would be the next queen's weapon until he died.

His last task for Endellion was to be sure that the diamonds were in the tabloids. There were innumerable pictures, not only of him and Alkamy but also of Lily and Creed. Often Vi was with them. Sometimes Roan and Will were as well. Zephyr could see the logic: Endellion wanted the public adoration secured before their true heritage was revealed, but he didn't think it necessary or useful. Opinion changed as quickly as it formed. Being adored today meant nothing about tomorrow.

Today those pictures hurt.

Zephyr stared at the photographs in one of the magazines he'd had delivered earlier that day. The diamonds stood like guards around Lily in them, not a proper formation of any sorts but clearly surrounding her protectively. Across the top of the two-page spread, the magazine asked: NEW STARLET? SINGING SENSATION? MODEL? Behind her, Alkamy was smiling.

She'd never do that again.

"Are you okay?" Lily said as she walked into the common room of the suite.

He'd slept there, claiming Alkamy's room as his own. If Lily and Creed slept in Creed's room, Zephyr would sleep in his own. If they were here, he'd sleep in Alkamy's bed. He hadn't told them as much, but he couldn't protect her if he wasn't there.

Right now, everyone was watching him like he was going to shatter. He wasn't. He was going to do his duty. He would keep the future queen safe.

Lily glanced at the now-closed magazine he held in his hand.

"You avenged her. The one who killed her is dead. That is the *right* and *good*," she said, and maybe it was simply because he knew the truth now, but he could see the queen in her expression. It was more than a little disconcerting.

"She's still dead."

Lily dropped into a chair across from him. "You aren't."

He shrugged. With someone not fae, he might pretend. Lily was the single most fae person in the human world. She was *also* the daughter of Nicolas Abernathy. The head of the nation's most influential crime syndicate had kept her face out of the news for her whole life, had kept her hidden away in his fortress, and until she'd suddenly come to St. Columba's, she'd been thoroughly unreachable. The Abernathy security was almost impenetrable.

And his sole duty in life now was to keep her safe. Nothing else mattered. It never would again. Alkamy was gone.

"I don't know what to say," Lily admitted. She tucked her feet up in the chair as if she were a mermaid curled atop a rock. It was not an unfitting image, considering the family affinity for the sea.

"There is nothing," he said baldly. "Humans can utter words of comfort, but they are lies. Nothing can be said to make this not hurt. No words matter now."

"I wonder sometimes what it would be like to be all human," Lily murmured. "Do you ever wish that?"

"No. Not even now. All I wish was . . ." He shrugged again. They both knew what he wished.

"Tell me how to help you."

Zephyr looked at her. She was the person he'd sought for years, the fae-blood who would lead their cell with him, and right now . . . he'd trade her in for Alkamy in a blink. "Be the queen our people need. That is all I ask. I will dedicate my life to your safety, Lily. I will guard you as my father has our grandmother."

"That's not what I mean!" Lily touched his arm. "You're my family, Zephyr. How do I help you?"

He was saved from a reply when the door to the suite crashed open. Creed was all but running as he entered their room, and Violet *was* running fast enough that she ducked past Creed. Tendrils of fire glimmered on her skin as she came into the room, making it clear that she was either furious or terrified.

"Get up!" Violet exclaimed.

"What?" Lily asked, immediately looking for a threat behind them.

"We have twenty-five minutes," Creed said.

"For?"

"Being where we intend to greet Lily's grandparents," Violet said in a voice still too emotional. "Messenger said . . . they'll come to where we are at that moment. I don't know that school—"

"Not here. Belfoure," Lily interrupted, standing with a fluidity that seemed to be more and more undeniable every day. "I want water, air, and earth near me. St. Columba's lacks water. If the others are coming, meet at the pier."

"We all go," Zephyr announced.

"They have a choice to—"

"We *all* go," he interrupted.

"Twenty-three minutes," Violet announced. "If we *are* going to Belfoure, we need to move or we'll be running the whole way. We might any—"

"Get the others, Vi," he ordered.

Violet glanced at Lily, who nodded once. Then Violet took off in a run.

"They could stay hidden," Lily said calmly as she pulled off her boots. She needed the touch of earth. "You both could too."

"No!" Creed glared at her.

Simultaneously, Zephyr said, "I am unable to stay behind, and if the others tried, there would be consequences."

It was the closest he'd come to admitting that the queen, their grandmother, had given him orders he'd not shared with them. Lily stared at him, hearing his unspoken admissions. Undoubtedly, Creed had heard as well, but his sole focus was on Lily.

Silently, she walked into her room, grabbed her sheathed sword, and then left the suite without another word.

She didn't head to the vine-covered wall that hid a secret exit. Instead, she descended the stairs and walked toward the main door. Zephyr and Creed walked behind her, trailing her like guards—which was a fairly normal position for them to assume these days.

She had her sword, still in its scabbard, hanging from her hip now. It wasn't the way she usually strode across campus. As she walked, Lily seemed to become *more*. Hair normally chestnut brown seemed to shift in tone and texture until it more closely resembled the rich dark of freshly turned soil. Skin that had looked no appreciably different from most of the students of St. Columba's grew starker, lightening into bone white.

"Did you see—"

"Yes," Creed said, stopping the question before it was fully formed. Softly, the words barely a whisper in a drift of air that seemed to slide directly into Zephyr's ear, he added, "She doesn't notice it though."

They had reached the door. Lily glanced at them. "You're sure?"

"Yes." They both swore.

"So be it." She paused as people looked their way, and then LilyDark Abernathy—heir to the Hidden Throne, daughter of a crime lord and the missing faery whose disappearance had started a war—cleared a path to the doors of St. Columba without moving another step.

twenty-nine

EILIDH

Eilidh wanted to argue that she should be allowed to attend the coronation, but she was worn out from the conflicts in the Hidden Lands. Her affinities seemed to be tearing her apart lately, and her people weren't much better. Finding Calder at her side as she walked through the caves was a shade past too much. She stumbled to a stop.

"At least we look like siblings finally," he said, gesturing to his scars.

Her Seelie brother didn't reach out to steady her, but he didn't shove her to the ground either.

"I am glad you aren't dead," she told him carefully. There were times that blunt statements were best, times when the fae need to speak truth served them well. This felt like such a time.

It also felt like a time when her recently increased

training was an asset. Her hand went to the hilt of the sword she wore at her side. She didn't draw the weapon, nor did she feel inclined to do so yet.

"Afraid I've come to pay you back, *sister*?"

Eilidh's heart hurt. He'd never called her that, and hearing it said so venomously stung. "No. I did as the lands allowed. You know that I was taking fair blood rights for—"

"No one does that. Not anymore."

"The law exists. The land and sea supported it," she reminded him.

"You're not Seelie. Maybe my father isn't even—"

"Do not even suggest such lies," she hissed. "The king *is* my father."

Calder stared at her, unable to refute it. "You are more like her. *He* was never one to torture."

Eilidh sighed. "And who do you think did so for him? The queen. Even before they were wed. Both have told me so."

Her Seelie brother stared at her. His lips parted as if he would argue. There was no argument that would be truth, however. Instead, he asked, "If I were to hurt Torquil again, what would you do?"

"Hurt? With cold words or slight? Nothing. Hurt with a weapon? Hurt with intent to kill him?" Eilidh weighed out the words she could use, trying to be as precise as possible. "Torquil is mine. To try to take him from me is to know that death will follow. No one, not even the queen or the king, would be spared."

"You would kill your parents?"

Eilidh nodded once. "If they meant to take Torquil from me? Yes, I would."

Calder paused at the end of the tunnel, staring at her in a way that was unfamiliar. It was almost as if he'd never seen her before that day. "And what of the new heir? Would you kill for her?"

"I would."

Calder studied her. "You *are* very much like the queen, aren't you?"

There was no need to offer an answer to that. They stood, her with hand on her sword hilt and him watching her, for several uncomfortable moments.

"Calder?" she said quietly.

He paused and looked back at her.

"I would kill for you as well," she said. "You are my brother, whether you choose to accept me or not. I may no longer be heir, but I am still their daughter. I was raised to believe that no act was too far to protect my family, no sacrifice too great to protect our homeland. You *are* my family."

Her Seelie brother nodded. "Nacton, Rhys, you . . . do you realize that all three of you were promised thrones that your parents took away?"

Eilidh startled at that. She hadn't thought of it, not so clearly. Calder was the only of the royal children never destined to rule. He was . . . the Seelie King's spare.

"I never wanted it," he said, as if hearing her thoughts.

"Me, either."

After another uncomfortably long pause, Calder said, "Nacton did. He still does."

Eilidh knew there were more things said than she was hearing. If her brother intended to clarify, though, he would've done so. Instead, he straightened, as if the bones in his spine were all suddenly lengthened, and he added, "I admire your willingness to draw blood for your beliefs and for the lands, but if you ever raise a blade to me again with such intentions, I won't forgive it . . . and you should know that my brother has not forgiven you *this* time. Not you. Not Torquil. Not the queen or the king."

Then he left.

Eilidh knew that Calder hadn't outright spoken his forgiveness, but it was there in the words he had spoken all the same. He'd sought her out, and he'd given her a warning.

Torquil.

The air in Eilidh's lungs escaped in a rush. Her feet were moving before she could allow further thoughts to form. Being with him, seeing he was safe, was suddenly the single most urgent thing in her life. A quiet voice reminded her that Torquil and Nacton had been friends, but she'd had more lectures on political maneuvers and machinations than anyone needed. Nacton had undoubtedly had many of the same ones.

By the time she found Torquil, her fear had grown into a heavy weight in her stomach.

There he was, swinging a sword in a meadow. He was untouched and safe. The sheer relief made her sag against a tree.

"Patches?"

Eilidh shook her head. She simply didn't have words enough for her feelings, so as it tended to do more and more, her affinity was speaking. The earth surged toward him as if the roots of trees had become hands and the soil flesh. Fire shivered, tilting toward him. Air slid over his skin, seeking surety that he was well and real. "I love you, and I was afraid that . . ."

"I am safe," Torquil told her as he crossed to stand before her.

Earth twisted, as water flooded the surface. Fire dropped to the soil, heating the churning ground. Eilidh couldn't find more words though. She stared at her betrothed, needing to know that he was whole and well and here.

"I have you." Torquil's sword fell to the ground. His arms wrapped around her, clasping her to his chest, steadying her. "*We* are safe, and we will stay so."

Still she couldn't speak. She was afraid to open her mouth, as if parting her lips would call rain down or pull the sea too far inland. She'd done that once after a particularly frightening dream. Instead of wanting her laughing father or her fierce mother, she had called the sea. It came crashing on her home, and only the foundational magic the queen had used in building it preserved the glass tower.

The fae who had still been in the streets near her home had not fared as well.

Eilidh shook her head. She wasn't ready to speak. The fear of unleashing the sea was too much.

Torquil looked at her, sighed softly, and covered her lips with his.

She felt some of her fire slip away to him, knew the coals inside her were being banked, heard the earth sigh in response. He took in her fears and gave her peace. He'd often done so, but with the touch of his hand not with a kiss.

"I don't deserve your love," she whispered when he pulled away. "Sometimes, I think there is a madness in me."

He laughed. "You are foolish sometimes, Patches, but not mad. You are everything right in my life."

"Sometimes the way I love you chokes me," she admitted in a still-low voice. "I am my mother's daughter. If you were taken from me—"

"I wasn't. I *won't* be." Torquil stroked her cheek so tenderly that her eyes drifted shut. "And you . . . made it clear enough that doing so again would be unwise."

This time it was Eilidh who laughed. She was about to speak when she felt the earth shudder. The gates between worlds had been opened, and she knew that her parents had left the Hidden Lands. She could feel their absence. The queen and king had *never* once gone to the human world during Eilidh's life. It was unprecedented.

But since Lily had become known to them everything was unprecedented. The soil, the roots, and the squirming things within the soil and among the roots chattered to her. *The regents. Leaving.* The words were few, but the cacophony with which they all spoke at once and repeatedly made Eilidh wonder how anyone walked with their skin touching soil. If this affinity were to lead to madness, she would be unsurprised.

"We don't speak the same to all and each," one of the willows told her with a fluttering of branches.

"We don't think they *all* need to know," another tree whispered.

The willow added, "But you do."

"I'm not the fae heir now," Eilidh pointed out, only to be reminded that the laughter of trees is a beautiful thing. The sound of it rose up inside her, filling her until her rage and fear had nowhere left to hide.

"Fae words," the willow said lightly. "You are ours."

Eilidh didn't understand, but communing with the earth wasn't the same as comprehending it. "I am yours," she agreed. "And you are mine."

The surge of love from the soil made her tremble. Much as the sea calmed her in her pain and rage, the earth filled her with contentment and acceptance. There was a part of Eilidh that felt sorrowful that anyone had to exist without affinity for sea and soil. For her, they were all that stood between her and the inferno that fire created inside her. They were her parents in a way that the fae who were her literal mother and father had never been.

"I am yours," Eildh repeated. "And I will keep you safe at any cost."

Eilidh meant those words as surely as she'd meant it when she said she would kill for her loved ones. The earth was beloved to her as well.

The queen's rage had been at the loss of her child. So many people—fae and human alike—forgot that before the rage was the fear. Fae were connected to the elements, and humanity had been destroying nature. Eilidh understood that.

Earth and sea called her, and she couldn't find the words to make those instincts comprehensible. The best she could do was to kiss Torquil and hope that her touch made sense in ways that words didn't. She tugged him to her, and let the instincts of nature reign over them both until he pulled away.

"We can't," he whispered. "Not here. Not in this world."

Eilidh swallowed, trying to ground herself in this world, but more and more she felt like earth and sea had sway over her in a way that grew stronger whether she willed it or not. "I need to . . . go."

Torquil nodded.

"I will come back," she added, feeling the waves in her words. "The sea needs me."

He stared at her, as if there were questions she could answer but with every moment, she felt less anchored in the body she wore. She was salt water and current; she was vine and soil. The body was the form that held it, and right now, the sea was calling her.

Without another word, she turned and ran until there was no land, only a smooth slide of soil and sand. She leaped, and the waves surged up and plucked her from the air. Eilidh was barely airborne before she was rolled under the surface, and the shimmering song of water dancing took her every worry away. Here, things were right. Here, her emotions were washed away.

Wave after wave drank her worry and fears. Droplet after droplet carried them away. No one would take her family from her; no one would stop them from coming home where they could be safe. The sea would serve her until she needed soil to anchor her.

thirty

LILY

In the main building at St. Columba's, the stone floor under Lily's bare feet spoke in heavy slow words, telling her that she was safe here. It insisted that there was *no need* to speak with the leafy things when rock was here for her. Stone could rise, could lift at her word and will, could terrify these people who had no fae blood.

"You are kind," Lily said carefully to the stone, speaking in a voice inside her where only things of the earth could hear.

Shattering the floor of the school seemed an extreme way to make her first statement, too bold by far. She was fae-blood, but she was her father's daughter first. *Abernathy Commandment #7: Secrets are valuable. Don't part with them for free.* If she was going to be outed not only as something illegal, but as the daughter of the missing heir to

238

the Hidden Throne, she wasn't going to reveal the full extent of her strengths. She hoped not to need them, but she might.

"Stay as you are in this moment. Stay whole," she spoke to the stone. "I don't want their fear, and you are too much for them to understand."

She sent her continued words of gratitude to the stone that hummed under her feet. Their words had never been so clear. Talking to them used to require touching them with bare skin, but since she'd donned the crown, will and word were enough. Ever since her trip to the Hidden Lands, she'd had a better ability with all of her affinities, but it still astounded her that she could hear and speak so freely to earth and sea, that she could still the air and summon fire. The reason for that improved skill, of course, could be as simple as that she was using her affinities more often or that she'd admitted things to herself that she'd not even known before. Or, it could somehow be the queen's doing. There were several possibilities, and Lily wasn't sure which was truth. She didn't even know if she wanted to be sure.

What she did know was that she wanted to make a statement here to the assembled crowd. She'd had no real warning, no proper time to prepare for the future. The queen had determined that today was the day that Lily would be exposed. Lily hadn't been consulted.

The news was full of attacks by fae-bloods.

Lily herself had been photographed at the fire that

destroyed the Row House.

And now she was to be exposed as a fae-blood, no longer just the daughter of a criminal but also the grand-daughter of the being who terrified almost everyone in the human world.

Lily would start the statement on her own. Her hand dropped to the hilt of the sword hanging at her hip.

Abernathy Commandment #5: Be bold.

As the stone reassured her that it understood her wishes, Lily called out to the vines that clung to the walls in the foyer of the building. She'd paused and touched those many tendrilled plants every day, drawing comfort at their presence within the building. Now, at her request, long green vines shot out, growing, uncoiling, releasing the walls where they clung and lashing out to grab the doors.

Gasps and murmurs rose behind her. A few screams twisted into the growing noise. She hadn't been here long enough to earn anyone's trust, and her familial name had always heralded trouble. This—her fae ancestry—could only confirm whatever suspicions she'd already elicited: Lily Abernathy was someone to fear.

Without thinking long on it, she used the vines to jerk open the doors and hold them fast. Sunlight and air spilled into the hall. More than a few students and faculty took advantage of those yawning doors, fleeing into the world outside as if being in nature would make them safer. Lily meant them no harm, but if she *had*, they were reacting exactly the wrong way.

Even after literal lifetimes of war with the fae, of imprisoning and killing them, of films speaking of the "faery menace," of songs romanticizing them, humanity was still as clueless as when the war had begun. The fae were aligned with varying elements, and short of technology's vile weapons, they were unstoppable when they had nature at hand. The only thing that had saved humanity from the true horror of the queen's rage was that there were simply so *many* people. Eradicating all of them had proven impossible.

Lily watched her classmates run from her, and she couldn't blame them for their fear. Unfortunately, she couldn't run—not from the fae, and not from the fear or anger humanity would bestow upon her.

Creed's voice rose up over the panicking students and staff. "History is about to happen. LilyDark has sacrificed herself for *you*. If you want to see, come with us."

She could feel him tugging the air, all but taste the water it pulled with that heat, shimmering above them like steam from the earth after the rain. A not insignificant part of her wanted to answer that air, to take it from him, to let loose the fire and water that she could summon. Being freed to act, to revel in her fae affinities, was intoxicating.

"Is this wise?" Zephyr asked, interrupting her urge to turn a small gesture into something grand.

Lily glanced his way. A part of her wanted to put this all aside, to let Zephyr have time to mourn. She couldn't though. The regents had spoken. He had to know that, but expecting him to be at his best the day after Alkamy's death was unrealistic.

Zephyr clarified, "Having *these* humans there? St. Columba's students?"

Lily couldn't swear to anything, but she doubted that even the Queen of Blood and Rage would slaughter humans on the day she entered this world to declare peace.

"Endellion will not hurt them," Lily said, certainty in the words growing stronger as she spoke them.

"She's not the only threat," Zephyr reminded her.

But the stone rumbled inside Lily's mind. "Endellion comes! We hear her."

There was often something steady and sure that only the oldest of stones could express, a weight and slowness of revelation that was the precise opposite of the way water spoke. The thick bass of stone's speech was not harried, but it was quicker in what Lily recognized as excitement.

It made her walk a little faster.

"The queen comes. Words for the queen. Stories for the queen. Truths to tell." Stone's words dropped like weights into Lily's mind. There was a heaviness there that made her steps seem to need more effort, and again she sped up.

She wasn't ready for more truths. She wasn't entirely convinced she was even ready for what was about to transpire. There were no other choices. Lily had made a bargain, and as a result, Endellion would announce that LilyDark was the next ruler.

"She comes for me," Lily spoke, both aloud and in that quiet place where stone and soil heard her. "The queen of the Hidden Lands, my grandmother, comes for me. She means you no harm. *I* mean you no harm."

Suddenly, Creed and Zephyr were at her sides, steadying her, as she stood forward to face the sheer enormity of her new life. They were silent, but she had no need for speaking. Words weren't what made a difficult thing more manageable.

In barely a heartbeat, vines reached out and made barriers between Lily and the growing number of people flooding into the hall. She hadn't asked them to do so, but Zephyr was earth too. It was his words they'd heeded.

"They are our classmates," she whispered. "Why would you think they mean us harm?"

Creed pulled air like a cushion around her, keeping anything and anyone from touching her. He said nothing, but his arm came round her waist. Between the two boys, she was protected by earth, air, and their physical presence.

"Your safety is everything," Zephyr said in a mildly chastising tone. More and more, he was as protective of her as an older sibling would be. They'd only just met a few short months ago, but when they'd returned from the Hidden Lands, he'd taken to his newfound familial relationship with zeal.

"Foolish, deadly girl," Creed murmured. "The media

has taught them that you could slaughter them as they stand. You stride through their space, armed, daughter of a criminal, and announce that you are blood to the queen. Why *wouldn't* they wish us ill?"

thirty-one

LILY

Lily walked past faces filled with open horror and awe. It wasn't the first time she'd been watched with such expressions clear to see. The children of her father's associates either were baffled by her or feared her. In the Hidden Lands, fae knelt before her, yet her own uncles had drawn swords on her. There was no place where she wouldn't be loathed by someone. St. Columba's had briefly offered that haven, but too soon, it was already at an end.

It made her want to hide away.

But she was LilyDark Abernathy, daughter of a crime lord and granddaughter to the regents of the Seelie and Unseelie Courts. She wasn't someone who was meant to bow her head. Doing so was disrespect to her family. Daidí had taught her that. He might not have admitted that he'd done so because of *both* sides of her ancestry, but the result was the same.

Tilting her chin upward, she quashed her hurt at the reactions all around her and feigned the confidence she should be demonstrating. What she *actually* felt was far from it. Fear thrummed in her skin, not just of the people who had been friendly strangers a few moments ago, but of the things yet to come.

She kept her doubts under the surface and walked toward the little harbor town adjacent to the school. As she walked, the plants and rocks under her feet hummed with excitement. Their vibrations battered her skin and sunk to her bones until Lily felt vaguely queasy from the bombardment of sensations.

Endellion did not walk freely here. Years past, she had. The fae had lived and thrived in the same world as humanity, but over time, humans had built machines that belched poison into the sky. They had created factories spilling noxiousness into the sea and soil. Time and again, year upon year, humanity polluted the earth.

Endellion and Leith had protected the fae by withdrawing from humanity. That was the all of it . . . until careless humans crashed their ship into the then-pregnant Endellion, spilling poisons into the sea and beginning the queen's childbirth. That one act of recklessness had been the last one. Endellion slaughtered tens of thousands of humans because she had believed that those few sailors had cost her the child she'd carried, Lily's mother.

It was no wonder that the people feared, or that the earth and sea rejoiced.

"I am afraid," Lily said quietly to her companions.

Neither boy spoke. To deny that she should be afraid would be to lie. To admit it wouldn't help. Sometimes silence was the only answer.

With Zephyr and Creed at her sides, Lily arrived at the same pier where she'd first met Zephyr. That day, a ship had exploded in the harbor. Today, there were no explosions. It was almost comically quiet. No news vans were on site yet; no crowds awaited the queen's proclamation. They would come. They would *all* come once the first pictures went live on social media.

First, though, Endellion would arrive in this world with no notice, no fanfare, no negotiations. She'd step into enemy territory with her consort at her side. Entering *her* realm the same way was impossible. Attempting it would result in bloodshed, but Endellion had begun the war. She'd fought it on her own terms. She'd declare a cessation to it the same way.

Lily couldn't blame her. Warning one's enemies wasn't a wise strategy, and the queen was nothing if not wise.

"She comes," the air whispered.

"Our queen among us," the waves murmured as they writhed and rolled.

And so she did. Endellion stepped into existence, rising from the sea as if she did so daily. She looked upon them as if she was somehow peering down at each and all. Using his affinity for air, Leith floated down from the sky to stand beside her, dressed in regal garb and a friendly smile. He gave a cheerful wave to the people, and more than a few responded. The magic of it was enough to bring a smile to Lily's lips.

Her grandparents, the most feared beings in either world, had exited the Hidden Lands and arrived in the tiny seaside town of Belfoure. The regents watched, waiting for the crowd to gather. A proclamation required an audience.

There was a palpable ripple among the people starting to fill the streets of Belfoure. They exited buildings and gathered. Voices lifted and grew sharp.

Lily had never seen such a crowd in town; it felt as if the entire population of the city of Belfoure was assembling to watch. People continued to arrive. Not only were the students from St. Columba all there, but the streets filled with groups of families.

Leith wore his traditional crown of white diamonds. Endellion wore black ones. The queen hadn't dressed meekly, but to any who knew fae tradition, her attire was meant to calm the throngs who would, no doubt, watch and re-watch the footage already being gathered by the shocked masses who shivered in her presence.

The Queen of Blood and Rage had not tied back her hair. This alone spoke of her peaceful intent. When she wielded a sword, she twisted it or coiled it up, but right now, it spilled like darkness over her shoulders and back. There were moments of light in the curtain of shadow, as if it were scattered with stars. Those lights were not dimmed for stealth. Likewise, her blood-colored armor had been replaced with a formal gown, a heavy red and black brocade creation that was cinched at the waist. Her arms were covered, but slits revealed a black underdress. It was not a gown made for combat. Her hands, throat, and face were the only exposed skin. Even her often-bare feet were hidden, this time under delicate, ruby and onyx covered shoes. All told, she looked regal, but still intimidating.

The king, of course, was equally beautiful, but unlike his wife, he looked jovial and as approachable as a faery king could be. His attire was mild, a simple tunic, trousers, and boots. They were well made, but his clothes weren't something that drew attention. His attitude was. He seemed biologically incapable of appearing anything other than some manner of joyous. Lily had to wonder if he was jocular even while ordering murder. Somehow, to her way of thinking, Leith's cheerful mien was less comforting than the queen's default demeanor of barely concealed aggression. Either Lily was more Unseelie than Seelie or her slight comfort with the queen's attitude was a result of a childhood spent with human monsters.

Unlike Lily, neither regent wore visible weapons. They appeared . . . almost harmless. She had no doubt that it was intentional.

"LilyDark," the king said, voice carrying over air so those humans who stood transfixed could hear.

Lily did the same with her voice. "Grandfather. Grand-mother."

Endellion's imposing expression faded briefly. "Grand-daughter."

The queen hadn't left the Hidden Lands in centuries, not since her daughter had been presumed dead as a result of human action.

"We've waited for this day since we conceived your mother," Leith said.

Looking first at her grandfather and then at her grand-mother, Lily told them, "I am sorry I did not know that I was your heir."

Leith nodded, but Endellion said, "It wasn't your fault. You were hidden, but now you are found."

Creed and Zephyr were motionless at Lily's sides. Behind her, she could feel Violet approaching. Since she'd declared fealty, Violet was like a fiery beacon, easy to locate by some intangible cord that linked them. Lily imagined that if there were hundreds of fae who declared fealty, that thread would become a great tapestry. For now, it was only a few single strands. She could feel fae blood, but not with the kind of solid knots that would pull them unerringly together. Not yet.

"I believe my mother's crown should be placed by the one who would ask me to wear it," Lily said, her voice still carrying over the people. "I think she would've liked that."

Endellion peered at her, fondness blossoming in her expression. Her words were still mild, however. She merely murmured, "Indeed."

It was an expression Lily remembered from her childhood. Her mother wasn't nearly as reserved as she would act around others. She certainly wasn't as regal as the queen.

Lily barely remembered her mother, and she'd certainly had no idea that her mother was far older than she'd appeared. All Lily had known was that when she was a child her mother had died. The things Lily had known were small in comparison to the depths she hadn't known.

Carefully, as if she were unaware that the group of humans who stood watching was growing by the moment, Lily walked away from her friends and down the pier to where the king and queen stood. It was a rickety thing, not exactly majestic in location, but the air was around them and seawater flowed under the boards, and the boards themselves were real wood that had been weathered with age. It was fitting for the fae.

As she approached her grandparents, she kept her gait even and her gaze steadfastly fixed on them.

"I am fae-blood, raised human," she said as she stood in front of them. "Daughter to Nicolas Abernathy and his wife Iana."

Leith nodded. "And I am sworn to protect the fae, including my daughter Iana, long thought lost to the sea."

"For that loss, for the loss of my first daughter, I have exacted blood," Endellion added, her gaze moving past Lily to take in every assembled person. "I have killed humans and caused still more to be killed."

The queen paused. There was something feral in her expression and voice, as if a spirit of vengeance would take shape from the sea and air at the queen's will, but it faded as quickly as it had come.

"Only for a worthy reason, for *you,* granddaughter, would I cease bathing my hands in such blood," Endellion said levelly and clearly.

"That is the cost of my accord," Lily said just as calmly. "These are my people, as much as the fae are. If you declare peace, I will be the heir to your throne as Iana once would have been."

She reached up and touched the tattooed circlet in her skin. It rose up to the surface, taking shape again as a serpentine necklace of black diamonds that burned on Lily's skin.

"I would wear my mother's crown," Lily said with a small shiver in her voice.

The King of Fire and Truth reached out to touch the necklace-shaped crown, and it released from around Lily's throat. As if alive, it slithered into his grasp, and he held it up where it seemed to glow, lit by some internal fire. The rope-like crown took shape then, looking more and more like a royal circlet.

The Queen of Blood and Rage withdrew a small dagger.

It didn't even occur to Lily to reach for her sword.

People gasped as if the queen who had decimated so many lives in her rage and grief could easily hurt the child of her lost daughter. It was foolishness that spoke of how much she'd been painted a monster over the decades. Lily wanted to point out their idiocy. She wasn't *immune* from injury at the queen's hand, but she wasn't likely to be hurt when offering to do as the queen willed.

Endellion frowned at the crowd, but the king merely extended one hand over the crown, which he held loosely in the other hand.

"I choose this," Lily whispered.

The queen's expression cleared and her focus returned to her husband.

"By my blood and will," Leith said as Endellion cut his palm.

His blood dripped onto the center of the crown. Then, she put her dagger—hilt first—into his bleeding hand.

She extended her wrist over the crown. "By my blood and will."

Leith sliced across her wrist, and again, blood dripped onto the crown.

The blood of the regents seemed to shimmer there, as if fire and sea and air all somehow twisted and danced in the glowing droplets. As they watched, it took the shape of a ruby, gleaming in the center of the crown.

"LilyDark, daughter of Iana our daughter and Nicolas the Abernathy, granddaughter to Leith Once-Seelie King and Endellion Once-Unseelie Queen, do you accept this crown and all it signifies?" Leith asked in a booming voice that rolled over the crowd.

"I do."

"LilyDark, do you accept your duty to protect the Hidden Lands and guide the fae?" Endellion asked, her voice filled with the lilt of wave and the weight of stone.

"I do," Lily repeated.

Endellion looked out at the people, staring into eyes and camera lenses unflinchingly, and announced, "So be it. Thus, I present the heir to the Hidden Throne, future ruler of the Hidden Lands as well as anyone in this world with a single droplet of fae blood."

Leith lowered the crown onto Lily's head. It felt much heavier than it looked, or perhaps its weight came from what it signified.

"To cause harm to her is to ask to die," Endellion added in a mild voice. "As a coronation gift to the future queen of the Hidden Lands, I hereby declare peace between the people of her father, the humans, and the people of her mother, the fae."

Every camera caught that pronouncement. Every eye was fixed on them. It was a moment of peace, of possibility, of a future that could be.

It was worth the sacrifice of Lily's freedom. Lily looked

to Creed and Zephyr, who were watching her. Behind them stood the remaining Black Diamonds. She might be afraid, but she wasn't alone—and she'd done the right thing. A part of her wished her parents had been present for her odd coronation, but she was grateful that they weren't witness to the fear on the faces of the watching humans.

Despite the fear in more than a few faces, in that instant, Lily honestly believed that things would be different. The war was over. This was the start of a new era.

But then the pier burst into fire around them. Humans fell into the sea, some burning. Screams of pain and fear erupted from those jumping into the sea.

At the same time, the sea rose up behind the faery regents.

Lily felt it, the surge of sea as it gathered and grew larger and taller by the instant. It hovered there, a tsunami wave about to break, and Lily only had a heartbeat to try to push it back.

Fire threatened her on one side, water on the other. There was no answer she could think of, no explanation that would turn this moment into something other than chaos. The queen was aligned with the sea; the king was most renowned for his affinity with fire.

"Help me," Lily said.

Even as she spoke, she could feel the gust of wind from both regents as they called the air to them to shove the waters back. At her back, the flames grew painfully close.

Pushing back the water was feeding the fire.

There was no way to stop both.

There was no solution to the disaster.

The wave fell. It swallowed them and many of the assembled crowd, toppling bodies into the murky waters.

And all Lily knew was the sea.

thirty-two

LILY

The Queen of Blood and Rage was livid when she surfaced from the sea. Her jewel-encrusted shoes were gone, sunken to the depths to be gathered in a fisherman's net and sold for the stones or the significance. Her heavy dress was gone, too, undoubtedly stripped off to keep the weight of it from keeping her submerged. Seaweed clung to her like a sentient thing, twisting and writhing, fashioning itself into a garment of sorts. Without her formal attire, the queen looked like a spirit of nature come from the depths to wreak havoc.

"Lily" was her first word as she stood aloft on the waves. The few simple letters felt like the full depth of the sea was encased within them. The queen's terror was clear in that one word.

The sea roiled, but the queen was motionless save for

her eyes. She surveyed the chaos, not pausing at the sight of the king in the sea or of the drowning and screaming humans. She didn't seem to be stirred by anything, not yet.

"Lily," she said again, her words more order than plea.

"Here!" Lily swam through the churning water, trying to reach a human woman who was faltering. "I'm here."

As Lily moved she tried to help people, finding them bits of the pier to use as rafts or simply pulling them out of the depths.

Roan had shifted into a seal, and he was steadily towing people to safety. Will and Creed were swimming out and hauling people to a section of the pier that bobbed but wasn't completely severed from the rest of the structure. Violet was drawing the fires that were erupting on the shore, pulling flames into her skin to siphon them off so the firefighters could try to combat the blazes.

Everyone but Zephyr was accounted for. Lily started to panic. "Creed, where is he? Zephyr!"

She looked around, diving under the water and asking the sea to help. "Where is he?" She concentrated on his image as she spoke to the sea and the plants that lived there. She held his face in her mind as she called down to the rocks. "He is my blood and family. Return him."

Lily surfaced and scanned the water again.

There wasn't even a glimpse of Zephyr.

Pulling the whole of the rush of her unfettered affinities to the surface, she started to send a call to any of the fae who might be near. Suddenly, the water around her took the shape of a massive hand that grabbed her and jerked her into the air. She floated there, aloft, water like solid ground under her feet. It shouldn't have been possible, but it was. The queen had willed it. That was enough.

"Where's Zeph—"

"Rhys," the queen spoke over her, cutting off her words.

Lily hadn't even known Rhys was there, but as she looked around, she saw him. He stood on the wreckage of the pier, balanced atop stone and board, sword in hand. Next to him was a very wet Zephyr. Seeing him made something relax inside her. She worried that losing Alkamy would make him reckless.

Rhys didn't offer any spoken reply to the queen. Instead, he pulled back his arm and threw his sword. It cut through the air toward her.

Endellion snatched it and in barely a heartbeat, she looked more like herself. Leith was with the humans helping those struggling in the water, but the queen stood peering around as if she expected another attack. Her attention continued to flow over the pier and those who were there. Now, though, instead of the regal fae monarch, she resembled nothing so much as a thing in nightmares. *This* would be the vision on the news. This would be the face of the fae that would be broadcast round the world—a terrifyingly beautiful being wrapped in seaweed, her sword upraised.

"Grandmother," Lily said softly, trying to find calm

around her lingering tendrils of fear. "The humans will never accept peace if there are so many dead today. We have to make sure there are *survivors*."

At that, Endellion nodded. Lily felt guilt at the way she'd had to phrase the truth. Death was a lot more than a public relations worry, but putting the situation in terms the Queen of Blood and Rage understood was necessary.

Endellion looked toward the shore and stared at the burning buildings. Clouds gathered and rain began to pour, aiding the firefighters.

Then the queen made another seemingly careless gesture with her hand, and the waves grew thick enough that there was a translucent bridge. She met Lily's gaze. "They can walk to safety."

"It will hold you," the King of Fire and Truth said cheerfully from where he bobbed in the water as if it were all a great game. "Up you go. Come on now."

He boosted people onto the water-wrought bridge. He was sopping wet, royal garb clinging to him, but he retained his cheerful mien. Lily found herself smiling briefly. It wasn't her nature to be like him, but just now, she could appreciate his willfully optimistic attitude.

The Queen of Blood and Rage, however, was as tense as a warrior between bouts.

"Summon your sword, LilyDark."

Lily wasn't attuned to metal, had no affinity with it, but she was adept at earth, and the metal was melded with deadly hemlock. She called to it, drawing hemlock, but instead of her sword, her first answer was from a water-rooted plant. She released it and tried again, not wanting to fail, not wanting to disappoint the queen.

The sword she'd lost in the sea came at her summons then, cutting through the water and flying toward her hand. That, too, would be news footage. The new heir calling a weapon to her hand didn't exactly proclaim "peace is here."

"Love?" Leith called up to them. "Can you add a bit of width to the bridge?"

Endellion pressed her lips together. The only other movement was a widening of her eyes. Quietly, she said, "Relying on affinities is never enough, LilyDark. I use them as tools, but they do not bring me the fear or respect that a bloodied blade will. Let them see me as I am, and they will remember it when they consider crossing me."

"Someone *has* crossed you," Lily pointed out. She hated speaking that truth, of giving voice to the undeniable fact that they had been attacked just as they declared peace.

"I know." Endellion scanned the shore again, her gaze pausing on the onslaught of vehicles rushing toward the pier. "And at least one of my own was involved."

The whole chaotic affair had taken so few minutes, but in those minutes, everything Lily knew had changed. She'd become a fae princess in the eyes of humanity, and someone had attempted to either kill or harm the witnesses. She was either a target or an innocent bystander.

The queen was correct: the attacker was obviously not human. Only fae could bend waves into weapons. Someone was angry enough to want to continue the war.

As Lily stood on the waves next to her grandmother, she watched police and militia on foot start to surge toward the sea, toward them, like a warring army. They wore battle regalia, heavy vests and combat boots, and they had weapons in hand. Nothing about this moment spoke of peace. Buildings burned. The dead floated in the harbor. Corpses were plucked from the water. This was a disaster.

"A fae attack on us and them." Lily nodded toward the shore. "Humans *about* to attack us. Where is the peace I'm trying to buy?"

She stared out at the crowds. Cameras were everywhere now, and there was no way that she was going to be able to step onto shore anytime soon. The crowd looked fearful, ready to erupt into violence at the slightest provocation, and all she could think of were Daidí's warnings. The world was more of a tinder box now than it had been before she'd negotiated for an end to war.

"I can't stay here," Lily announced.

Endellion glanced at her, but she said nothing. Her expression was blank.

"I'm not giving up," Lily swore. "I want peace, and I want to live in this world *and* the other. For now, though, I would go with you."

Endellion smiled slightly. "I am pleased that I don't need to force the matter."

Lily sighed as the truth of it settled on her. They were *all* at risk if they remained here. There was nothing to do but go to the Hidden Lands and figure out where to go from here. She hoped they'd all cooperate gracefully.

thirty-three

ZEPHYR

"Did *she* do that? The wave?" Zephyr asked bluntly. He was far past being shocked by the machinations of the queen. There hadn't been a time in his life when he had been unaware of the ruthlessness of the Queen of Blood and Rage. Perhaps as a small child, he might have had a degree of ignorance, but he wouldn't even swear to that.

"It would not further her primary goals, so it is likely an attack *on* her rather than by her." Rhys had a sliver of anger in his voice.

As Rhys spoke, he didn't pull his gaze from the increasingly large crowd of humans on the shore near them. Although he was armed only with a short sword and they were brandishing guns, Rhys was not as unevenly matched as he might appear. Humans had no skill with affinities. That was a purely fae ability, and Rhys was the eldest child of the Queen of Blood and Rage.

"I would rather you are unharmed. Stay at my side," he added as he motioned toward the crowd with a peculiar gesture, as if he was drawing in the empty air with the blade in his hand. In the next heartbeat, Zephyr could feel the air grow thicker, as if the molecules were slowing and drawing together. It was as if Rhys was building a wall in front of them, a shield that would protect them and yet not be visible to any of the watchers from the shore.

The pier was destroyed. They were standing atop some of the planks and rubble that had toppled to the shallows. In the near distance, fins cut through the choppy water as sharks were drawn by blood. It was not the fae who were at risk.

Zephyr glanced toward the queen and his cousin. As Lily stood there dripping wet, with her sword in hand, she was as alike to the queen as a person could be—regal and commanding. She looked terrifying.

But LilyDark had surrendered everything to end war between the worlds. If the human governments were wise, they'd realize that the new heir was someone they should endorse. Embracing her would lead to the peace they'd all sought. It seemed an obvious choice.

Politics, however, were no longer the future Zephyr would have. He'd be Lily's guard, no more or less political than his father. There was a kind of peace in that. He'd have rather had the future he imagined with Alkamy, but without her, a life by the sword was all he could fathom.

In the midst of the chaos, Zephyr looked down to see a familiar body floating under the waves.

"Father?" Zephyr gestured. He had no words to tell Rhys that his sister was dead. Her eyes were closed, and she was not moving or swimming.

"Eilidh?" Rhys said, voice cracking in apparent worry.

At his voice, the former heir opened her eyes and surged upward. The waves shaped into a watery chair that drifted in the shallow edge of the waves. She walked out of the sea and to Rhys' side.

"Eilidh?" Rhys repeated.

She stumbled briefly, and Zephyr leaped forward to steady her.

"I wasn't feeling well, so I went to sea, and . . ." She shook her head, paused, and then said, "And now, I am here."

Frowning, Rhys motioned for them to walk farther ashore. "You are not to be here, Eilidh. You know as much. There are risks and"—he motioned toward the chaos on shore—"these are not calm beings. They are a danger."

Zephyr agreed, but telling the princess not to be here didn't change the fact that she *was* here. There was no way to undo things, so the only option was to go forward with what was. He kept his sword in hand, but his focus was also on Eilidh.

"I feel peculiar," she said quietly. Then she drew a shaky breath and slumped into him, almost taking him to the ground.

Zephyr barely managed to hoist her into his arms. "Rhys!"

Rhys started to turn toward St. Columba's where there was a pathway to the Hidden Lands. "We will take her home."

"No," Zephyr corrected. "Not until the others are with us. I need to know they are safe."

Rhys brushed the princess' hair back and felt her head. "There are no bumps." He glanced at her seemingly without emotion, although Zephyr knew better, before pronouncing, "There is no blood."

Zephyr saw Roan and went toward him with a barely muttered, "This way."

There was a part of him that felt uneasy leading the Unseelie prince, but he needed to see the rest of the diamonds. He'd already lost Alkamy, and he wasn't sure he'd be able to handle losing anyone else. "Where is everyone?"

"Lily went with the queen," Roan said, but his gaze was fixed on Eilidh.

"My father, Rhys, son to the Queen of Blood and Rage . . . and his sister, Eilidh." Zephyr sounded more formal than he'd intended, but there were phrases that were hard to make casual.

The usually calm Roan, however, was oblivious. He scanned the remaining groups of people. "Right. Have you seen Will?"

"No . . . and I haven't seen Creed or Vi either."

"Vi must be with one of them if she isn't with Lily."

Zephyr looked around, but the crowd was a mess of bodies. There were a lot of injured people. Emergency vehicles and armed officers added to the chaos rather than quelling it.

All Zephyr wanted was to find the others and get everyone to safety. Focusing on that mission was the clearest he'd been since losing Alkamy. It wasn't undoing the pain in his chest, but it allowed him to ignore it briefly. That was what he needed: reasons to concentrate on anything other than his gaping wound.

"I need to find him," Roan said.

He turned and walked away, and although Zephyr might have criticized him for impulsiveness a few days ago, he understood the fear Roan had to be feeling in that moment. Roan and Will had loved one another before Zephyr had realized his feelings for Alkamy. They were together, and the war was ending. To lose that *now* seemed cruel.

Then Zephyr spotted a familiar figure, the arsonist from the club. "Father! Over there." He pointed at the smirking fae-blood. "There! The one from the fire."

Even as he spoke, the fae-blood turned and faded into the swarm of people. There was no way that they could catch him, even if they could move through the panicking and angry humans. "We need to follow—"

"No. You take Eilidh home. Keep her safe," Rhys ordered as he walked away, too, striding into the crowd as if he wasn't surrounded by humans who found his very existence a crime.

Zephyr was left holding an unconscious princess.

There were hundreds of people milling around. Guards and police mingled in the crowds, seemingly interrogating everyone. Journalists were recording clips. Former classmates from St. Columba were staring at him. He had to trust that Roan would be safe, that his father would see to it.

That left Zephyr to get himself and his aunt to safety. It was a massive amount of trust that his father had placed in him. Zephyr looked down at his aunt. She was obviously fae, in a crowd of people currently terrified by their kind. Whether or not peace had been declared, the resulting events felt nothing like peace. He had declared himself to the new heir, his cousin, but he still had the fae loyalty to family first.

He carried Eilidh away from the crowd and to—he hoped—some measure of safety.

thirty-four

WILL

Will looked around for the others as best he could with a
police officer holding on to him. He wasn't sure whether
it was better that he'd been separated from them or not.
Somehow, he couldn't picture Violet or Zephyr taking
well to being arrested—or Roan coping well with the way
the policeman was manhandling him, especially not while
everyone was still grieving over Alkamy. Will wasn't sure
any of them would deal with his arrest particularly well.

Being arrested was not an experience he'd ever *sought*,
but it was certainly one he'd pondered often enough. He
was a fae-blood, a mercenary for the queen, and the son of
an outspoken human politician. His odds of running afoul
of the law weren't negligible.

"We have flex cuffs so you won't get burned by the
metal," the officer said, not unkindly. "The car isn't

avoidable though. Are you one of the ones who get throwing up sick from it or just weak?"

"I'll be fine," Will said, quite truthfully. The humans' belief that steel sickened those with fae blood was both wrong and persistent.

The officer, a man who had the sort of round face and fluffy hair that made him look like he shared close genetics with koala, stared at Will in silence. His hands trembled ever so slightly as he slipped cuffs on Will's wrists.

"You are making a mistake," Will said.

"Is that a threat?"

"No. I'm not who you think. My mother is Senator Parrish—"

"You're fae," the officer interrupted. "You and your actress friend."

"Violet?"

The officer tightened the cuffs just this side of too painful. He pushed Will toward the back of the cruiser. "Some of the others said I should gag you so you don't trick me. I don't want to, but if you keep talking, I will."

Will sighed. There wasn't a lot he could do. Attacking the man seemed stupid—not that being caged seemed particularly smart. Unlike some fae, he had no gift of charm or persuasion beyond that which any person might have. He was well-spoken, reasonably attractive, and his family had influence. In truth, he was not so different from any politician's son in that regard. His affinities were, of course, an exception, but they didn't lend him charisma.

They simply meant he could work with the air around them.

He'd done so on the queen's orders, but he wasn't going to attack these people for doing their job. If he could avoid it, he would. If his mother got word of his imprisonment, she'd come for him.

"*He's* not fae," Creed said, his voice making Will spin halfway around. "I am. I am the faery king! I am the rightful king!"

Will's mouth dropped open at the ludicrousness of Creed's words. The idea of declaring himself a faery king was dangerous at every corner. The *actual* faery queen was vicious in her best of moods. The former heir wasn't much better, and one of the Seelie princes had stabbed Creed not too long ago. Plus, of course, possessing any faery blood at all was illegal.

"You'll see! They all act like they're someone, but I'm the real thing." Creed was playing it crazy, looking around at everyone with a strange madness that seemed far too realistic.

"You're insane," Will said loudly.

He saw Erik in the crowd of onlookers too. There was a moment where Will thought Erik was going to draw the weapon he had hidden under his jacket. He glanced at Creed, who obviously was watching Erik too.

"Get out of here," Will said, staring back at Erik as he spoke although he used words that could be thought to be in response to Creed: "You need help."

Erik faded into the crowd. That, at least, was a crisis averted. There were enough human deaths today, and having a criminal firing bullets at officers would be a step too far.

"I don't need help," Creed replied, as if Will had been speaking to him. He stumbled forward as the officers rudely jerked him. "It's not like I haven't been hassled before."

Like him, Creed was bound and being dragged toward the opposite side of the car. Unlike him, the cuffs on Creed's wrists were obviously metal. There was no pretense of kindness in their treatment of Creed Morrison. His swelling eye and split lip made obvious that the officers were not above excessive force. For all of Creed's recent progress with being more tractable in general, he was still who he was. The whole "rock star with a bad attitude" thing wasn't an act. Creed was often a jackass. They all acted like he'd only turned to drinking because of the things that they'd done for the queen, and Will could allow that Creed's swing to *heavy* drinking was due to that, but he'd always been the one in primary school who was last to volunteer, first to test a rule, ready to raise a fist, quick to deliver cruel words. It was as if there was an edge of darkness in him that could only be restrained, not eliminated.

"He's probably drunk," Will said. "Drunk or looking for headlines, as if his new girlfriend's lineage isn't enough."

Creed grinned, looking vaguely grotesque because

of his split lip. "Yeah, and you were just hanging around me trying to get attention. Now you're trying to pretend you're *fae-blood*? No one's stupid enough to believe that."

"Shut it." The officer restraining Creed jerked open the cruiser door and shoved him inside.

Before he could reach for Will, the other officer opened the passenger door and nodded. Will slid in as carefully as he could with restraints on him. "Can you remove these while we're in the car?"

The kinder officer said nothing; he simply closed the door.

Creed was trying to kick the officer who had shoved him into the car. "Screw you."

Once the officer had managed to get Creed's feet in the car and the door shut, Creed looked at Will and winked.

"What are you doing?" Will asked in a whisper so low that only another fae-blood with an affinity for air would hear it.

"Keeping their attention."

"Because . . . ?"

Creed smiled. "She's my girlfriend, man. You think they'll believe I'm *not* fae-blood? You can get out of it if we stall long enough to keep them from testing you."

Will stared at him.

"I don't have a problem with it being crystal clear that I belong to her," Creed added, rolling his shoulders. "Old man can hit fairly well. Guess they don't worry about bruises on anyone with skin as dark as mine."

"Bruises still show," Will muttered.

Creed twisted his lips into a wry smile before pointing out, "I resisted arrest. Got injured as a result."

Will leaned back in his seat and shook his head. Antagonistic or not, Creed was trying to look out for him, and he was willingly sacrificing himself in the process. Will wanted to argue, to suggest that it was a huge mistake, but that wouldn't undo what was already done.

Then he heard words spoken so softly that they could be mistaken for a breeze drifting into Will's ears. "Don't let her come after me. You need to make sure of it when you get out, okay? She storms in here after that coronation, and *she'll* be in a cell."

Will glanced at him and nodded once. Creed was taking the weight, but he'd asked Will to do an impossible task. Lily was going to be a nightmare once she found out that Creed was in jail.

He closed his eyes and whispered a prayer to St. Ninian that there was a way for this not to be a complete disaster.

thirty-five

EILIDH

Eilidh woke to the strange sensation of being kept away from sea and soil. Neither waves nor plants were holding her. Instead, she was held in someone's arms, cradled as if she was a small child. She was going to choke if she didn't get to either earth or water immediately.

"Down. Now." Her eyes were unfocused, even as she tried to look at the face of the person holding her. She blinked and squinted. "Rhys?"

"Close." The voice was one she'd only heard a few times, but it was familiar enough even so.

"His son," she said. "Family."

To the fae there was an order. One's family was the most important. After that, it was one's land—or perhaps one's birth court. The opinions varied there. For Eilidh, as she was born of both courts, she ordered it as family, fae, and land. It was often all one and the same, but family was still somehow *more*.

"*Soil.* I need the soil," she told Zephyr.

Carefully, he lowered her legs so she could stand, but he kept an arm around her, steadying her. The moss under her bare feet was like medicine. For a heartbeat, she could've sworn that she had roots as a tree or vine would, sinking into the soil, sliding past rock and creature, winding toward trickles of water that flowed deep in the heart of the earth.

"Princess Eilidh? Can I . . . what should I call you?"

As the soil nourished her, flooding her with strength and stability, she felt her eyes come clearer. She'd changed. There was no other way to say it. Over the last few weeks, she'd become something more . . . primal. Today made that exceptionally clear. She had no memory of what happened when she let the sea take her. *Eilidh* had simply ceased existing. There was only the sea. She was just a part of it, drops of water within the waves under the surface.

"Eilidh," she echoed. She could feel the sea tugging her back, but she was separate now. "Yes," she told Zephyr, reaffirming her name, needing to hear it and speak it. "Eilidh."

She stepped away from him so she could fold herself closer to the earth. She collapsed onto the ground, gracelessly enough that Zephyr lunged to catch her.

"I'm sorry. I thought—"

"I'm fine," she interrupted. "Where is my brother?"

Zephyr scowled and glanced at the stone wall. As he did so, Eilidh realized that she was on the campus grounds, near where she had met Zephyr and discovered that she had a nephew, that Rhys had a son. That meant there was a gate home nearby. A part of her wanted to refuse it, to stay and give herself over to nature. That part of her grew louder and more constant with every dawning day.

Was this, she wondered, the cost of nature giving her life when she was first born? Was that life somehow not wholly her own?

"He went to find Creed and Will, and I was left to guard you," Zephyr said, leaving Eilidh to try to remember the question he was answering. That very little bit of focus was nearly too much to ask. Words were not clear for her right now. The act of speaking felt like it took all of her mind to complete. It was not uncommon to struggle so, but typically, once she'd been released from sea or soil, she could regain some measure of clarity.

"We should . . . go home," Eilidh said carefully, stretching each letter over her tongue and teeth, making them sound as they must.

Eilidh was unsteady as she walked to the gate. Earth and air offered her support. Soil and stone tethered her, reminded her that she was solid. They also reminded her that the human world was tainted. The sea she fell into in her own world was clean and pure. The water on this side of the sea gate was sickening.

As she led Zephyr into the Hidden Lands, she felt the

change in the air like weight falling from her chest. This was as it should be. The purity washed over her, and every one of her natural affinities pressed against her. This was the world all should be like.

She could make it so.

With her affinities allowed full range, far more than those few at the pier would die.

She could wash them all away.

With her affinities guiding her, she could purify the earth, sky, and sea.

Shaking her head to find clarity again, Eilidh glanced at her nephew. Zephyr was looking at the twisted rock formations all around them. It was not shocking that they'd entered here. Both of them were earth affinity, and being surrounded by the towering rock formations was fitting. They were at the edge of the sea, but surrounding them on three sides were basalt columns. They stretched into the sky like steps for something too large to fathom.

Eilidh led him into the trail that twisted into a cave in the center of those columns. Inside was another sort of majesty. Stalactites and stalagmites reached toward one another like stony teeth in a wide grin. Eilidh could feel their hum of welcoming words and suspected that her nephew could too.

"I am sorry that you lost your beloved," she said.

He stumbled.

"War is not kind." Eilidh reached out and squeezed his arm. "I am grateful that you were spared."

"I'm not," he said, and she heard a thousand tears in those two words. She couldn't imagine the loss of Torquil, not truly. She'd sat at his bedside when she'd thought he might perish, and she'd run to his side in her fears. There was no reason to believe that Zephyr's love for Alkamy was any less true simply because they were so young. True love, the sort that made your hearts beat in perfect time, knew no age. When your souls touched, it was everything.

"I understand," Eilidh assured him. "And selfishly, I am still glad that you are not dead too."

Zephyr kept his silence as they walked. He neither agreed nor argued. There was no need. Family wanted family to survive; lovers being severed wanted to perish. Neither of these were new truths. In time, Zephyr would find ways to hurt less and less, or he would take the sorts of risks that let him cross swords with death. It was what her family did. Her mother had been ready to slaughter the world at the loss of her beloved child. Eilidh would be no different if Torquil were to perish. Asking other of Zephyr was unfair—but that was what family did. Eilidh had schemed to find a way to make her mother surrender her grief. She'd offered LilyDark to her as an appeasement.

If there were one to offer Zephyr, Eilidh would do so. For now, though, she would present him with a home where he could try to heal.

When Eilidh and Zephyr exited the cave and walked toward the area where the fae lived, he remained silent. He stared at their watchers with the same haughty assurance that his father wore like a mask. All he said finally was "I do not know where we go, but I would speak to the queen."

Eilidh let herself sink a little further into the hum of the voice of the land. It was harder to keep separate than it was to hear these days. "Mother is not here yet."

He nodded, and Eilidh led him through the Hidden Lands. Here, it was as the world had all once been. Here, the fae had kept the toxins out. It was the only space that was truly as nourishing as the world was meant to be.

When they reached the sparkling glass tower, Eilidh gestured for him to precede her into her home.

Still mute, he did so, ascending the stairs until they reached the common area, where they found Torquil waiting anxiously.

"You were gone, Patches. I thought I'd lost you. . . ." His words faded. Torquil walked over and wrapped an arm around her. She leaned into him.

Then, in a blink, Torquil had composed himself. "Zephyr."

"Torquil."

"What happened?" Torquil asked them both. "The sea is thrashing, and the earth is rolling. Something has happened, Eilidh."

Zephyr filled Torquil in, but they both watched her expectantly as Zephyr explained that she had appeared, floating under the waves after the disaster that had taken lives and endangered the heir and Eilidh's own parents.

"Eilidh?" Torquil asked. In that question were the fears and doubts she herself struggled to address. What had happened? Why was she there? Had she attacked her own family?

But Eilidh couldn't reply. All she knew was that the sea had taken her and when she had awakened she was on the shore.

She needed answers. *They* needed answers. She simply didn't have them.

thirty-six

LILY

Entering the Hidden Lands this time was a very different experience from the first time Lily had done so. This time, Lily wasn't being summoned there. She was entering as the heir, alongside the rulers of this strange land and one of the Black Diamonds who was there as *her* subject. Lily entered with a sword in one hand and a circlet seemingly affixed to her head of its own will. It was an overwhelming experience, one she wasn't sure she'd be so calm about later.

At her side, Violet was silent.

The first time they'd come here, Lily hadn't had any time to look around and enjoy the odd beauty of the world. She also hadn't realized that the doors didn't always open to the same place. When she'd come through before, the Hidden Lands seemed more like forest than anything else. This time, she'd stepped into a craggy landscape of exposed reef and crumbling cliffs.

"Is there a pattern to where we enter?"

"Bloodline," Endellion said simply. The Queen of Blood and Rage walked at her left side, as if they were equals or perhaps friends. "You are more *mine* so you will enter through my gate more often. Sea or water will often be near you."

"Oh, Dell." Leith sigh-laughed. "She isn't more yours. She was in the *forest* last time." He increased his pace so he was on the opposite side of Lily. "A lot of times, it's affinity. With you that gives a few options, of course, but there will be spaces that call to you more. There are those bits of air—"

"Or sea," Endellion interjected.

"Air *or sea*," Leith continued with barely a pause, "that will call to you, as if they are solid space where you can anchor yourself. Dell is fond of these sharp rocks of hers. I like the softer moss of the forest. Our daughter tends to mix the two. She has a little spot she slips in and out of, as if we don't notice, where there are trees, but she crosses through the caves. The girl's always had a thing for the caves."

Lily tried to ignore the oddities of the moment. She and Violet exchanged a look, but neither of them spoke. Lily wasn't sure there was an appropriate response *other* than silence. These were her grandparents, talking about her aunt, but they were also the two single-most powerful creatures in either world. In the moment of crisis at

Belfoure, she was grateful for their power and presence, but now that she was beyond that moment, she had to admit that there was a trickle of terror.

The regents of the Hidden Lands were pleased with her, and as such, she was cherished, but the truth was that the fae were capricious. The queen had waged war, using children as soldiers. The king had sat back in his throne and let her do so with full knowledge of her plan. Perhaps he was simply pleased that she wasn't waging war on *his* court as she'd reputedly done centuries ago when the fae were divided. Lily might have been raised around guns, arrests, and the occasional assassination, but that was mild compared to the ways of the fae. She couldn't forget that. Ever.

The Hidden Lands themselves inspired a fair degree of awe as well. There was something almost alive in the fae lands, as if they were sentient. Lily felt like there were invisible fingers reaching out to her, trying to touch some part of her where her affinities were surging. Briefly, she wondered if she'd felt it the last time she was here, but the fear of Endellion had subsumed everything and she'd not noticed. It was the fae that worked and lived here in the Hidden Lands. This was the land itself stretching toward her.

"You need to do something about them. Today was to be a celebration. I wore queenly clothes. I had *shoes* on my feet." Endellion's words were accompanied by a large root snapping to the surface where the king almost stumbled over it.

As the root tried to trip him, Leith merely floated upward as if on a draft of air. "It wasn't the boys, Dell."

"So say you."

"I do, and you know I'm right." Leith pushed warm air currents toward the Queen of Blood and Rage and ruffled her primitive sea-grass dress as if he were a boy trying to flirt with her.

Endellion let out a grumbling noise that rolled through the trees and soil like a small earthquake. The ground shuddered under their feet, and seams cracked in a nearby rock. It wasn't deadly, but it felt a lot like a warning.

Violet and Lily exchanged a tense look, but neither spoke. The fae regents were seemingly oblivious to the girls' presence as they bickered—or so Lily thought until Leith winked at her. He sent a gust of wind to shape fallen leaves into two clashing swords in front of the queen. "Calder has only air. Nacton has fire and compulsion. No water for either, my love."

The queen called a gush of water to drench him up to his hips. It surged across the forest floor like she'd summoned a river to form. In truth, it was a beautiful bit of magic, especially as it curved around them and only doused the king.

Laughing, Leith hopped out of the suddenly appearing creek, somehow managing not to look ludicrous in the process. He continued to speak as if his wife hadn't just tried to injure him . . . *again*. "Calder is still recovering from torture."

The queen was silent for a brief moment before saying, "It obviously wasn't Rhys."

Leith guffawed. "That boy wouldn't cross you for anyone but our daughter, or possibly"—he gestured at Lily—"our granddaughter. He might be Unseelie, but he's loyal to his family."

"And what, pray tell, is wrong with being Unseelie?" Endellion seemed to grow taller in her anger. Trees shivered, dropping leaves in a sudden shower. The water that the king had just stepped out of turned toward him as if it were stalking him now.

"Nothing. Someone has to take on the task of being temperamental and violent, and I've never been fond of it." He eased closer to Lily and Violet and said, "It was the most difficult flirtation of my life. Always with the insults and crossing swords. A few centuries ago she almost had me convinced she disliked me."

Endellion said levelly, "Sometimes I *do* dislike you."

"You see?" Leith said, levitating a long strand of spiderweb, shaped as a heart, in front of the queen and setting it afire.

With an audible sigh, she drew water from the creek she'd just pulled to the surface and drenched both the flaming heart and the king.

He wiped the water from his face. "My sons suspect she's a sorceress, bewitched me to madness."

"You were mad before I decided to wed you," the queen muttered.

"Mad with love. You know I love you, Dell . . . anyone with sense knows that."

Endellion glared at him, but she was smiling slightly too. "Fine. I will allow that it wasn't your Calder or my Rhys, and it might not have been your other son."

She fixed her husband with a pointed stare. "Who was it then?"

He didn't answer, but Lily saw a glimmer in his eye that made her suspect that he had a theory. Whatever it was, whomever he suspected, the King of Fire and Truth wasn't sharing. He turned to Lily instead and asked, "Do you want to visit my court? Your grandmother will want to check on Eilidh, pretend she's not worrying over Rhys—"

"There's no need to worry," the queen interrupted. "He can handle himself."

The king smiled at her kindly, and then he turned to Lily. "That boy got injured once, and she trained with him from that point forward till he was likely to expire out of sheer exhaustion."

The queen said nothing.

"So," the king continued, "I would love to offer you both rooms at my palace."

Lily glanced at the queen, who did nothing other than swish her hand toward the king. Apparently that was as close as she was going to get to an assent. Carefully, Lily said, "If it would be okay, I'd also like to stay with my grandmother for a few days."

Endellion didn't say anything, but a look of pleasure

crossed her face before she spoke, "You keep her safe. Do you understand? I won't have those cretins upsetting her again, and the dissenters need to be kept in line."

"Yes, dear."

"The dissenters?" Violet asked.

"Some of our kind would want to kill LilyDark so she can't be queen, the few who want to once again separate the courts, but it's folly to even entertain it. . . ."

Lily sighed. Of course some of the fae wanted her to die. Humanity wanted to arrest her. A declaration of peace was a massive change. To accept it, laws would need to be rewritten. Tolerance for fae-blood would need to be mandated, and the gates between the worlds would need to be cracked open. It wasn't a process that would go easily or quickly—especially with rogue fae out there burning places down and attacking the coronation.

Lily glanced at the king. He'd begun humming again, seeming as if he was as content as anybody could be. A small voice reminded her that he was the King of Fire and Truth, and he'd not only ruled the Seelie Court but found a way to forge peace between the courts—and now had angled the queen toward peace with humanity. He winked at her, and she shook her head. It was easy to forget that there were ways to achieve your ends that required no bloodshed. It wouldn't do to underestimate the king.

thirty-seven

CREED

Inside the police station, Will and Creed were separated. Will had apparently been determined not to be a threat. Maybe it was because they realized who his mother was and that they'd arrested him with cameras rolling. The senator undoubtedly knew by now—as, most likely, did Creed's fans and manager.

And because of Erik, Lily's dad undoubtedly did too. If they were supremely unlucky, Lily did too. Creed *truly* hoped that wasn't the case.

He found himself inside what was more or less a terrarium with foot-thick glass walls as if he was a bug in a jar or—

"You must release the singing boy." The oddly worded proclamation interrupted Creed's thoughts.

"Noxious plant in a bell jar," he said quietly to himself. He wasn't sure any of this was actually the start of a song, or if he'd ever get to sing on stage in this world again. Before Lily, music had been his only love. If he had to choose between them, Lily would win every time. First, though, he had to get out of a cage with walls so thick he couldn't crack them.

A wiry officer stepped toward the door. "Sir, we—"

"He is to be released," the voice repeated.

Creed walked to the edge of his cage, trying to see who had come seeking his freedom. Everything was distorted though. He *had* expected someone to come after him. He'd hoped that Erik had called for a lawyer when he'd seen him being arrested. His own manager wasn't as quick at bailing him out these days. Honestly, Creed needed to fire the woman, but his career hadn't been his top priority of late.

"He is not yours to keep." The person who was demanding Creed's release moved forward even as various officers tried to reach out and grab him. It was as if the air around him were impenetrable.

"Rhys?" Creed winced at the realization that the Queen of Blood and Rage's *son* was in a police station because of him.

"The boy belongs to my queen," Rhys pronounced, drawing a sword from his side.

Guards scrambled toward him, trying to halt his advance.

"Step back," Rhys ordered.

This was about to become an incident, the sort that wouldn't foster peace. The fae were rarely so bold out in public.

"Rhys!" Nicolas Abernathy's voice at the door made the faery turn and scowl. "You cannot do that. There are *laws*."

"My queen's laws are clear," Rhys began.

"We are not in her territory," Lily's father said.

Rhys kept his sword in hand, but an officer moved toward Lily's father and that was enough for Rhys to leap over a desk, knock down two other officers and one prisoner, and step in front of Mr. Abernathy. Mildly, as if his actions were mundane, Rhys said, "This is my niece's father. Blood of she whom I've sworn to keep safe." He let his gaze drift over the room menacingly, but he continued to sound conversational as he added, "I've killed more than a score of men in an afternoon after I'd already sustained a grievous wound. I have no doubt that most everyone here will die if you draw weapons."

"And if we don't draw them?" one of the officers asked.

"Then you don't bleed," Rhys said. "My blade is currently clean. I'd rather it stay that way. I do not relish killing, and my queen has declared peace with your world this day."

Uncharacteristically, Lily's father addressed the assembled group of officers. "This man—"

"Fae-blood," interrupted one of them.

"Fae," corrected Rhys. "I am but a weapon created and wielded by the queen as needs be."

"Not helping, man." It was Erik. He had followed Nick into the station. He shook his head.

"This *fae man*," Lily's father said, almost as if he hadn't been interrupted at all, "has broken no law yet."

"Being fae is illegal . . . sir," said an officer cautiously.

Nick waved his comment away, sounding more and more like his attorney. "Nonetheless, there were no other laws broken."

"Yet," muttered Erik quietly.

"Brandishing a weapon," interjected someone from Creed's left.

When Nick started to turn to glance behind him, there was a moment, a split instant when Creed knew that something very bad was about to happen. He heard the air, but being in the glass cell meant he couldn't bend it. He couldn't solidify it or reshape it.

"Move!" Creed yelled as he slammed both fists on the glass.

Before the word was fully formed, a bright red blossom covered Nick's chest. Someone had fired a bullet and hit Nicolas Abernathy, crime lord and father of the new heir to the Hidden Throne. The shot wasn't from inside the station. Creed could hear enough of the displaced air to know that the bullet was fired by someone outside.

"Nick!" Erik lunged toward him and tried to steady him.

And at that moment, Senator Parrish's voice carried over the room and she shoved past several guards with a loud, "Unhand me right now!"

Within moments of stepping into the melee—even with an officer holding on to her arm—she looked as composed as she always did, right up to the point when she saw Nick bleeding, Creed in a glass cage, and a faery with a sword standing in the midst of it all.

"Put that down," she ordered Rhys. She glanced around. "And *you* . . . the one still seated . . . call for an ambulance. There's a man down."

Her very sensible black pumps clacked on the floor as she walked farther into the room.

"And you." She pointed at an officer. "Fetch my son."

"Your . . ."

"William Parrish. My son." The senator leveled a glare at the officer and extended a folded batch of papers. "You have him held wrongly. His test results are very clear and *public*."

The officer she was browbeating stepped forward when she shook the papers in his direction like she was summoning a recalcitrant pet.

"Ma'am?" another officer started.

"Senator," she corrected in that same barking voice. "I am a senator, not a *ma'am*."

"Yes, Senator, ma'am." The officer accepted the papers

and scanned them quickly. After he read them, re-read them, and nodded to himself, he said, "The nice one is free."

Then he turned to glance at Creed. "But you're staying. Anyone that's got a thug . . . and one of *them* coming to free him is right where he ought to be."

The senator said nothing. Her lips pressed tightly together, but Creed wasn't sure whether that was in disapproval or if she was weighing her options. Her hands shook so slightly that it would take a slow motion camera to see that she was nowhere as confident as she was pretending to be.

Rhys watched everyone, as if he were trying to decide whether he could start brandishing the sword that hung loosely in his grip.

"My cage is comfortable enough." Creed shrugged as if it was fine. He could pretend too.

He couldn't help but look at his girlfriend's father though. Nicolas Abernathy was bleeding and on the floor. Erik had shrugged out of his suit coat and given it to Nick. Rhys stayed there as if he were a statue guarding the fallen man. Nick himself had slid to the ground, but he'd managed to stay in a half-sitting position. He surveyed them all, speaking quietly to Erik, and holding the balled-up jacket to his own wound.

Creed didn't want to imagine Lily's wrath if she knew what was happening here. Obviously, he wasn't the only one thinking that way either. Nick coughed and winced at the pain it caused before saying, "Lily is not to find out *that* one"—he inclined his head toward Creed—"is in here or that I have had a bit of a complication, do you understand?"

Erik frowned, but when Nick stared at him, he gave a curt nod.

Rhys said, "She will be displeased at the deceit."

"And if she *is*, what's that going to do for the peace accord?" Nick asked in a wheezy voice. He was either struggling with the pain or blood was getting into his lungs. "Creed, I'm trusting you. She comes here and all hell will be breaking loose."

"*Abernathy Commandment #4: Weigh the consequences before beginning a course of action*," Creed told Nick. "You have my word."

Nick nodded once and after a visible shudder he said, "Erik."

"Yes, sir?"

"Handle it." Nick closed his eyes then.

And Creed wasn't sure if he was dead or not.

"If you let me out, I'll do whatever I'm told," Creed said, realizing he sounded desperate but unable to help himself. "Just let me out to help him."

No one even deigned to reply. They simply ignored him. His girlfriend's father was unconscious or dead on the floor, and he was unable to do a thing.

Erik's hand went to Nick's throat to check for a pulse. He resumed holding the jacket to Nick's wound to staunch the blood and told them, "He still has a pulse."

"Where's the fucking ambulance?" Creed punched the glass again. He couldn't help, couldn't do anything but sit in a cell and watch Lily's father bleed.

thirty-eight

WILL

Will wasn't surprised to see his mother when he was escorted out of his cell and into the police station. He wasn't even surprised to see Creed still in his glass cell or Erik Gaviria there already. What *did* shock him was seeing the man bleeding on the floor . . . and the realization that the man in question was Lily's dad.

"Who shot him?" Will asked softly.

A fae man with a sword turned and studied him. "I do not know. A human."

"Who are you?"

"I am Rhys, son to—"

Erik coughed loudly, eliciting a frown from Rhys. The faery had been on the verge of admitting that he was the child of the faery queen who had been waging war on humanity. It wasn't the sort of lineage that would encourage the police to ask questions first, and today of all days, it might incline them to shoot.

"Is the ambulance coming?" Erik asked, worry obvious in his voice.

"Yes," an officer answered.

"I will keep him safe," Rhys said in a voice that would not carry. "Go seek the shooter."

With a single nod, Erik turned and walked outside.

As the guard released Will from his cuffs, his mother walked toward him, her pace a little closer to hurrying than she ever allowed in public. She stopped in front of him and reached up. Her hands stroked his hair back and cupped his face, tilting his head from side to side to examine him.

"I'm fine," he told her truthfully. "Creed took all the attention off me."

"Indeed," she said with an assessing look at his often-belligerent friend. "What are the charges against the other boy? He goes to school with my son and—"

"You're not Mr. Morrison's mother, now are you?"

Will watched his mother's shoulders go back in the way that usually meant she was about to dig her feet in and be difficult. He reached out and put a hand on her back. "He'll be fine. Please, we should go. Whoever shot Mr. Abernathy . . ."

. . . *was still nearby.*

It didn't need to be said aloud. His mother let him lead her away.

Rhys was still standing guard over Lily's father, and

in that position it was abundantly clear that he was so far removed from human that he was as different as lions are to house cats. "It is best to not tell my niece of any of this. We don't know who did this or why. Until we know more, we have no need to inform her . . . as long as he is alive."

"Lily will be furious," Will pointed out.

"Lily?" his mother asked.

The air around them grew solid, creating a barrier that allowed them to speak safely. No one addressed it aloud, but Will suspected that the only one not to feel it was his mother.

"The new heir to the Hidden Throne," Will told her quietly. "Lily Abernathy."

His mother startled and glanced at Lily's dad. "He's . . ."

"Nick Abernathy," Will supplied, knowing full well that she was quite aware of who he was.

"Oh, William," she sighed. She gave him a small sad smile and patted his cheek in that affectionate way that she rarely allowed herself. Then she straightened again. "I knew the day would come when my life and my career would be at odds. You're not going to jail, Will, because of a gift from Mr. Abernathy years ago."

"Oh."

She glanced past them all to the paramedics coming into the building with Erik. "Over here, gentlemen." Professional mien fully intact, she gestured at Nick. "I am Senator Parrish. This man is under my direct care. No one sees him or moves him without my authority."

"Is he dangerous?" one of the paramedics asked.

"No, but *I* will be if he's injured or imperiled during his convalescence," the senator said.

Will smothered a smile.

Erik nodded and said quietly, "My family is in your debt."

"Gaviria, I presume?"

He bowed.

"Criminal syndicates and fae guardsmen," she murmured softly. "This is why I've kept my legal credentials up to date."

"She was an attorney first," Will explained to Erik.

They escorted Lily's father to the ambulance, creating an odd procession of sorts: the Unseelie prince, the senator, the criminal, and Will. Everything felt far more manageable, though, when Will saw Roan standing at the edge of the crowd. He felt like a thousand weights fell from his shoulders. Roan was alive and uninjured.

He started toward him, but saw Roan's eyes dart toward the others. It wasn't exactly a *secret* in either of their families that they were a lot more than just friends, but there had always been an unspoken accord that they would not be demonstrative. After Alkamy's death, Will couldn't continue to do so. He pulled Roan in for a kiss as soon as he could reach him.

For a moment, the world—*both* worlds—and the troubles at every corner vanished. The boy he loved was safe. They were alive and together, and maybe that was all they had, but as they kissed, it felt like enough.

"I love you," he said as they separated.

Roan grinned. "You too."

They interlaced their fingers as they walked over and waited for the stretcher to be loaded into the ambulance. Cameras were turning their way.

"You sure about this?" He squeezed Roan's hand.

"Completely. It's far from the biggest scandal of the day," Roan said lightly. "How's she going to be with this?"

"*She* is not deaf, boys." Senator Parrish was clearly in full presence. That was the way Will often thought of her—there was the senator and his mom.

Smiling broadly for the cameras, she leaned in and kissed both of their cheeks. Then she told Roan, "My son has excellent taste. I can give you the 'don't hurt my child' lecture later. I've been practicing it, so it's quite intimidating."

No one seemed to know what to say, though, until Erik spoke. "I will escort the senator to the hospital and summon our attorneys to meet you here." He looked at Will and Roan. "Tell Rhys the gunman was long gone."

The ambulance doors closed.

Erik was clearly hesitant to go, but he was a human. Someone ought to be at Mr. Abernathy's side, and Erik would be safer at the hospital, where it was easier to avoid both bullets and fae. Will and Roan, while not exactly immune to bullets, were in the company of a faery who was more than adept at protecting them.

Will wasn't sure whether they were going hunting a shooter or trying to rescue Creed. Either way, it was best that the three humans weren't there. He met Rhys' gaze and asked, "Do we have a plan?"

thirty-nine

ZEPHYR

Zephyr had stepped outside to give Eilidh and Torquil privacy, as much as they could have in a glass tower. In part, he had left because seeing them together made the stabbing in his heart grow sharper. It wasn't that he wanted everyone else to be miserable. He simply didn't want to see what they had and he had lost.

Several fae were waiting outside the tower, some boldly watching him and others staring upward. They weren't reacting to his presence any more than they had when he and the others had arrived, and it occurred to him that this was . . . *normal* for them.

"Do you do this often?" he asked.

"Watch?"

Zephyr nodded.

The faery shrugged. "We all do sooner or later. She

was going to be our queen. Now, she is one with the sea." He gestured to the water. "When she is angry, it roils in temper. When she is calm, it moves like music."

"The land too," a female faery added with a nod toward the rose and vines that seemed to be twining around the tower and the jagged rocks below it. They were things that should not survive under an onslaught of salt water, but the blooms were as big as dinner plates.

"Once, before these regents," a new voice said, "the land chose the ruler."

Zephyr glanced at the new arrival. The Seelie king's eldest son stood there. He wasn't any more intimidating than Zephyr's father, but he was Seelie-born. And Zephyr was the Unseelie queen's grandson.

Without hesitation, Zephyr drew his sword. He didn't raise it in confrontation, but he held it in his hands. There was no way he'd have the skill to best the Seelie prince, but that didn't mean he wouldn't try to defend himself.

"Ah, yes, Rhys' human child," Nacton said in a dismissive voice. He lifted his sword into a high guard, a *vom tag* position, not quickly or even with any degree of concern. He moved as if there were exactly no chance that Zephyr would know how to respond.

The attacks he used were the standard master cuts that any proficient swordfighter would know. The *zwerch hau*, the crosswise strike, was the master cut intended to "break" that guard. Four of the five master cuts were the logical offensive move against an individual strike. The fifth, the *zorn hau*, was arguably viable against all of the guards.

"Not completely useless, then," Nacton said musingly.

Zephyr was debating whether or not there would be reason to engage when he realized that Nacton was merely provoking him. He felt a bit like a mouse, toyed with by a bored cat.

Then Nacton swung.

The fae who had been watching the tower were silent as Zephyr and Nacton crossed blades.

"My father has been training me." Zephyr didn't feel compelled to add that he'd been taking lessons since he was a small boy. That was obvious. Admittedly, though, he had only lived less than two decades. Nacton was centuries old.

"You are not incompetent."

"And you aren't as bad as Rhys implied." Zephyr grinned, despite himself. This was what he needed, this clash of steel and surge of fear. It made him feel less broken. Provoking the Seelie prince was admittedly stupid. He knew it as he did so—and perhaps that was part of why he did it.

Nacton lowered his sword suddenly and voided the attack.

Zephyr stumbled slightly when he swung to find only air meeting him. He started to ask, "What . . ."

Torquil stood there. "If you hurt this one, you will not be so easily forgiven. Eilidh tortured your brother. Do not think she would be hesitant to do the same to you."

Nacton spoke a word Zephyr did not know, or even know the language of, but it was obviously rude if his tone was any indication. Then he added, "So this is what you've become? You are no longer Seelie if you can speak so easily of torture."

"Zephyr is her nephew. His beloved was Seelie-born, and she was killed. He mourns, and Eilidh is not calm of late," Torquil said, as if Alkamy's loss was so easily mentioned. It hurt.

"She was Seelie then," Zephyr said.

"She was *very* Seelie." Torquil stared at Nacton.

"His?" Zephyr asked, with a horrified glance at Nacton.

"No," both Torquil and Nacton said in unison.

Zephyr's relief was short-lived, as Torquil added, "Family to him, though." He met Nacton's gaze again. "Did you know you had a sister, Nacton?"

The Seelie prince pivoted and walked away.

To his back, Torquil added, "She loved Zephyr. Your *sister* loved Rhys' *son* despite their separate courts. Surely, your spies knew as much. Surely, you knew."

Nacton continued on, and Zephyr stared at his departing form and then at the fae watching them as if this were a pageant for their amusement. They had watched the brief swordfight, and they had watched Torquil threaten and then chastise Nacton. There were politics here, but Zephyr wasn't sure what exactly they were.

"Come, nephew," Torquil said gently.

That, too, was politics. Torquil had reminded all and sundry that Zephyr had the protection of the former heir, that he was the son of the Unseelie prince, and that he had been beloved by . . . the King's daughter?

"Alkamy was . . ."

"Leith's child," Torquil finished.

Zephyr scowled. She'd had a father, a powerful one, and she had felt alone but for the diamonds. "He never thought to claim her or bring her home?"

Torquil sighed. "My king had plans. He liked the possibility of the queen's grandson wedding his daughter. Her missions were light in order to keep her safe, and he lobbied the queen to allow you to wed the girl when she was of age. She would've allowed it, I believe."

For a moment, the possibility of a future with Alkamy made Zephyr smile. They'd wanted that, but the thought of it had seemed like an impossible dream. To think that it could've been reality was almost too much now. The pain in his chest doubled over on itself. Alkamy would never know how close they'd come to claiming their dream, and he did know. Right then, he wasn't sure which of those facts was worse.

Silently, he turned and walked inside. If he couldn't fight with weapons, perhaps he could ask the questions that had been forming as he'd thought over the events at the pier.

"They said the land responds to her more than to any

other. That the sea does," Zephyr said baldly as he returned to the living quarters where his words would not be overheard. "The queen and king, Lily, all of us were swept under by massive waves at the coronation. People died."

"Are you accusing Eilidh of treason?" Torquil asked derisively. "She's the heir of—"

"Former heir," Zephyr cut in. "And she was at the coronation, possibly trying to drown the queen or Lily or . . . I'm not even sure."

Eilidh stared out the window of the tower, ignoring them.

The tower was truly a magnificent place. The view stretched forever, and the sea appeared to want to reach up to touch Eilidh the more upset she became—and she was becoming upset. Zephyr hated doing it, but he'd seen those waves. They were immense. If they hadn't been created by one of the fae regents, that meant that either there was someone powerful hiding there at the coronation or that the chaos was caused by Eilidh.

"Was the idea of a new heir that unpleasant?" he prompted.

Zephyr watched as the sea started to twist. He could see a funnel forming in the distance, and Eilidh seemed to not notice. She had the same vacant look that she'd had when she came out of the sea.

Quietly, he said, "She really doesn't remember, does she?"

Torquil looked at him. "Nature is more a part of her than most of us . . . or she's a part of it. I have never understood which direction it flows."

"Did she create the waves today?"

Torquil lifted one shoulder in a half shrug. "Perhaps. Or the sea was strengthened by her presence. It's impossible to know. Nature speaks to her and through her."

The princess walked past him as if she was being summoned by a voice he couldn't hear. She stopped at the wall, but he suspected that was only because she could go no farther. Whether it was wind or water, something in her affinity was speaking to Eilidh.

forty

WILL

When Rhys hadn't replied to Will's query, Roan looked at him and prompted, "So? Creed now or something else?"

Will nodded to himself. "Creed."

Rhys scowled. "I thought we were leaving him there? Was that not the plan you pressed for?"

"Only while Will's mother and Lily's dad were there," Roan pointed out. "For all their bluster, they were still in danger. Can you use the air as a shield?"

"Of course." Rhys looked affronted.

"Good. We'll go in, open the cage and remove Creed," Will announced. He glanced at Roan.

Roan shrugged, relaxed in a way that was contrary to logic for most people, but he was often relatively calm.

Will was elated to be doing something so impulsive. He looked at Rhys. "We are aiming not to kill anyone."

Rhys deflated the smallest bit. "At *all*?"

Roan and Will exchanged a look before Will carefully said, "At all. If possible, we would like that."

Roan added, "But if it's that or us getting killed . . ."

Rhys nodded and withdrew a couple smallish daggers. "You may use these."

The boys took the weapons and stepped so they were both slightly behind Rhys, and then they went into the police station.

It wasn't the worst plan, all things considered. They were outing themselves as fae sympathizers, but the fact that they were openly friends with the new heir of the Hidden Throne and several of their friends were likely outed made that more or less immaterial.

Rhys pushed open the door, and they followed him inside.

Creed's expression as he saw them could only be described as alarmed. Will felt compelled to say, "It's fine."

Creed frowned. He could probably feel the solidified air, and as he saw their weapons, his frown grew. "Bad idea."

Roan shrugged.

"We require him to be set free," Rhys announced. "Uncage him."

Will glanced over at Roan, who grinned at him. It was as good of a way to get a reaction as any. Police officers swarmed toward them. They ran up against the wall of air that Rhys was maintaining as a transparent shield. The initial sight of grown men running into seemingly nothing was funny, although it highlighted how little the things humanity knew would prepare them for dealing with the full fae—or even with a strong fae-blood like Lily.

Several officers drew weapons.

At first they simply brandished them, but eventually one the men fired. Rhys' wall stopped the bullet. It simply thudded into the air and then dropped. Will felt Rhys flinch though. There was a limit to how long anyone could hold the air around them like a protective barrier, especially after the day they'd had.

Will looked at Roan. "Stay close to him. A shield like this works better if it's very small in space. It easier to hold. *Stay* with him."

Then Will walked through the shield and toward Creed's prison.

"What are you doing?" Creed and Roan both asked at once. The nearest guard asked the same thing. It was an odd series of not quite simultaneous voices asking the same question.

He didn't answer. He pulled air to him, not in as thick or wide of a shield as Rhys had done, but enough that the air vibrated an exhalation away from his skin. Then he walked over to the still-locked cage.

"What are you doing, Will?" Creed asked again.

"Something good." Will concentrated on feeling the air inside the cage. He closed his eyes. Sometimes that was the easiest way to see everything, by not using his eyes.

The air around people touched every surface, every shape, flowing around everything in constant vibration. It was the inverse of water in a container. Water took the shape of the vessel. Air was everything inside, outside, over, under, and around an object—be it vessel or solid.

And that air could be agitated just as it could be slowed to be as a shield.

As soon as Will could feel the air starting to respond, he dropped his shield for the moment it took to set the air *inside* the cage to manic motion. It was only a moment that he was vulnerable.

The walls of Creed's prison started vibrating from the air's battering. At first, Will thought he'd made a mistake. He'd never tried this on anything this large or complex. He could feel the walls rattling, shuddering, trying to come apart.

The sound was like a gasp, air moving faster and faster until it felt like he'd created the center of a tornado in the cage. There was no way Will could've tried this with his mother in the room. It was too dangerous for humans.

Creed was an air affinity, too, so Will had no worry that he would be injured. If anything, Creed could protect himself from the currents circling him and pressing away. It felt like every molecule of air, every exhalation in the room wanted to run away at once.

"Duck," Creed called. "Everyone *down!*"

The air pressure grew until Will could think of nothing else and then the air screamed, a shrill noise that grew louder as the glass shattered. The pieces ricocheted as they blasted outward.

The sudden sting in Will's arm surprised him. He'd never been hit by the explosions he'd created. Will glanced over at his arm, seeing a gush of blood. Absently, he reached out to touch it.

That was when Creed knocked him to the ground and snapped, "Focus before you get shot a second time!"

"Shot?"

Creed jerked him to his feet, shielding Will with his body as he propelled him toward Rhys and Roan.

Once they were beside the Unseelie prince, Rhys said, "I stopped most of the bullets. I apologize that I missed that one."

Roan wrapped an arm around Will's waist. "That was your plan? Expose your affinity and get *shot*?"

Will grinned. "It worked. I wasn't sure if it would on something that large."

"Rhys could have done—"

Rhys interrupted. "The boy did well."

There was something wonderful about having extracted Creed and done so with his affinity. Later, Will would ponder it.

"Roan?"

"Yes?"

"The ground. It's shifting," Will said. "But you're not earth and neither am . . . I . . . or . . ."

Words were getting more difficult as exhaustion and

blood loss combined to make everything seem suddenly fuzzy.

"Ground . . . ," he added, trying to explain.

But then the ground seemed to vanish—or maybe *everything* did. Will couldn't keep his eyes open to figure out exactly what had happened. All he was sure of was that Creed and Roan were holding on to him, but he still felt like he was falling.

forty-one

LILY

"Violet will come to my palace," the king pronounced. They had stopped, and Lily realized that they were at a crossroads leading to the regents' individual homes.

"I'm not *your* subject." Violet tilted her chin upward. "My vow is to her."

There was something argumentative in Violet's every move. Even when she wasn't being confrontational, her tone was one that invited trouble. Lily had the same instinct, but she repressed it unless she needed it. Violet never seemed to do so, except on the rare occasion that she offered calm obedience to Lily.

Leith's smile was all teeth. He reached out and tousled Violet's hair. "Oh, I like this one."

Violet growled. "I am not a pet to be—"

"Vi! He is the *king*." Lily stepped close to Violet. She

didn't expect her grandfather to react poorly, and in truth he was still smiling in that absurdly cheerful way of his, but he was also the same affinity as Violet. That meant his temper could be volatile too.

The queen said nothing. For a woman who usually seemed imperious, her silence was unsettling. Her lips were pressed together as she looked at Violet, and that made Lily all the more uncomfortable.

"Oh, come now, Dell! She's the daughter of our daughter's betrothed," Leith pointed out in that merry voice of his. "She's protective of LilyDark. . . ."

Endellion said nothing.

"She's a fine granddaughter," Leith added.

The weight of that sentence seemed to toll through the forest around them.

"Granddaughter?" Endellion and Violet said in tandem.

"The daughter of our son-in-law, so . . . granddaughter by matrimony." Leith seemed to tower over all of them, joyous in his pronouncements. "We have gained two granddaughters, and you have gained a grandson too."

At that the queen tensed, as if she heard other words not spoken. As with the rest of their peculiar interactions, this was one fraught with things that neither Lily nor Violet understood.

"I'll treat the boy as gently as I've treated Rhys," Leith said, sounding deadly serious for a moment.

The Queen of Blood and Rage exhaled sharply before saying, "I'd have been kinder to your sons if they were . . .

not hateful to me and mine. They've tried to start troubles, attacked Lily, and—"

"Nacton," the king interjected. "Nacton was the one doing that. You know that as well as I do. Calder simply follows."

"He chose to follow."

They scowled and stared, seemingly forgetting that Violet and Lily were there. And Lily wasn't interested in whatever decades or centuries of conflict they were trying to sort in hidden words. She cleared her throat gently and asked, "But aren't Vi and I *both* your grandchildren? That's what it sounds like you're saying."

Leith gave her an approving look, and Endellion merely took another deep breath. Then she looked at the king and said, "Fine. As long as any of your get aren't troubling—"

"Intentionally troubling on major issues," Leith cut in. "If they are unsupportive of a unified throne, you are free to be difficult."

"*Fine*," Endellion bit off. Another deep breath followed before she resumed in a milder voice, "If any of your children or grandchildren are supportive, I will be . . . polite to them. Better?"

"Violet?" Leith prompted. "Do you support a unified throne?"

For a moment, the weight of both regents' gazes seemed to quell Violet's naturally bold temperament. Then, she glanced at Lily and grinned, "I support Lily. I support the world not being so nasty. I support a good sharp blade applied to anyone—relative or not—who threatens me or my friends." She crossed her arms and looked at first the king and then the queen. "Or my father."

Endellion looked increasingly happy as Violet spoke. "You sound more Unseelie than Seelie."

Violet's fire came to her hand in the form of a short knife. "As long as you and yours aren't a threat to mine, I have no issue with anyone, any court, any unity or separation. I would like to know who attacked us though."

At that the King of Fire and Truth was preening and the Queen of Blood and Rage was staring at Violet with obvious interest. "As would I."

Violet glanced at Lily.

"If it wasn't my Seelie uncles, who was it?" Lily prompted.

"I will ask those in my court," Leith said.

"Go with him, Vi." Lily met her grandfather's gaze. "I want to know what he discovers."

Lily had just challenged one of the fae regents. The reality of that was not settling on her yet, and before it could, she added, "And I will learn what I can in the Unseelie Court."

Her grandparents exchanged a smile, and then Leith shrugged and walked away.

Violet followed.

She *was* Seelie, and if the queen thought that her temper was Unseelie, she wasn't paying enough attention to the actual true nature of the Seelie-born fae. It was obvious to anyone without bias that fae of both courts were more similar than not. There were minute differences, primarily in skin color, but in truth, any other differences were merely a subjective opinion that said more about the speaker than about the object.

Once they were alone, the queen looked at Lily and said, "Nacton might not have caused the wave or the fire, but he knows who did. The king knows more than he's saying too."

Lily gaped at her briefly.

"I've been quarreling with Leith for centuries." Endellion shook her head. "He has his tells. I do too. He answers by omitting things."

As Lily played over what she could remember, she couldn't figure out what her grandmother meant to say. It felt very much like a test she was failing. The king had defended his sons, flirted with the queen, and spoke of family.

"He didn't mention our daughter," Endellion said after a moment.

"Eilidh?"

"Yes." Then the queen's voice grew less conversational: "Weapon."

A sharp whistle cut through the air a split second before the queen stepped backward abruptly. Three more whistles followed. Lily realized a moment later that they were arrows. One nicked her shoulder.

"Who *dares*?" Endellion's voice crashed through the

forest as she saw the blood on Lily's shoulder.

"I'm fine." Lily dropped and tried to figure out where the shooter was. She had no long distance weapon with which to defend herself. Swords weren't much use against arrows, and Lily had none of her guns because of the incident at the pier.

As more arrows came toward them, Endellion disproved Lily's theory on swords. She moved quickly enough that she cut down a number of them as they flew toward her. Earth and air both surged toward Lily like shields, but Lily brushed them back. "Let me help."

Endellion didn't reply, but she didn't overpower Lily either.

"Where are they?" Lily asked.

"Moving." The Queen of Blood and Rage started to stalk toward the attackers. Soil lifted like a shield in front of her, rolling forward like a vast invisible plow was gouging the earth. There was nothing in either world that would make Lily want to be in the shoes of the fae who had attacked the queen.

There was a seeming blindness to the queen's temper as she went in the direction of the last volley of arrows. They hit the soil and jutted there only to be buried in the earth as the moving shields shifted around the queen. It was akin to the waves that had towered over them at the pier, but this was the obvious extension of Endellion's affinity.

Lily kept her sword aloft as she followed the queen.

Without warning, an arrow came from behind Lily.

It pierced her upper leg, sinking deep into the flesh, and causing Lily to scream. Unlike the one that had grazed her shoulder, this one had embedded in her skin.

The Queen of Blood and Rage spun to face Lily. Her hand lifted and the earth around Lily rose up to shield her. As that happened, the shield that had protected Endellion dropped—and a blur of arrows flew toward the queen.

"Grandmother!"

Endellion stayed in front of Lily. Earth flew around them, encasing them in a mound akin to old burial cairns Lily had visited with her father on holiday. The earth hardened like stone, sheltering them from further attack. The queen, however, only looked at Lily, smiled, and said, "You're safe."

Then she closed her eyes.

Lily crawled toward her. Blood was soaking the ground, and broken arrow shafts were crushed under them. The queen was alive but not moving.

"Help," Lily asked the earth.

Instead of protecting herself, the Queen of Blood and Rage had defended Lily, and now there were several arrows protruding from her body.

323

forty-two

EILIDH

Eilidh could hear Torquil and Zephyr speaking, but their words had become nothing more than cacophony. It was as if they'd slipped into a tongue she didn't recognize. She could hear the earth and sea though. They were growing louder, beckoning her.

Her mother and her niece were wrapped in soil where no air could find them. Someone had taken their blood and spilled it in earth. Without a word spoken, Eilidh turned and started to descend the stairs of her tower.

Torquil took her arm in his hands, holding her back.

"Release," she managed to say as she shook him off and continued down the steps. Something was wrong.

Or perhaps everything was wrong.

As her feet touched soil, she heard her mother cry out in pain. Her mother's voice had joined with the soil. Both of her mothers were hurting. The earth was sick. The coronation had been threatened by human and fae alike.

Eilidh had gone to sea, felt the water beckoning, and when she'd given over to it, the waves tried to bring her family home to her. The sea had pulled Lily, Endellion, and Leith under where the poisons and humanity couldn't destroy them. And Eilidh herself had gone to Rhys and Zephyr.

Still, they were not safe. No one was safe. Her *mother* was in pain, blood soaking soil. Eilidh had to protect them. It was why she had been given life—to protect.

Eilidh's body felt like it was fracturing. Earth reached through sea, sending tentacles of vines to ensnare her and working with fire to create lava tubes to imprison her. She was theirs. Belonging to no one or nothing but the Hidden Lands. It was foolish to think elsewise.

Not safe, not good, not pure. The Hidden Lands were speaking, and finally she understood them. The world was too poisoned. They were protecting her, as she was a part of them. *Need. Stay. Need. Safe.*

She didn't resist. The elements were a part of her, had always been within her, and she was of them. If she sickened, so too would they. Of course it was right that they hold her.

"Eilidh!" Torquil spoke. She knew him even now, but the name-word seemed less familiar than before now. That was what she'd worn as a name. She knew it. It was wrong though.

Steadily, she walked past the fae who were reaching out to her. They were hers. They were all hers. This was her duty. She would protect them all.

"Land," she whispered.

"Sea," she sighed.

"Fire," she screamed.

Her body was one with the elements that had given her life as an infant, and she could feel her seams, all of the cracks within her body, starting to vanish. She would come apart. She would give the Hidden Lands the strength and health that she'd been lent by the elements.

"Air . . ." She exhaled the final word, the piece of her she had barely known. It was all there. Other affinities were in her bones and blood. Healing, dreams, compulsion, they were inside her because the Hidden Lands were rooted in her every fiber. Metals were there, letting her draw sword and knife, dagger and ax. The thought of it brought weapons singing through the air toward her body where it was suspended in a fiery, sea grass–wrapped cage. Waves circled her. The *corrywreckan* became even more vast than it already was.

"Home," she told them, her voice echoing across the Hidden Lands. She felt them all, her family, her fae, Seelie and Unseelie. They would be safer now.

"No!" Torquil tried to pull her back, to separate her from the Hidden Lands.

"Come," she said, wrapping herself around him as she told the lands, "He is of me. He must be safe."

The elements allowed her this, and her last thought was of gratitude as Torquil was completely wrapped in vines. Thorns jutted from them. No one could harm him now.

Then Eilidh let her affinities control her, gave over everything that was thought, and she went to find what belonged to her and those who had tried to take it away.

forty-three

CREED

They'd only just entered the Hidden Lands when Rhys stiffened as if he, too, had been shot. Will was alert enough to walk, but he leaned heavily on Roan and Creed both in order to do so. Rhys was obviously more than able to keep them safe in this world, so it was as fine of a plan as anything could be.

"What?"

"She's missing." Rhys inhaled sharply, turning as he did so. "She can't be missing. She's—"

"Who?" Creed's panic was starting to feel like it had reached a critical level. Alkamy was dead; Lily's father was shot. Will was shot. He couldn't bear the thought of Lily being hurt too.

Rhys ignored him.

Creed grabbed his arm, and immediately felt stupid for

thinking that would be a threat to the queen's son. "Who's missing?"

Finally, Rhys seemed to gather enough focus to say, "The queen."

Then he changed direction and ran.

Creed turned to Roan. "Can you do this? Lily was with her and . . ."

Roan shook his head. "We'll be fine. Go."

And Creed ran as fast as he could after the Unseelie fae. He wasn't sure he'd ever moved so quickly in his life, but seeing the seemingly imperturbable fae so panic-stricken was terrifying. Whatever had happened was dire, and Lily was with the queen as far as anyone knew. If the queen was in peril or dead, Lily . . . was . . . Creed couldn't even allow himself to think whatever would finish that thought.

He ran.

They crossed unfamiliar landscape and eventually entered a vast palace. Rhys didn't look back at him, and Creed didn't have the breath to run and speak up to say he was still there. He was simply grateful that he had air as his affinity because without that, he wasn't sure he would be able to breathe at all by the time they reached a garden where the Seelie king and his guards all spun to face them.

Swords were unsheathed in a symphony of slithering sounds.

"Where is the queen?" Rhys stalked past them all until he stopped directly in front of the king and added, "I can't find her."

"Did you look at—"

"I *can't find her,*" Rhys stressed. "No air can touch her. Wherever she is, I can't find her."

"I left her with our granddaughter." Leith frowned.

Creed felt his heart sink further at that. It didn't mean that Lily was hurt too. It couldn't. She had to be fine.

Rhys repeated again, "There's no place in the Hidden Lands where I can't find her. Ever. In my life."

The king scowled. "Obviously . . . she's . . ." His words drifted. "That's not possible. I can't find her. The only reason for that is . . ."

The king and Unseelie prince exchanged a look, but neither finished the sentence. There was no real need. Creed could only think of one possibility: the queen wasn't in this world. That meant she was in the human world or dead. It was the only logical answer, and Rhys had already said he'd looked in the human world.

"You looked over there," the king half asked.

Rhys didn't dignify that with an answer. He just stared at Leith. "The air touches everything. The only place I've ever not been able to find her is under the sea, but after today, it would be peculiar to take LilyDark for a swim when they've only just arrived here."

The King of Fire and Truth was suddenly as terrifying as any being could be. "We will find her."

He looked around, seemingly sizing them up, and pronounced, "I need water affinities. Ask the sea. If she's in . . . if she and my granddaughter are in the sea . . . *Find them.*"

Leith bellowed, "Where are my sons? And where are my loyal fae?"

The line he drew between his sons and his loyal fae struck Creed, but he said nothing.

"What are your friends? My other granddaughter . . . Violet? She's only fire. You are not water either." He glanced at Creed, paused for a heartbeat to smile. "Air and compulsion. My court. Welcome, boy . . . but not what I need right now."

"Her affinity is earth too," Creed ventured. "Like Lily."

"Earth . . . maybe they're under the earth," Leith echoed in a shaky voice. "Water *and* earth affinities too. Where are my loyal? *Find my wife.*"

The realization that there were few reasons to take Lily to sea and fewer still to be under the earth where no moving air could touch their skin was settling on all of them. If they were swimming, they would surface to breathe. If they were in an earthen space exploring, air would still move there. There were no good reasons for the queen and Lily to be unable to be touched by air.

"Father!" Calder ran toward them with the sort of fright in his expression that made Creed want to learn every prayer in every tongue.

"Wh—"

"Eilidh," Calder interrupted before the king could

finish a single word. "She's . . . you need . . . *come*. Just come, and quickly."

Leith was moving even as Calder spoke. He gestured to Creed and Rhys and ordered, "Come."

forty-four

EILIDH

Eilidh had left her beloved in a shelter of vines. It was not enough, but he would be safer there. She was going to make them *all* safe.

As she walked, fae after fae whose impure thoughts she heard by way of soil or air were imprisoned or struck down. They were her enemies if they did not want peace. They were imprisoned in cages of vines and serpents if they had doubts. Those few who had worked against peace were simply ended. Air stopped flowing for them.

They would learn to obey or die. The humans at the pier who thought ill were not released from the waves. She'd asked the sea to keep those who were *hers* safe.

Her affinities needed her to be as blade severing the weak or diseased. It was like the purifying fire in the forests. The deadwood was turned to ashes that would strengthen the soil. That was what Eilidh had to do. She had to protect the strong, to create a world where her family was safe.

But someone had hurt her family.

She walked through the Hidden Lands until she felt them there—and she helped. She could feel the earth hardening over them like a shell. Soil was pressing together as tightly as any stone could be.

"Stop," Lily implored her. "Please. We aren't safe in here either."

Eilidh heard the words, the plea for safety. She would keep them safe. It was her duty.

Serpents came from the corners of the land. Thornladen vines twisted over the hardening mound of earth that sheltered the queen and the heir.

Not our queen. Neither. Earth and air objected to her naming of those in the safety of soil.

"Mine," Eilidh argued. It didn't matter who or what they were. All that mattered was that they were her own. They were two of the fae Eilidh had held before herself. They were those whom she sacrificed and bled for, and they had to be kept safe.

Another, one who did not wish them safety, tried to come near. He brought with him other despoilers. They claimed to want the safety of the fae, but they were traitorous in their selfishness. They were shedding blood, opposing peace. Eilidh sent a thunderous wave of air outward, knocking them backward, sending them far from the place she now guarded.

Within this earthen mound were the two who could make peace happen. Eilidh would let no one near them.

"You are safe," she told them, words dropping through the soil. There were few words she could speak, but those, those words were sacred. "You are safe."

The rain fell from the sky, dampening earth, and wind brushed her skin. "Safe," she told the Hidden Lands as she summoned fire from her body.

She would destroy any who opposed the peace she sought. The Hidden Lands demanded her protection. These fae women who shared her blood required her protection. Eilidh would keep them all safe.

forty-five

CREED

Why fae ever believed themselves subtle was beyond him. He could follow what they were saying with their pauses in place. The queen and Lily were either under the water or earth. They were unconscious or otherwise trapped because no air was touching them.

Whoever was opposed to Lily's coronation had gone even further than he had in the human world. At this point, Lily's father was in the hospital, and Lily was trapped. She wasn't dead. She *couldn't* be. He refused to believe he could be alive in a world without her. The thought was too much for him to even consider—but if that *were* the case, he was going to find the person responsible and destroy him.

The king, who was leading their peculiar group, seemed to be of the same mind. Anyone who thought that the Seelie King and Unseelie Queen were only married for political reasons would quickly revise that stance if they saw his current rage. Perhaps the queen was usually the one who handled matters of violence, but there was no doubt that the King of Fire and Truth was quite capable of it.

Of course, so too was the Unseelie prince. Rhys looked like he was ready to slaughter even those with him. Creed couldn't determine whether it was worry over his mother or duty to his people or fury that anyone would strike the queen. He suspected it was all of the above.

As they walked, the first group of fae who'd answered the king's summons assured him the queen was not in the water.

"Neither is the new princess," one added hurriedly.

The king and Rhys didn't slow their steps. Creed kept pace.

"Earth!" said several fae as they ran toward the small group. "They're in the earth."

"Well, get them out then!" bellowed the king.

The eight faeries who'd all joined the group began to speak at once. All Creed could get out of the sudden cacophony was that the earth was refusing.

"The soil won't turn," said one.

"Try harder." Rhys lifted his sword, tip scraping the faery's throat and drawing drops of blood.

They all continued on. No one seemed able to get the earth to release the queen or Lily, and both the king and prince were increasingly loud in their demands to do so.

"Is everyone inept?" the king finally yelled. "Find me fae who are capable, or I will make the queen's rage seem like laughter."

By the time they reached the spot where the queen and Lily were entombed, Creed thought that tempers could rise no higher. He was only holding on to his because there was nothing he could do to make anything happen any faster than an irate faery king and prince could.

That changed when he saw the mound.

In front of him, the earth was littered with arrows. Blood darkened the soil in several places. Lily's sword was half-buried in a giant hill of soil that was covered with still-growing plants. The plants twined together into a treelike structure that was almost as wide as the mound itself. Still, it grew.

Among those plants, a veritable knot of hissing serpents writhed.

"They're guarding it," Creed said.

Whatever had happened here, the earthen mound was either a trap or a shelter. Either way, it was secure, and the earth seemed unwilling to release its captives even as the earth-affinity fae who had come tried to force it to do so.

Creed shoved air at the snakes, knocking them away as best he could. They gripped the plants as if their sinuous bodies were tentacles. It was unnatural.

The king made a gesture with his hand and exhaled, and a cloud of fire torched the plants atop the mound. As they burned, Creed saw the shape of a woman in the fire.

She was at the center of the plants, had been hidden by the greenery and size of the still growing mass.

"Stop!"

Even as it burned, the vines and branches grew. The woman inside them didn't seem to notice. She stood as the fire ignited her.

"Eilidh?" Rhys stepped closer, walking near enough that the fire flared out at him like a hand to shove him back. He stumbled. "Eilidh!"

The king stepped around him and strode up to the fire. It was his affinity, flames of his own making. They retracted into him in a blink as if they'd never been there.

Creed didn't know what else to do. He dropped to the ground and started clawing it away with his hands. It was slow, but it was working. "Help me!"

Faeries joined him, scraping the dirt away with only their hands as tools.

One faery tried to use his affinity, and the mound started growing larger. Dirt they'd removed raced toward the pile. Half of their small amount of progress was undone in a heartbeat.

"No magic! Use your hands only," Creed ordered.

The king and prince could figure out what to do about the snakes and plants and silent princess. Creed was going to get to Lily. That was all he could think to do.

forty-six

ZEPHYR

When Eilidh had encased Torquil in plants and fled, Zephyr was torn between following her and trying to free Torquil. He let out a cry of frustration. Everything was going wrong of late. He wasn't sure where Lily was, and he was sworn to protect her. He couldn't keep Eilidh safe, and his father had tasked him with that duty as well. And, in all truth, he wasn't sure he could stop the princess. Getting Torquil free was the only answer he had in that moment.

He reached out to touch the plants, calling upon his affinity and asking them to release their captive. Nothing happened. He drew his sword and tried to sever the vines. Between affinity and brute force, Zephyr managed to free a now-scratched and bleeding Torquil.

"Are you—"

"We must get to Eilidh," Torquil interrupted in a grim tone.

They followed Eilidh until they found a bunch of fae-bloods and several full fae in the forest. Not shockingly, Nacton was there. Oddly, though, he was reprimanding several fae and fae-bloods who had appeared to be trying to leave.

They still stopped Zephyr and Torquil, but they appeared reluctant.

"Why?" Zephyr asked. There were a number of questions bundled into that question—Why was he here? Why was he killing humans?—but at the bottom of it all, they all boiled down to *why*.

Torquil's hand was unsteady as he lifted his sword. There was little chance that he could best Nacton and the fae strangers with him. As Zephyr glanced at them, he saw many of them retreating. Others were looking around in fear.

After a moment, Nacton raised his sword to Torquil. "I don't have reason to fight you, Torquil."

Torquil shrugged. "You are standing in opposition to what is best for our people. I have reason."

Nacton looked down for a moment, as if he were considering options.

"She tortured Calder," Torquil remarked in a mild tone. "Do you think you would be safe from her temper?"

As Nacton lifted his gaze, he seemed unsteady. "In her state . . . I'm not sure any of us are safe."

"What do you mean?" Torquil asked.

Nacton glanced behind him. "She'd not Eilidh anymore."

Torquil swung his blade as Nacton did the same. There was little chance of even identifying the attacks they were exchanging. The clash of steel on steel seemed nonstop, with barely a moment between strikes. Both fae were aggressive, and there was nothing Zephyr could do but hope or try to get free of the other attackers to try to find Eilidh.

The others all appeared to be leaving or hanging back.

Zephyr looked away from them just as the fae-bloods who had set fire to the Row House tossed a ball of fire at him. It was showy and petulant, a blatant look-at-me move, but it was also effective. This fae was not so hesitant to fight. He had Zephyr's full attention.

Unlike at the Row House, however, here Zephyr was far from unarmed. He lifted the sword his father had given him. "I'm not going to stand here and play games."

Zephyr kept his gaze on the fae-blood. "Did you know about the attack on Alkamy?"

Nacton was the one who answered, "My sister was to be safe. They were to kill *you*."

The shock of his revelation made Zephyr swivel to look at the Seelie prince. The bullet had been meant for him. Alkamy was dead because they were trying to kill him. He froze.

And in that moment, the fae-blood kicked Zephyr in

the side of his knee. If his reflexes had been much slower, it would've taken him to the ground, but he'd been training with Rhys. As it was, it still made Zephyr stumble into a tree.

"Why?" The fae-blood repeated the earlier question. "Not all of us had the good luck you did. You want us to declare peace with humans? You wouldn't be so willing to do so if you had to truly deal with the poisons they pour into the earth."

There was no rational way to discuss any of it with him tossing handfuls of fire at Zephyr.

He dodged them, trying to get close enough to knock the fae-blood down. Both of Zephyr's affinities—earth and water—were useful in combating fire, but he wasn't sure about drawing on them while keeping an eye on the other fae-blood.

He reached to earth as he twisted to avoid another flame, but when he did so, he heard words he was hoping he misunderstood.

"Ours," the soil insisted.

"Let me go," Lily's voice argued.

"Endellion called. We protect," stone and soil said in a heavy rolling voice that called to mind mudslides.

"I need air," Lily's voice rumbled through the soil like a yell. "*She* needs air."

Zephyr heard enough to call to Torquil. "I know what Eilidh is doing. The queen is trapped. With Lily."

Nacton looked at Torquil for a moment longer than

343

necessary. "I didn't mean to strike the queen." He lowered his sword. "Only the girl."

"No!" the fae-blood yelled. "What are you doing?"

The Seelie prince ignored his son and told Torquil, "If I stop you, Eilidh will kill me. If I don't, my father will when he learns that I shot the queen."

"You shot the *queen*?"

"It got out of hand, Torquil." Nacton sighed, but he lowered his sword.

Zephyr walked past all of them. He understood the hesitation at accepting peace. The world was being destroyed, and there was a part of him that fundamentally understood the urge to destroy those responsible for the destruction. But there wasn't a cause he'd ever put ahead of his family.

He shoved through the trees and followed the sounds in the earth until he came to a mound. Creed was on his hands and knees with a bunch of faeries scraping away at the dirt, and Eilidh was on top of the mound dressed in fire. Rhys was trying to talk to her without getting burned. From the scorch marks all over him, that wasn't working very well.

"Zephyr," the king greeted.

"Torquil has stopped Nacton back there. He shot the queen and Lily," he said bluntly, looking from the king to Creed to his father. "They're in there. Suffocating. I can hear Lily."

Creed dug faster. The faeries all did.

"No affinity," Creed said, not looking up from the hole

he was digging. "It makes the earth mound up further."

Rhys looked torn between going after Nacton and trying to continue to reason with Eilidh, who was staring blankly at him.

The King of Fire and Truth looked even angrier than he had when Zephyr approached.

Zephyr's sword hung loosely in his grip. There was nothing here he could do, no enemy to battle. "She's hurt."

The king stared at the earthen mound, at his daughter on it, and he yelled, "Endellion! What are you doing? Get up here, woman. Do you hear me?"

For a moment, faeries paused, glancing at their king. Zephyr wasn't sure if he truly thought it would work or not. It didn't.

"Eilidh," Zephyr began, walking toward his aunt and father. "Can you hear me?"

The broken princess didn't respond.

"Go after Nacton, Rhys," the king barked. "Don't kill him though. Your mother will be in a snit if he's dead when she gets out."

As much as Zephyr appreciated the optimism in the king's voice, he wasn't sure it was warranted. There was only so long anyone could go without air, and from the sounds of Lily's voice, they didn't have much longer. That wasn't even taking into consideration whatever injuries made them take to ground.

Rhys went after Nacton, and the king's cheerful tone vanished as he said, "Can *you* reach them?"

Zephyr tried to talk to the earth, but it ignored him.

"No one can get an answer," Creed said. He nodded toward the fae digging next to him. "They all tried."

So Zephyr tried to read Lily or Endellion instead. "Lily? Your majesty? Can either of you hear?"

All he heard was silence.

The faeries were scraping away. The king was alternating yelling for his wife and trying to talk to Eilidh. Creed was clawing at the ground frantically, undoubtedly realizing that Zephyr not answering was bad.

Zephyr debated using his sword for a shovel. He didn't know what else to do. He jabbed it into the mound and started to pull back dirt, and he heard the queen, "Family. Blade."

"Yes!" Zephyr answered. "Family. Blade. *Our* blade."

The sword had the ability to find the ones whose blood was fed to it. Zephyr had taken that literally, but it was more than that. It could find her. With it in his hand, Zephyr said, "Let me reach you. Please!"

The queen didn't answer, but Eilidh walked to him. She looked like clarity was returning to her. Whatever had driven her was releasing.

"Your mother needs us. Lily needs us," Zephyr told her.

"Safe."

Torquil walked up to them and reached out as if he'd embrace her. "They are not safe, Patches. Not under the earth."

346

For an instant, she stared at him. There was something alien in her expression that was receding. Then she started to cry as she flung her arms open. At her gesture, soil and plant and serpent were tossed aside in a veritable explosion.

The earthen tomb was unsealed, and Zephyr could see its inhabitants.

The queen and Lily were there, both mud and blood covered. Eilidh dropped to the ground between them and gripped one of each fallen woman's hands. The earth bubbled around them. Fire danced from Eilidh's body to theirs. Water surged through the ground from the not-so-distant sea, and breezes battered them.

As Zephyr watched, both the queen and Lily opened their eyes at once. They seemed to be healing. Lily was breathing, and arrows were being plucked from the queen's body as if by invisible hands.

Eilidh smiled and then all three women closed their eyes simultaneously. They were alive. All three were alive.

Zephyr watched in a mix of relief and pain as each of the three had someone to pick them up and carry them to safety. He glanced at the assorted fae who were watching the trio of fae royal women being pulled from the ground.

"Come," he ordered. "We will guard them."

This was his future now. His duty was to these women, to guard them as they ushered in a new era of safety. It was enough.

forty-seven

LILY

Lily woke in a room that looked like neither her bedroom at home or at St. Columba's. Her father was sleeping in a bed on one side of her, and the queen was propped up watching them both in a bed on the other side.

"What happened?"

"We were attacked," Endellion said simply.

"Daidí?"

"Was attacked in the other world, visiting your . . . Creed." Endellion looked as though she wanted to wipe something unpleasant from her hands.

"What?"

The Queen of Blood and Rage sighed. "He was useful. I do not approve of a Seelie-born with you, especially as it appears that your father is also fae-blood with Seelie associations. My great-grandchild will already be more Seelie than Unseelie."

"Great . . . grand . . ." Lily blinked at her. "Not pregnant."

The queen waved her hand dismissively. "You will be eventually. The point of a unified throne was balance."

Lily wisely decided not to point out that *anyone* she wed in the far distant future would be more one court or the other. She suspected her grandmother knew that, but was simply objecting to which court had more blood on the ruling throne. "I think there are plenty of years to sort that out."

"Or," said a cheerful voice from the doorway. "We could let your grandson marry Violet? Seelie and Unseelie. Fae and human. There's potential there, Dell."

Lily looked around quickly to make sure Zephyr wasn't there. She couldn't imagine him ever being ready to move on, but she was, at least, relieved to hear him mentioned. That meant he was alive. She shook her head at her grandfather and then glanced at her bruised friends behind him. "What happened to everyone?"

"Shot," Will said.

"Snake bites," Creed said in an equally mild tone as he came over to her side. He leaned down and kissed her.

"I see you," Daidí muttered in a raspy voice.

Lily glanced his way. "Shot, Daidí?"

He shrugged and then winced. "It's healing."

"Zephyr is fine. He's with Eilidh," Creed said quietly. "Everyone's fine."

"Who attacked us?"

Endellion folded her arms and glared at Leith. "Tell her."

The King of Fire and Truth sighed. "I was wrong, Dell. I should've listened, but I'm telling you, he's sorry."

"Nacton?" Lily asked. "But . . . why? Okay, he doesn't want me on the throne, but he shot the queen?"

The queen snorted. "He never liked me. Hated me before the courts were unified, and afterward . . ." She narrowed her eyes and stared at her husband as she said, "Do you know that petty fool started all those stories of wicked stepmothers in the human world?"

Lily laughed, despite herself.

"You threatened to drown him," Leith said lightly.

"He stabbed my son!"

Leith shook his head, but he was smiling at the queen. "He's been sentenced to work toward peace in the human world. If he fails, he'll die."

"Die?" Lily echoed.

"Treason results in exile. He attacked the queen and the heir." The King of Fire and Truth sighed deeply.

It made a certain sort of sense, really. Nacton wanted the peace accord to fail. He wanted the courts divided. He thought himself safe from retribution because he was the king's son.

Unfortunately, it wasn't a recipe for the sort of peace

she'd traded her freedom to buy. "So we're trusting *Nacton* to move forward in peace negotiations?"

Leith laughed. It wasn't as disconcerting that he was jocular in the face of her temper now that Lily realized that it was likely that a few centuries with Endellion as a wife and Nacton as a son and . . . well, ruling faeries meant that he could either find amusement or be surly. The queen had opted for that approach. She ruled with fear, whereas the king ruled with smiles. Lily had begun to suspect both were somewhat feigned.

"The humans want a diplomatic liaison," Daidí said.

Lily glanced at him.

"Apparently, being raised by an amoral criminal means that you would be able to understand the fae," he continued.

The queen snorted.

Daidí kept explaining. "And the media is charmed by your romance with the rock star." He paused to look at Creed. "So if you two are willing to take the task . . . Your friends Violet and Erik are already there, and both are sworn to keep you safe."

"As is Nacton," Leith added.

Endellion laughed again.

"Dell, he'll *die* if anything happens to her," Leith said in a tone that was painfully patient. "Do you think he wants to stay in the human world forever or die? Those are the results if LilyDark is injured or the peace process doesn't go well. He *hates* it there."

At that, Endellion smiled contentedly. "There is that."

Through almost all of the discussion up to this point, Creed was silent. Finally, he said, "I'm in. If you want to go back, I'm in. I'd like to sing, but I'm sure I can sing here too. It's not the same, but . . ." He shrugged.

She could hear it though. It was what he wanted. It was what *she* wanted too. Not forever, but to move freely in the world, to be able to be in charge of working on the peace negotiations and fae-human relations. That all sounded far more appealing than being a figurehead here for court events. She glanced at her father.

Daidí shrugged with visible effort. "I agreed to be one of the human liaisons. There are others, but I said I would do it since I am not as likely to get killed because of my connection to the newly crowned faery princess."

"And I could still spend time here?" Lily asked her father and grandparents. "I can do that, but I don't want to not be able to come here. I want to see you, and the others." She frowned. "What about Will? With the senator, isn't he going to be a good choice to help?"

"He and Roan want to stay here," Creed said. "Zephyr is undecided."

Lily thought about it, all of them having a *choice* to do what they wanted. It was what she'd wanted, what they'd all wanted. She'd been willing to sacrifice her own choices so the rest of them had theirs. She wasn't going to begrudge them that now, especially as she'd unexpectedly received a fair degree of control over her own life too. It was good, not perfect, but certainly far more than she'd dared to hope possible.

There was still a lot wrong in both worlds, and she didn't trust that everything would go perfectly. That was life though. It was messy and complicated. She squeezed Creed's hand and said, "I'm in."

Creed kissed her. "My clever, deadly girl."

Her family and friends were safe right now, and they were at the start of a peace between the worlds. They'd figure the rest out as they went.

acknowledgments

All books require a lot of support, even when the support is simply to keep the author from crippling self-doubt or fits of mad research. Sometimes it's a few people who are always there, and other times, new voices arrive. In no particular order, the support team for *this* book is:

Bill Grandy, for being such a patient and talented longsword coach. Thank you for lessons and answering a thousand questions.

Tera Latendresse, you're somewhere between a bad influence and a great influence. Thank you for both sides.

Jeannette and Asia, thank you for reading and shredding this and for moral support when I'm struggling.

Neil, you really are my faery godfather sometimes. So much love to you and yours.

Kelley, from books to cons to travels, you've been an

awesome coconspirator. Thank you for the plotting and for the steadiness.

Youval, thanks for the longsword . . . and everything else.

Rachael, after twenty-four *years*, I still think you're perfect—and more essential than air. I'd have been broken in a corner a long time ago without you on my side.

And to my family, it's been a rough year. I'm grateful you're rowing this boat with me.

WHEN THE CAR HIT Eva, the thump of her body was louder than I expected. It reminded me more of hitting a deer than a possum. I'm not sure why I was surprised. Girls aren't the same size as possums, but I suspect I thought more of her nature than her size. The initial thump of her body was followed by a thud as she fell against the car hood. I've dreamed about it twice since I hit her, since I thought I'd killed her.

I swallow and keep walking toward the entrance. No one looks at me any more than they do the nurses and techs that fill the halls at Mercy Hospital. I'm part of the scenery here. I'm nobody important.

Neither is she.

I can't tell anyone that though. They wouldn't understand. It's not that I need approval. I don't. I don't need a lot of things.

What I *do* need is to see Eva. I've been thinking about it—thinking about *her*—since she fell. I have to know if she's really alive.

The article in the *Jessup Observer* says she is. I carefully clipped it out to save for my book, but after the fourth read, I needed a second copy because the ink was smeared and the edges were crumpled. I was careful with the second copy. Now, though, I hold the original clipping in my hands.

Eva Tilling, the granddaughter of both Davis Cooper IV (Cooper Winery owner and CEO) and of the esteemed Reverend Tilling, suffered multiple serious injuries after a hit-and-run earlier this week.

Miss Tilling, 17, underwent surgery this week and remains at Mercy Hospital in Durham, where she was transported after the incident. She is in critical but stable condition.

The victim was walking unaccompanied when she was run down by an as yet unknown vehicle. Authorities believe Tilling was only alone for moments after being struck when another passing vehicle saw her unconscious along the road and called 911.

The Jessup sheriff's office is looking for witnesses to the incident. They said evidence has been recovered but declined to discuss specifics.

An arrest has not been made at this time.

The staff at the *Jessup Observer* would like to

extend our prayers and thoughts to both the Tilling and Cooper families during this difficult time.

I know the staff writer has to suck up to the Cooper-Tilling family. No matter what *They* do, they're always thought innocent. The paper is only one of the many things They control. I didn't realize it a few years ago, but I see it now: Jessup is owned by Them, the ones who support the crazy rules that govern every interaction in Jessup. I'm not ruled by Them, not now, not ever again. Eva wasn't either, but that changed. She became corrupt. I have seen it, dirt on her flesh where the corruption has begun to take root. She was the shining light, the proof that not everyone believed Their lies. Then she fell. She became just as guilty as the rest of Them, so I had to act before the corruption consumed her. It's like a disease, eating away at all that's good and pure.

I ran over her to save her.

I was willing to let her die in order to save her. I'm like Abraham with Isaac, willing to sacrifice the one I love above all others. Like Abraham, I lowered the knife—or car, in my case—but God spared my beloved one. Now, I am waiting, hoping, *praying* for a reward for my faithfulness.

I'm praying that her acceptance will be my reward.

As I approach the metal detector at the hospital, I wrap my arm around the large arrangement of flowers as I fish out my wallet with my other hand. I don't have an ID in it, but I brought an empty one so as not to draw attention. I drop it and my clipboard into the bin, and then I step through the arch with the flowers. The guard barely looks at me.

I look a little older than I am, and with the scruffy facial hair and hat, the guard probably assumes I'm in my early twenties. He sees the flowers and uniform, and he fills in the rest of the facts to match the image. It's enough for him to shift his attention to the next person. I gather my items and keep moving.

The flowers aren't ostentatious, but they're still large enough to be believable as a gift from the paper. My clothes are nondescript enough—black trousers, navy button-up, and a navy-and-white ball cap. My shoes are plain black, too. Nothing here stands out. Still, I tug the ball cap down a bit farther to shade my face and hold the floral arrangement up and to the side. I stopped in earlier to get a look around the lobby. A camera aims at the door, and another sits in the back far corner of the ceiling behind the reception desk.

A bored woman glances up as I approach the desk.

"Pediatrics," I say.

"Fourth floor." She motions toward the elevators.

A second security guard stands nearby, but he's not here to stop deliveries. Being the intersection of the east–west I-40 and north–south I-85, Durham has long been a high drug-trafficking area. It's not as bad as it once was, but the hospitals have security due to drug-related crimes.

Inside the elevator, I look at the flowers. We talked about

the language of flowers in one of our lit classes because of *Hamlet*, so I know that Eva will figure it out. The flowers I picked are yellow roses (for apology and a broken heart), white roses (for silence and purity), red carnations (for passion), and white daisies (for innocence). The daisies were in *Hamlet* too, so I know she'll see them as a clue. She'll figure it out.

I've already removed the Harris Teeter grocery price tag, but I check again to be sure there are no other identifying marks that will ruin my disguise. I keep my eyes downcast in case there's a camera in here, too. By the time I reach the fourth floor, where Eva is, my hands are trembling a little, not noticeably enough that strangers would see, but I feel it. Intentionally, I step on the long piece of my shoelace as I walk, untying it as I approach the desk. I tied and retied it repeatedly to get the length right. I'd practiced as I walked around at home, too. Today, I'm doing everything right. Today, I'm not going to get impatient. It's hard though. I didn't think I'd ever see her again—aside from her funeral. I knew what I'd say *there*. I'd planned it. The words, the pauses, I practiced. I may change it some now that I have more time.

Maybe I won't have to say the words at all.

When I saw the article, when I found out she was alive, I knew it was a sign. God doesn't want her to die yet. I understand that now. I was hasty. I have spent the past three days thinking about the right path, praying for clarity and considering my options. He's giving me another chance, giving *her* another chance. Maybe I can make her see, and she can be redeemed. If I save her, she can live, and she'll be so grateful for all that I've done to save her.

I stop at the desk and tell the receptionist, "Delivery for"— I glance at the clipboard as if I don't know her name, as if I could ever forget her name, and read it—"Eva Tilling."

"That girl gets more flowers than the rest of the floor combined!" the woman says as she signs on the clipboard where I silently indicate. The sheet is very convincing. I ordered my own flowers so I could have a good model for my form.

Once she walks away, I glance at my shoe as if I am just now seeing that it's untied. No one seems to be watching, but you never know. I crouch, my posture allowing me to use my hat to hide my face as I watch her carry the flowers to a room. She taps on a door, and I finish tying the shoe as I watch her go inside.

Straightening, I glance around. No one pays much mind to delivery people. So many flowers arrive at the hospital. Why would they look at us?

I force myself not to hurry. We wouldn't be in this situation if I had practiced patience in the first place. Hurrying is dangerous. Slow and steady wins the race, especially in the South. My grandmother told me that so often that I'm sure she'd take a switch to me if she knew that I'd messed everything up by being impatient.

I glance inside Eva's room as I pass it. It's only a moment, a split second, but she's there. She's awake and speaking softly. If I didn't know better, I'd swear she was an angel. She's not though. She's one of Them. If I can't save her, she'll have to die. She's been spared for now, but I need her to understand. If she doesn't, she'll be a sacrifice at the altar of venality.

Like the rest of Them should be.

My mouth is dry at the thought of how close I am to her now. I could walk straight into her room and visit her, but I'm not ready to talk to her. Still, I needed to see her.

I wonder if she'll notice my name on the card. I listed several names—the editor, a few staff writers, and then I added my own in the middle. *Judge.* It's not the name I was born with but it's my true name, my *soul* name. I'm not really an executioner yet, and without Eva, I'm not a jury. Together, we could be a judge, jury, and executioner.

I'd despaired when I realized that she was one of Them. On the night I tried to kill her, I thought I would be always solitary. Now that she survived, I have hope again.

Outside, I pause to breathe the already thick air. Early summer in North Carolina isn't as humid as the heat of July and August, but the air is heavy already. The sweet taste of wisteria fills my mouth, and I wonder if Eva likes the flowers. They're not as sweet as the pale purple clusters of wisteria clinging to the trees. For her, I brought common flowers—like her, not truly special. That was my mistake before: I raised her up like a false idol. I know better now.

I cross the parking lot to the car I have today and slip on my gloves before I touch the handle. Like my uniform, it's not memorable, a dark blue, four-door sedan. I'll park it beside the one that has Eva's blood on it.

JOIN THE Epic Reads COMMUNITY

THE ULTIMATE YA DESTINATION

◄ DISCOVER ►
your next favorite read

◄ MEET ►
new authors to love

◄ WIN ►
free books

◄ SHARE ►
infographics, playlists, quizzes, and more

◄ WATCH ►
the latest videos